The sound was ghostlike...

...an eerie moan emanating from the darkness. Though Ann was halfway down the barn, the unfamiliar noise caught her attention.

In the pasture several horses cried, then ran. Sudden panic swept through the barn as the stalled horses screamed and kicked in answer.

For the first time since she was a young girl, Ann was scared of the dark massive structure of the barn. She couldn't shake the sensation that someone sinister was waiting for her. Her fingers on the light switch, she paused. And where was Matt? She had seen him enter the barn, but then he'd disappeared.

Suddenly a strong, leather-gloved hand covered her mouth. She struggled, fighting the sense of blackness that swept down over her... until something heavy struck her head and it suddenly ended.

ABOUT THE AUTHOR

Horses have always been an important part of life for Caroline Burnes. She has two—Miss Scrapiron, a Thoroughbred, and Mirage, a half-Arabian. When Caroline isn't writing, teaching or working, she's usually riding. *Measure of Deceit* is a spinoff from her earlier Intrigue, #86 *A Deadly Breed*, and features one of its secondary characters, Mississippi horse breeder Ann Tate.

Books by Caroline Burnes

HARLEQUIN INTRIGUE
86–A DEADLY BREED

Measure of Deceit

Caroline Burnes

Harlequin Books

TORONTO • NEW YORK • LONDON
AMSTERDAM • PARIS • SYDNEY • HAMBURG
STOCKHOLM • ATHENS • TOKYO • MILAN

This book is dedicated to my horse-loving friends
in Mississippi—Gloria Howard, Karen J.Pate and
Pam Dattilo. Without their help and friendship I
would have lost my horses. Also to Dr. Karl
Smith. Through fat and lean years he has cared
for my menagerie.

Harlequin Intrigue edition published October 1988

ISBN 0-373-22100-2

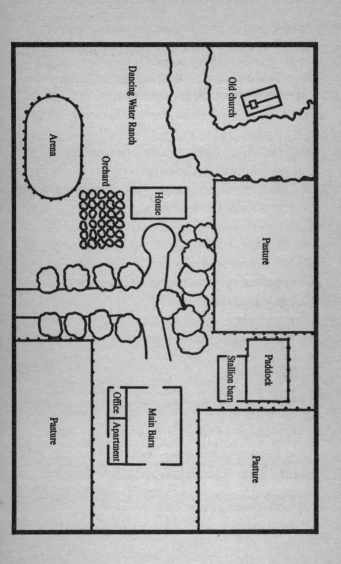

Dancing Water Ranch

Old church

Arena

Orchard

House

Pasture

Pasture

Stallion barn

Paddock

Office

Main Barn

Apartment

Pasture

CAST OF CHARACTERS

Ann Tate—Trying to save her stallion, she found herself a victim of the past.

Matt Roper—When he came to Dancing Water Ranch, trouble began.

Freddie—His loyalty couldn't be questioned, but his life hung in the balance.

Bill Harper—Greedy and mean, he seemed the perfect villain. Or was he only a foil?

Cybil Matheson—Longtime friend and veterinarian, she showed up at every emergency.

Robert Tisdale—Ann's ex-husband, he disappeared three years before, along with a valuable horse.

Dawn Markey—She had opportunity to create trouble, but did she have motive?

Chapter One

The gleaming, silver Featherlite trailer and matching pickup pulled down the white shell drive. Ann Tate watched the slow, careful progress of the rig as she sipped a cup of black coffee in the shelter of her front porch. The truck and trailer were immaculate—a good sign—and the driver was cautious. Her phone conversations with Matt Roper had left her with more than a little curiosity about a man who so thoroughly took care of his horse. Curiosity and approval. As owner of one of Mississippi's finest breeding farms for Thoroughbreds, she was learning that many horse owners were more interested in winning races than in horses. Roper, though, sounded like a man who cared about more than money. At least he'd asked hundreds of questions. She smiled as she put the coffee cup on the rail and started down the steps to greet her newest human boarder and his mare.

Brittle pecan leaves crunched beneath her boots as she cut through the orchard. The driver of the truck parked at the smallest of her two barns. Before she could attempt a hello, an earsplitting whinny issued from the silver trailer. Several horses in the west pasture bucked, reared and ran to the fence, answering the call with shrill cries of their own.

"Easy now, Blue Chip." A deep voice, soft and comforting, came out of the back window of the truck. The darkened glass shielded the man from Ann's view, but she liked the tone of his voice, the soft command and comfort that mingled so easily.

"Mr. Roper?" She walked beside the trailer, automatically taking note of the shiny mahogany coat of the mare that continued to whinny loudly. Ann watched with interest as a tall, dark-haired man opened the truck door and leaned out. His direct gaze caught hers and held. The overriding characteristic of his face was intelligence blended with humor.

"Pleased to meet you, Ms. Tate." Matt Roper eased out of the cab, followed by several empty sacks from fast-food outlets. The quick February wind whipped the paper and sent it flying around Ann's immaculate barn area. He made a grab for the litter, but it was in vain. "I'm sorry. I hope the litter patrol doesn't believe in capital punishment." He nodded in appreciation at the perfection of the grounds. His first impression of Dancing Water Ranch far exceeded his expectations. Ann Tate had been inordinately modest on the telephone. The place was very impressive. But he'd been warned by his clients that she would attempt to hide her financial distress, would attempt to put up a front. He was to walk cautiously and keep his eyes open for signs of incompetence and inefficiency.

"The wind is hungry today." Ann extended her hand. "Don't worry. We'll catch up with it when it tangles in the pasture fence. Welcome to Dancing Water Ranch. That's a good-looking mare you brought with you."

Matt stepped forward and accepted her hand. "It's good to arrive finally. It was a long drive from Georgia."

"Let's get Blue Chip settled in her stall, and we'll go into the house and have a cup of coffee. It may be the sunny south here in Mississippi, but there are a few cold days, and you picked one to arrive on." Ann did up the top button of her fleece-lined jacket as she spoke. Her business was judging horseflesh, but she couldn't help appreciate the casual grace of the man. He had none of the slackness of muscle she'd come to associate with desk jockeys. Far from it. Matt Roper gave the distinct impression of a physical man. Even though she'd decided to put men behind her after her disastrous marriage to Robert Tisdale, she could still appreciate Matt's catlike, understated masculinity.

As Matt walked around to open the back door, Ann noticed his long, athletic stride, the casual grace he wore as nicely as his jeans.

"You don't look like a stockbroker." The words flew from her mouth the way the paper had flown across her yard.

Her reward was an amused grin. "You're right. I haven't pulled out a prospectus or quoted any figures in fifteen minutes. Maybe I'm not a stockbroker. Maybe that was all a bad dream."

His warm laughter ignited her own. "There's someone in the barn I want you to meet. I can see that the two of you have a twisted sense of humor in common. Jeff Stuart also has a mare here, and a yearling. I'll introduce you when we take your horse to her stall."

Like a well-trained dog, Blue Chip backed carefully out of the trailer at Mark's command. She was an exceptionally well-put-together mare, with a wide chest and long legs. Ann was fond of her own mares, but Blue Chip was a stunner. The idea of a foal that combined the good qualities of Blue Chip and her stallion, Easy Dancer, made her tingle with excitement. Derby quality.

"She looks like a runner." Ann ran an appreciative hand down the mare's glossy neck. "Good shoulder depth. She's a real beauty." Ann straightened the edge of the animal's heavy, red traveling blanket and felt Matt's eyes on her. She looked up, and he was smiling.

"You're a fine judge of horseflesh, Ms. Tate." Matt was assessing her, taking note of her open and friendly blue eyes, her confidence as she looked at Blue Chip. There was no hint of worry or concern. Had he been misinformed?

"And you, too, obviously. You picked my stallion to breed your mare to." They laughed together and started to the barn.

The horses at the fence, now a herd of ten, whinnied a collective tooth-rattling welcome, and Blue Chip danced nervously under Ann's hand. The mare sniffed the air, nostrils widening to pull in every scent of a new and strange environment.

"This is her first time away from home," Matt explained. "I've always been hesitant to send her away for breeding."

Ann nodded toward a large, well-lighted barn. "Her stall's in there, and the stallion is in this smaller barn." She pointed to the sturdy wooden structure where Easy Dancer ruled. "I'm sure you'll want to make a thorough inspection of him before you leave."

"Oh, I'm in no hurry—" Matt flashed a mysterious smile "—to leave. Now let's find this girl a place to stay." Matt was eager to see the stallion. More eager than he'd admit, even to himself. He had to find the perfect stallion for Blue Chip. His future, and his children's future depended on it. But his dreams and hopes were something he couldn't easily trust to a strange woman. Especially one who might be hiding financial problems, the result of mismanagement.

Inside the barn, Matt was struck once again by the cleanliness. He took in the spacious stalls, the recently swept floors and the scent of fresh pine shavings, but his eyes strayed continually to Ann Tate. She was a tall woman with shapely legs, shown to advantage in snug, faded jeans. He judged her to be near thirty, a mature woman with a wealth of happy experiences that showed on her bronzed face. A woman who met life head-on and liked the experience. He could tell that little bit from her firm, confident handshake. Nothing about Ann or her establishment indicated poor management or ruin. To his surprise, Matt felt a deep relief, along with slight puzzlement.

"This is Blue Chip's stall." Ann opened a stout wooden door and stepped back. Matt walked inside, sinking almost to his shins in clean shavings. The fresh pine scent rose up around him.

Blue Chip entered the stall willingly and allowed Ann to unbuckle her traveling blanket.

"You have a way with her," Matt noted as he watched Ann's facile fingers unsnap and unbuckle. Before he could offer to help, Ann had removed the blanket.

"If I don't get along with the horses, I'm in trouble," she said. "She's set for a little while. We should leave her alone and let her make the acquaintance of some of the other horses. In a few days, I'll turn her out in the pasture with one or two other mares. I want to give her plenty of time to adjust."

"Driving over here, I was a little on the anxious side. As I told you on the phone, Blue Chip is my only horse. I've raised her from a foal, and she's become a lot more than just an investment." Matt grinned sheepishly as he spoke, his teeth strong and white against his olive-toned skin. "After five minutes here, I know Blue Chip is in excellent hands. I'm relieved." After what his clients had indicated, he didn't add that surprise was his major reaction. He thought again of the last-minute inquiry he'd gotten from Gordon Boswell, the unofficial spokesman of a group of investment-minded men calling themselves the Winner's Circle. Since he'd already planned on bringing Blue Chip to Dancing Water Ranch for breeding, he had agreed to check out the premises as a potential investment property for the group. He was still amused by the specificity of Boswell's interest in Dancing Water, as if it were the only ranch in the world he would consider buying. It was almost as if Boswell had known Matt was bringing his mare to Dancing Water. The purest kind of coincidence? He shrugged. It only went to show how fast gossip traveled on the horse circuit—almost as fast as the horses.

"You can go back to Georgia with a calm mind to tackle the bulls and bears of the market," Ann said with a grin.

"All in good time." Matt looked around. "How about a tour?" If there was anything amiss, a close look around would be a good place to start, he thought, as he cleared his mind to listen for any hidden nuances, any discomfort on the part of his guide.

Ann found Matt an absorbed listener, eager to learn as much as possible about the breeding business. She showed him the vet area, the foaling stalls, the paddocks and the pasture of pregnant mares, all ready to foal in a few weeks.

"This time next year Blue Chip will be near term." He spoke with some trepidation.

"You can always bring her back here and we'll play midwife," Ann offered. "I love the whole business, but the excitement of a new foal arriving is my favorite part. Like children, they're wonderful—until it's time to start training them." Her blue eyes narrowed as she stared into the bright afternoon sunlight of the pastures.

"So the risks and gambles of horse breeding don't leave you insecure about your future?" Matt watched her closely. "You haven't even considered selling? For a good price?"

Matt's question was startling. She turned to face him. "No." For some reason she felt as if he were insinuating something. "Now, let's see about the stallion. Easy Dancer is the climax of the tour."

Without waiting for Matt, she walked away. For a second, he stood and watched her, then he quickly caught up. He'd expected some defensiveness, but he couldn't find a shred.

Ann was silent but very aware of Matt's presence as she entered the stallion's barn. Easy Dancer nickered, and his soft greeting put the smile back on her face. "I know all owners brag, but Easy is a remarkable horse."

She was cut short when a tall, muscular man popped up inside the stallion's stall.

"Jefferson Stuart, don't you have a dab of sense—playing in a stallion's stall!" Ann regained her composure quickly. Though her words were harsh, her tone was only exasperated.

Jeff's laughter ceased abruptly when he saw Matt standing in the doorway, a puzzled look on his face.

"Ronnie dropped her watch in Easy's stall and I was looking for it." He held up the watch as evidence, then turned to Matt. "Ann would have you believe she's the only person Easy loves, but he's as gentle as a kitten. He doesn't care what I do to him."

"You're worse than a plague of yellow flies," Ann threw at him. "I told Matt you had a demented sense of humor, but really, you'll give him the idea I let my boarders run wild." Her eyes were bright with pleasure. "Matt, this is Jeff Stuart, the husband of a good friend of mine—"

"I'm up here!" a feminine voice called from the hayloft. At that moment Veronica Stuart's happy face peeked over the edge of the loft. "I'm coming down." Her feet could be heard on the rungs of the ladder as she descended.

"Everyone calls me Ronnie." The pretty brunette took Matt's hand. "You're bringing in the mare from Georgia that Ann was so excited about. Good bloodlines. She's talked about you and Blue Chip for weeks now.''

''I'm flattered.'' Matt couldn't resist Ronnie's infectious smile.

''Watch out for these two,'' Ann said. ''First they flatter you, then they flatten you. Let's all go into the house and have some coffee. It's cold out here, and I can see now that putting Easy through his paces won't be possible with Jeff around.'' She turned back to Matt. ''Jeff comes in here and spoils him rotten and then laughs at me when I have trouble.''

Easy Dancer whinnied as if he approved of her statement and poked his head over the stall door. Matt could see that he was a beautiful creature with a finely controlled fire about him. When he walked over and patted the stallion's head, Easy Dancer nosed against him, rumbling softly with an inquisitive sound. He was friendly, but his warm brown eyes followed Ann's every move.

''Ann and Easy have a special relationship,'' Jeff commented.

''We respect each other,'' Ann said, walking to the stallion and stroking his velvety muzzle.

''I'm feeling better and better about my decision to come here,'' Matt said. ''My past experiences haven't left me inclined to trust my most valued possessions to a woman.''

Though he spoke with humor, Ann detected bitterness, which she filed away for later thought. Matt Roper wouldn't be the first man who needed convincing that a woman could run a business, especially one as demanding as a breeding farm. Somehow, though, she didn't think Matt's statement involved something as simple as business-related chauvinism.

Jeff secured the barn, and the four of them walked the thirty yards to the gracious old farmhouse, with its wide, inviting porch.

There was a large, comfortable den, but the kitchen was the center of life at Dancing Water Ranch. Ronnie and Jeff settled themselves at the table while Ann put the coffee on. Matt stood for a moment, then Ann signaled him to sit.

"Once we leave the barn, we're very informal. Most of the people who have horses here are friends. The kitchen is considered open territory. If you want something, come in and get it. No service and no charge."

"Sounds a lot like a family," Matt said.

"Ann's wayward clients," Jeff said, laughing. "Believe it or not, at one point in my life I was a respectable businessman. Then I became friends with Ann Tate and everything changed."

Jeff and Ronnie were red with suppressed laughter. Matt looked questioningly from face to face. His business mind rose at the hint of some unsavory secret, but his intuition told him Ann had no sordid past.

"Don't believe anything he says," Ann warned him. "Jeff isn't even forty and he's already a retired politician. Does that say anything for his character? He's a lawyer and a scoundrel. His only redeeming qualities are that he was smart enough to marry Ronnie and he likes horses."

Jeff adopted a wounded expression. "We were friends before you even knew Ronnie."

"That's true," Ann conceded, walking over and patting his head. "And Jeff did sacrifice a brilliant political career to see that horse racing was legalized in this state. But that's all in the past. Now he's practicing law and letting Ronnie teach him the art of civilized behavior."

Matt leaned back in his chair and watched the three friends banter and tease. It had been a long time since he'd seen such deep friendships, and once again he contrasted what he saw with the things he'd been told to expect. Ann Tate did not appear to be the greedy, desperate woman Gordon Boswell had described. And he liked Jeff Stuart and Ronnie. She was a real beauty. But he was drawn to Ann Tate. As she put mugs on the table and poured the steaming coffee, he began to think that his stay in the rural stretches of Mississippi might be a lot more pleasant than he had ever anticipated. A lot more pleasant, but not nearly as profitable.

"What delightful thought has you grinning like the cat that got the canary?" Jeff watched him with interest.

"He's just thinking what a lovely foal Blue Chip and Easy Dancer are going to produce," Ann said, stepping in to rescue him. "Now let's drink our coffee and try not to frighten him to death."

She sat down beside Matt. "This is your breeding and boarding contract. You'd better look it over carefully before you sign. We take every precaution with the horses, but accidents can happen, even at the best barns."

"I'll look it over." He tucked it into the pocket of his coat. "I won't be leaving immediately. I want to make certain Blue Chip is comfortable." Uneasiness returned with surprising swiftness at the mention of accidents. Blue Chip was more important than he cared to think about; she was his future. Was Ann Tate's statement a warning? "I've heard the coast has a number of excellent resorts. Can you recommend any?"

At the thought of Matt's continued presence, Ann felt an uncharacteristic flush tickle her skin. Her first reaction was pleasure that he was staying. There was also a tingle of irritation at his lack of trust in her ability to provide professional care for his horse. Before she could recover, Jeff answered the question.

"There are a few along the coast, but that's something of a drive from here. I'll bet Ann could put you up for the night. Then you could get a fresh start in the morning. Right, Ann?"

There was a devilish glint in Jeff's eyes, and Ann realized that her flush had not gone undetected. She dropped her gaze to the table. "Of course you're welcome to stay here. Dancing Water Ranch has a long tradition of hosting clients, and it might make you feel easier about leaving Blue Chip if you stayed over." Looking directly into his eyes, she added, "Dancing Water also has a long tradition of excellent mare care. Not a serious incident since we opened."

Something unnameable flashed in Matt's dark face as he smiled. "I didn't mean to imply otherwise, and I certainly can't resist your gracious offer."

"Ann's father built this house with a separate wing for guests. He was a Kentucky breeder who was aware of the importance of entertaining his clients. He was also a man who enjoyed meeting and knowing new people. Ann inherited those traits, Matt. It will be wonderful to have you as a guest." Jeff spoke with warm enthusiasm, carefully avoiding the scalding look Ann directed at him.

Beside him, Ronnie's face glowed with mischief. She, too, could see that Jeff was setting Ann up, but she had no intention of coming to her friend's rescue.

"It will do Ann good to have some company," Ronnie interjected. "She works too hard. Maybe with you around she'll take a few hours off."

"Ann, are you sure?" Matt asked.

"Of course. And I'm sure Ronnie and Jeff will stay for dinner." She shot them a look of warning.

"Uh, sorry," Jeff said, looking at Ronnie. "We already have plans . . ."

"To have dinner at Judge Brackston's house," Ronnie finished, even though she knew Ann would know it was a lie. "He wants to talk with Jeff about prison reform. If it were anything else, we'd try to cancel, but we can't."

"Yes," Ann agreed with a low, throaty tone. "Jeff should surely be interested in prison reform. After all, he's certainly bound to wind up in a prison the way he's going today."

Matt took a sip of his coffee to hide the intensity of the gaze he threw at Jeff and Ronnie. Prison?

"Now, Ann," Jeff said as he stood and drew Ronnie up beside him, "Matt may not understand your tart sense of humor like we do. Thanks for the coffee, but we'd better get back to town."

Before Ann could say another word, Ronnie hugged her and they left her sitting alone at the table with Matt.

"Why don't we go look at Easy Dancer?" Matt suggested softly. "I didn't get much chance to see him earlier."

"By all means," Ann agreed, rising.

Matt followed her out of the house and across the yard to the small stallion barn. For a moment he was tempted to tell her of Gordon Boswell's interest in buying her farm. He felt slightly deceptive, especially since he'd accepted her hospitality. Before he could broach the subject, Ann was in Easy's stall.

Her gestures were sure and natural as she brought the big reddish-gold stallion out of the stall and hooked him into the cross ties. All traces of anxiety disappeared as soon as she touched the horse. "When he was younger Easy was a little unruly, but he's been the best stallion I've ever worked with since our trainer, Dawn Markey, started with him three years ago."

Easy pushed his head against her chest and rested there.

Matt slowly extended a hand and ran it over the soft, golden hide. "He is extremely well mannered, very fond of you," he agreed.

"He's very gentle with the mares." For the first time in her professional career, Ann felt a slight discomfort at her plain words. Breeding was her business, so why did talking about it with Matt Roper make her feel shy and awkward? She pushed through those feelings. "When he was racing, manners weren't so important. Now Easy is a gentleman, and we make sure he behaves like one."

Matt walked around the horse, surveying him from every angle. "He's everything you said he was and more. I know it sounds like a boast, but I have this gut feeling that Easy and Blue Chip are going to produce a Derby baby!" For the moment he was able to put aside his business observations and think only in terms of his personal goals. He was almost afraid to believe it. He'd thought so long and so hard for a way to get the money he needed. Now, possibly within a year, he'd have the foal that could change his future, bring his children home to him. A Derby baby!

Hearing her earlier thoughts brought to life, Ann felt a sudden chill. Whether it was anticipation or warning, she couldn't be certain. She chanced a look at Matt and found he was watching her intently. As she held Easy's grooming brush above his neck, their eyes locked and held. She had the distinct impression that Matt Roper was a man with many purposes, some of them deliberately unstated.

The sound of a loud musical horn broke the moment. From behind the barn three German shepherds raced out, tails wagging.

"Where's everybody?" Cybil Matheson called as she wheeled her veterinary lab truck into the yard. "This place is as quiet as a tomb."

"It's Dr. Matheson," Ann explained to Matt. "She's the best vet in the South."

Matt stepped away from the stallion. "Is she your regular vet?"

There was some doubt in his tone, and Ann smiled, remembering his earlier comments. "Cybil's the best in the business, even if she is a woman." She wasn't offended by Matt's attitude. It was obviously another area where stereotyping ruled, and though Ann didn't condone such thinking, she understood. Vetting large animals, especially high-strung Thoroughbreds, was a tough job. Cybil Matheson was a match for it. She'd cut her teeth as a veterinary assistant when she was a teenager and had paid for every penny of her education herself. She'd fought long and hard to attain her dream, and she was more knowledgeable, smarter and better with horses than any vet Ann had ever seen. Matt would just have to take her word for it.

Cybil parked her truck at the barn door. "What are you two doing in here? Planning a robbery?" she asked as she stepped through the doorway, a long blond braid swinging behind her square shoulders. "Where's that new mare?"

Ann introduced Cybil and Matt, and the three of them went to Blue Chip's stall. Cybil did the necessary work to ensure the horse was healthy and ready to breed in a few weeks. She talked quietly and assuringly to Matt as she examined the mare.

"Anything else?" she asked, stripping off the long glove and resting an arm across Blue Chip's back. "I hear Ben Johnson has a couple of new mares he wants checked, so I'm headed that way."

"Nothing here," Ann answered.

Cybil nodded at Blue Chip. "She's one of the best mares I've ever seen. Reminds me of Easy's dam, remember?"

Ann nodded. How could she forget Sky Dancer? The beautiful chestnut mare had been her father's favorite horse. He'd pinned a lot of hopes on her and her offspring. Then tragedy had struck.

Matt watched the almost-hidden pain sweep quickly across Ann's face. He didn't understand what it meant, but he saw her successful efforts to compose herself, and he wondered.

"You're right, Cybil, there's something about Blue Chip that brings Sky Dancer to mind. Something in her attitude and build." An uncontrollable shudder caught her. Sky Dancer's death from a rare blood disorder had been horrendous. It had also been only the beginning of a series of tragedies. Her husband left without warning, divorce papers from Mexico the only word she'd ever gotten from him. A valuable stallion, a full brother to Easy Dancer, had also vanished that same October night.

For a moment she was touched with an icy finger of dread. "Blue Chip is okay, isn't she?" She spoke before she could stop herself. The premonition of disaster was too strong to ignore.

"You bet," Cybil responded, gathering her tools. She looked up at Matt. "She's in top physical condition. She's the perfect age for breeding and I predict an exceptional foal." Cybil studied Ann. "What's wrong? You've never produced less than a healthy baby here."

Ann rubbed one eyebrow with the back of her hand and forced a lopsided smile. "I had the craziest feeling. You know, like a premonition." She turned to Matt with an apologetic shrug.

"Ann has a perfect record here, Mr. Roper." Cybil gave Matt a reassuring nod. "In fact, the only trouble she's ever had was theft."

"Theft?" Matt couldn't hide the worry he felt. "Was it recent?"

"No." Ann tried to maintain a calm front. "It was three years ago and it was one of my horses, not a boarder." She gave Cybil a warning look. When she looked at Matt, she could see he was not convinced. "Listen, Mr. Roper, my ex-husband left and took a horse. It had nothing to do with the boarders. It was personal."

"Robert wasn't the man we thought he was," Cybil agreed sharply. "But I hardly think he'll come back here. Not after everything that happened."

Matt's attention was on Ann. She looked distraught. So, she had an ex-husband. An interesting tidbit.

"Robert would never dare show his face here," Ann said grimly. "When he left three years ago, the road disappeared behind him. Whatever else he is, he isn't stupid enough to try to come back."

"Robert won't be back, but maybe one day Speed Dancer, the best stallion in the South, will come home." Cybil gave Matt a knowing look that held total sympathy for Ann. "This all happened in the good old days, Mr. Roper, before the wild South was won by decent women." She chuckled.

"I gather that Dancing Water Ranch has had an interesting past," Matt said, recovering quickly. "It sounds mysterious and fascinating. I'm just glad there are no current troubles. Right?"

"None," Ann answered, linking her arm through Cybil's. "It's the future we're interested in at Dancing Water, not the past."

"Spoken like a true businesswoman," Matt said, falling into step with the women as they walked toward Cybil's truck.

"Yes, Dancing Water has a glorious, exciting future." Cybil smiled as she slid into her truck.

"See you Saturday," Ann called after her. "We need to get our foaling game plan down."

Standing at the fender of the truck, Matt watched the exchange. Were Cybil and Ann hiding something? In one afternoon he'd found out about a horse theft, death, inheritance, insurance and divorce. Gordon Boswell's information might well be more accurate than he'd first thought.

Chapter Two

Matt poked the fire into a snappy blaze and returned to the sofa and his brandy. Curled across from him in a large overstuffed chair, Ann savored the warmth of her drink and the pleasure of Matt's conversation.

As they talked, swapping stories about horses, she studied his face, a dark stubble now showing on his olive skin. Tiny lines of fatigue were etched around his eyes, but she could see he wasn't quite ready to call it a day. And neither was she.

"Dinner was excellent," he said, stretching his long legs out a little further. "I'm almost ashamed I ate so much."

"Mannie's cooking is legendary. Like Freddie, my barn manager, she's been with me since long before my father died."

"That cake." Matt rolled his eyes and chuckled. "She could tempt a saint to consider the sin of gluttony. After riding in that truck all day, I need some exercise. What about a walk?"

"A walk? Tonight? Do you know how cold it is?"

Matt stood and extended a long arm to grasp her hand. Strong fingers curled around hers and he easily pulled her to her feet. "It isn't that cold and the fresh air will be exhilarating. We'll take a quick tour of the barns and make sure Easy and Blue Chip are fine.''

She started to protest, but his hand was compelling. She wasn't sleepy, and a walk might help remove the nervous tension that had haunted her all evening.

When Matt held her warm coat for her, she slid into it and went to the door. The brisk night rushed into her face, and she looked up at the stars, a mass of glitter across the sky. Matt's hand closed over her elbow, gently steering her to the main barn.

The soft noises of the horses greeted them, and Ann made no attempt to pull away from Matt's touch. Unexpectedly she was assaulted with a bitter thought. Robert's hand had once given her a sense of safety, too. That was before she'd really known him and his talent for deception. She edged away.

Walking down the center aisle, they were greeted on both sides by curious horses. There were a few soft nickers, and from the center of the barn, Blue Chip welcomed her master more loudly.

"She knows you," Ann noted. "That's a compliment."

"She's familiar with my habits," Matt explained. "I always check my barn before I go to sleep." For the past few years, Blue Chip had been his number-one priority.

"It's a wise habit." Ann bent to check the automatic waterer. "I have such wonderful help here that I'm afraid I've gotten dependent on them. Freddie always closes up the barn at night. He's the best help anyone could want."

"Good help is the key to success." Matt laughed at his pronouncement. "Now that sounded like something in a business textbook." He stopped at Blue Chip's stall and stroked her neck with one hand as she nuzzled the other for a treat. Like a magician, he drew a carrot from his pocket.

For a moment Matt and Ann stood silently in front of the horse. When Blue Chip returned to her hay, Matt directed Ann back into the night. Without the protection of the barn to block the wind, it was much colder. With gentle pressure on her shoulder, he halted their progress to gaze out over the pastures that ended in a tree-blackened border.

"It's so flat here."

"Not like northern Georgia," Ann agreed. Her heart was pounding in an unexpected and disconcerting way.

"More isolated, more remote, but I like it."

His hand tightened slightly, signaling his pleasure in the beauty of the night and the sounds of healthy, well-cared-for horses that came from the barn.

THE REAR DOOR of the stallion barn inched open, black-gloved fingers clutching at the wood to hold it just ajar. In the darkness of the night, the bulky figure was only one more shadow, slightly darker and denser than the others. Instinctively it sought the shadows, crouching as a low curse rumbled deep in the warmly clad chest. Angry eyes followed the leisurely movements of Matt and Ann as they looked out over the pasture. The powerful hands tightened on the door.

Ann Tate would never be safe again. The slow months of waiting had passed. Now it was time for action. She'd brought it on herself, of course. Everything was her fault because she was greedy. And selfish. And arrogant. Those things would be her undoing.

A moan escaped from the figure's open mouth. The cramped body shivered slightly, solid muscle and bone twitching with the need for action. The eyes narrowed on the couple that continued to stand and talk at the pasture fence.

The man Matt was an unexpected element. Nothing that couldn't be dealt with, but his interest in Ann was inconvenient, and wrong. He wasn't acting properly.

"They're acting like lovers," the figure muttered. "You'd think she might remember her husband, but I see my time is running out. She'll have that man caught in her web, tending to her every whim. She must lose everything, all of it, so I can have it."

The figure stood, brushing a cobweb from a leather bomber jacket, and crept farther into the barn, back toward the stall where Easy Dancer contentedly munched his hay. For a long moment one hand stayed on the stall latch.

"Such a beautiful fellow," the voice crooned hoarsely. "Too bad you belong to the wrong person. Too bad everything belongs to the wrong person. Life isn't fair. But judgment day is coming."

"THERE ARE SOME wonderful places to ride. If you can stay awhile tomorrow, I'd like to take you." Ann, speaking with unnatural shyness, felt as if the romantic winter night had invaded her brain. Jeff had tricked her into inviting Matt to stay, and now, stargazing with him at the fence, she didn't want him to leave. There was something disconcerting about him, and she couldn't be certain if it was her reaction to him or another, harder-to-define reason. The darkness hid her confusion.

"I'd love it." There wasn't a heartbeat of hesitation in his reply.

Anticipation and excitement mingled for a second of intense pleasure as Ann looked up to meet his gaze. A slow smile spread across her face, matching his.

"You're not as mischievous as your friends, are you? I don't want to find myself riding some bronc." What he didn't want were the thoughts that came into his head as he looked into her eyes. He'd never seen lips that tempted so unconsciously. He had to remind himself that his work didn't involve, and most assuredly should not include, romantic thoughts of the woman who stood beside him.

"We may cut up among ourselves, but none of us would ever endanger a person or an animal in a practical joke." She almost reached up to touch his cheek, but a shadow moving near the stallion barn caught her eye.

"What is it?" Matt had anticipated her touch and, when it didn't happen, felt a genuine stab of disappointment. Then he saw the look of concern that crossed her face.

"I thought I saw someone going out of the stallion barn." She hesitated a moment, reluctant to leave Matt's side but too concerned to ignore her intuition. "I know it's impossible. No one should be on the grounds at this time except Freddie. He lives in the main barn in an apartment. But if it was Freddie, he would be out here talking your ear off."

Matt's arm circled her shoulders, sending much-needed warmth through her. "Let's check it out," he said. "It was probably a trick of the darkness, but it's easy enough to investigate."

Ann's stride lengthened as she walked toward the barn with Matt beside her. Her first warning of danger was the sound of metal shoes on cement. Matt heard it, too, and they both rushed to the closed door of the barn.

With Matt's help, Ann threw the door open. Easy Dancer stood in the center aisle of the barn, his nose buried in a hundred-pound sack of feed.

Ann's heart froze, but her body reacted with calm deliberation. Like well-rehearsed dance partners, she and Matt separated. Matt moved to the left while Ann went to the stallion's right. They moved slowly, calmly, not betraying their concern.

"Easy, c'mon, boy," Ann soothed, as she unhooked his halter from the stall. Matt guarded the door as she moved to the horse and slipped the halter quickly over his head. Easy nuzzled against her, then tried to turn back to the grain that had spilled on the floor.

"How much do you think he ate?" There was quiet concern in Matt's voice. He'd heard enough nightmarish stories about horses that had somehow been allowed to eat unchecked. The result was often a painful, anguished death. Overeating could result in many problems, among them colic, the number-one killer of horses. Matt held back his own shudder as he looked at the magnificent stallion and thought of the stories of critically twisted guts and death that no veterinarian could cure.

"I don't know. We'll put the feed back in the sack and see how much is missing. I don't know how this feed got in here." Ann shook with fury. She walked Easy to his stall and put him in it. As she closed the door, she carefully examined the latch. It worked perfectly. There was no conclusion to draw except that someone had deliberately opened his door so he could get to the feed.

That someone could still be hiding in the barn. Trying to conceal her fears from Matt, she fumbled with Easy's halter.

Matt put his hands on her shoulders and turned her to face him. "If we hadn't come out here, he could have died. That's enough feed to kill him."

"I know." Ann's voice was shaky. Her eyes searched the darkest shadows at the end of the barn.

"How big was the shadow you saw?" Matt saw the worry on her face and knew she was afraid. Boswell had warned him about possible tricks and last-ditch efforts she might try to save the ranch, but watching Ann's raw fear, he didn't think this was one of them.

"It was just a shadow." She'd had only a sense of dark moving through dark. "I couldn't even guess."

"Well, maybe we should go have a talk with Freddie. Do you keep your feed room secured?"

"Secured, yes, but not locked. It has a wooden slide that can be worked from the inside or out. You see, Ronnie was knocked unconscious and almost burned to death in the barn last year," Ann said, the memory bringing on another case of trembles. "It was so horrible."

"Your barn burned?" Matt's face reflected deep concern. At least she was being open, not trying to hide a fact that some farm owners would have failed to mention.

"Arson, not carelessness," Ann emphasized. "Someone was trying to kill Ronnie, and she happened to be here. Ronnie was a reporter investigating the fight to stop the passage of the bill that legalized horse racing in the state. Anyway, when I had the barn rebuilt, I didn't want a single door that locked. No horse can work the slide, but anyone trapped inside can always get out."

Matt walked over to the spilled feed. The sack was split wide open, so obviously a very sharp instrument had been used. He carefully began to scoop up the scattered feed and refill the sack. After a moment, Ann joined him, moving as if she were in a trance. No one she knew would have hurt Easy. He was a favorite of all of her clients, and many of their mares were scheduled for breeding to him. It didn't make sense.

Together she and Matt cleaned up the feed. To Ann's immense relief, the hundred-pound sack was almost full.

"You were lucky this time." Matt lifted the edge of the sack and shook the feed back inside. "I don't think he could have eaten more than a few pounds. We must have gotten in here just after he got into it."

Relief spread through her. "Thank goodness."

Matt grabbed the end of the sack and pulled it out of the main barn toward the feed room. Ann slid back the wooden latch and held the door for him. Once inside, he stopped. "Let's leave it right here. When it's daylight I want to come back out here and take a look. There might be some clue."

"Who?" Ann's disbelief and misery were in that one word. "If anything happened to Easy, I'd be ruined. Three years ago when Speed Dancer was stolen, it was a blow that made my father give up. Now someone's trying to hurt Easy." As she spoke she drew away from Matt and examined the hayloft above the stallion's stall.

Matt's gaze followed the direction of her eyes. Someone could easily have hidden in the loft for hours. He made a mental note to check it out first thing in the morning. "Could Freddie have accidentally left the stall door opened? Maybe one of the grooms got careless and left the feed here. Maybe—"

"Freddie isn't careless." Ann wasn't angry, just unshakable in her faith in her employee. "Freddie might forget to eat his own meal, or take time out to sleep, but he'd never leave a door unlatched or feed out. And the bag was slashed open, Matt. It wasn't an accident."

He didn't argue the point. From the long, vicious slash he'd seen in the sack, he had to agree with Ann's assessment. The possibilities were so ugly, though, that he wanted to shield her from them.

"Let's go talk with Freddie. Maybe he can shed some light on this. There's a chance it isn't as awful as it looks."

Ann matched her step to his as they hurried to the main barn. Freddie Weston lived in small but comfortable quarters that Ann recently had built for him. After the past year's fire, she wanted someone to live in the barn area, and Freddie, a widower, had readily agreed to the arrangement.

He frequently enjoyed Mannie's delicious meals, and he was conveniently located for the long hours of foaling season.

Her loud knock on the door brought Freddie in a hurry. Like many horsemen, he was ready for whatever might happen on a large farm. "Somebody sick?" he asked, then cast a startled look at Matt.

"Did you close the stallion barn tonight?" Ann asked directly.

"As always," he answered, relaxing a little when he sensed there was no immediate emergency.

"Freddie, I know you wouldn't leave feed in the aisle, but—"

"Feed? In the aisle?" Freddie turned red. "I'm not so simpleminded or senile that I'd leave feed where a horse might get to it. Where was this feed?" He was reaching behind him for his jacket. "Let me have a look."

Ann stalled him with a hand on his shoulder. "It's okay, Freddie," she said, then gestured at the man at her side. "This is Matt Roper, a new client, and he and I took care of it, but tomorrow morning I want you to talk to the staff. There was a hundred pounds of feed, the sack slashed wide open, in the aisle. Easy was out of his stall munching away when we found him."

"Easy!" All signs of anger drained from Freddie's face, replaced by a fearful pallor. "How much did he eat?"

"He's fine, Freddie. Perfectly fine." Ann's concern for the horse shifted to Freddie. He would take this incident personally, as if he'd failed in some way. "There was no damage. Matt and I were out walking and I thought I saw someone near the barn. Just to be safe, we went in to check. I'm afraid..." She hesitated for a moment.

"It appears that the whole incident might have been deliberately planned and executed," Matt finished for her. His dark eyebrows hid the look of suspicion he cast at Freddie.

Perhaps Ann was an innocent victim, a woman who'd misplaced her trust in her staff.

Freddie stiffened, but some color returned to his face. "I'll tell you, if it was one of my boys being careless, he'll pay with his hide."

"I don't think it was anyone on the staff," Ann said. "Just talk with them, see if they can tell you anything. If someone has been hanging around here, then we need to stop it. If it was some juvenile prank, someone making trouble without understanding the consequences, then we'll have to find a way to stop it."

"Is there anyone who might patrol the barns, at least for the rest of tonight and maybe for a few days?" Matt asked. "If the intruder is still around..." He cast a worried look toward the area where Blue Chip was kept.

"I'll take the rest of tonight and set up a watch for a week. See how things go then," Freddie said. "In fact—" he was in his jacket and pulling on his gloves "—I'm going out to check on Mr. Easy right now. It might not hurt to give him a turn or two in the grass."

Ann started to protest that he hadn't eaten enough to warrant walking, but Matt's hand on her waist stopped her. All three were silent as they left the apartment. Freddie went straight to Easy's stall and began a soft, soothing conversation with the horse as he led him out onto the grass and let him graze.

"It's better to let Freddie work with the horse. He obviously feels responsible, and this is something he can do to help," Matt said.

"You're right." Ann shook her head. The fright was over, but a deep, nagging worry for the safety of her stallion had taken its place.

"Are you okay?" He couldn't help the concern he felt for her. It was clear she cared for her stallion in the same way he cared for his mare.

She nodded, unable to speak. The scare with Easy made it impossible for her to say a word.

"I think we should go back inside and warm up. Easy's fine, and he's in wonderful hands. I'm sure Blue Chip is fine, too. No one would be stupid enough to attempt a second 'accident' tonight."

Ann read his comment as concern for his horse. "Matt, this has never happened here before. I realize it looks bad, especially to someone who's leaving a horse here for care, but you have to understand, this incident is unprecedented."

"Let's talk about it inside," Matt responded, moving her toward the warmth of the house.

The fire had died almost to embers, and Matt stirred it back to life and added more wood. Ann started to pour them both more brandy, but Matt waved her back into her chair.

"Relax for one minute. I think I'm capable of pouring two small glasses of liquor." He was back at her side in a moment, brandy in hand.

"Who's the first person you can think of who means you harm." He meant to startle her. If this wasn't a setup, if this was a direct threat, Matt felt an obligation to help. Her answer would also give him something to go on for his clients' interest in her ranch. A person with enemies had weaknesses.

The directness of his question made her shudder, and his fingers closed over hers on the glass as he steadied her hand.

"This is going to sound like Pollyanna, but there isn't anyone. Not anyone who hates me enough to hurt Easy."

"No business competitors? Old enemies?"

"No one. Honestly." Ann's blue eyes were wide, showing her worry and fear. "If there was someone, I'd tell you. Easy's safety is the most important thing in the world to me. There are people who dislike me, I suppose. Everyone suffers that. But no one hates me enough to hurt Easy."

Matt was impressed with her forthright words, her honesty. But to protect her stallion, and his mare, she had to understand the possible dangers. "Ann, think. It could mean the horse's life. Next time."

The certainty with which he spoke made her heart pound. "Next time? What makes you think there will be a next time? It was probably a prank."

"Because I don't believe some high-school kid sneaked into your barn and dragged a hundred pounds of feed around to a horse in some sort of stupid initiation."

"Matt, kids are always doing wild things!" Her protest was too vehement.

"I'm not defending teenagers. God knows I did my share of hell-raising, but this wasn't a joke." It might well have been a very thorough setup, though, he thought. A person in financial distress might not have been above contemplating a little insurance money.

Ann shook her head stubbornly. "I can't believe that someone would deliberately do something that terrible. Easy could have been killed."

"Exactly. And if that's the case, Blue Chip and every other horse might be in danger." As soon as the words left his mouth, Matt wanted to eradicate the shock and hurt in her face. They didn't have to discuss the situation at that moment. Tomorrow, after he'd investigated the barn, he might have something more than his suspicions.

He cupped her face with his hand and then knelt down beside her chair. "You've had enough for one night." Their eyes were level and he was only a few inches from her mouth. Damn her vulnerability, the honest distress he read in her eyes. He took the hand that held her glass and lifted the drink to her lips. "Now take a sip."

She did as he told her, warmed by the fire of the liquor and by his gaze. "Matt, I . . ." His finger touched her lips.

"Don't talk." He smiled. "Don't talk or think. Take another sip." He nodded at her glass.

She started to argue, but instead took a small swallow of the brandy. It was fiery, soothing.

"Relax," he encouraged her.

A long moment passed as they looked at each other. Against all better judgment, past experiences and solid vows, Matt knew he was attracted to her. In only one short day, her intelligence, warmth and humor had won his respect. And she was damned attractive.

He stood, reining in the tender thoughts Ann kindled without even trying. He reminded himself that he'd come to Mississippi to see about his horse and a potential investment for his clients. His future depended on Blue Chip's safety. Involvement with Ann Tate would not be a smart move.

Taking his cue, Ann started to rise, but Matt's hand on her shoulder stopped her. From the floor by the chair he picked up her glass and gave it to her. "Finish your drink. You need to relax and then get some sleep. I'm going out for one more look at the horses."

The silence between them lengthened. She drew a determined breath and forced a smile to her lips. So, Matt Roper didn't feel his mare was safe. She could hardly blame him, but she also couldn't help feeling the sting that came with his behavior.

"Before you go, finish your drink, too." She nodded to the sofa across from her. "We've been so concerned with my reaction to what's happened, I haven't had a chance to ask you some questions I'm curious about. How did you get Blue Chip?"

He shifted so that he could look into her eyes. "Blue Chip is a long story, but I'll give you the shortened version. When my wife and I decided to divorce, she took the children. I had one small investment left, and I cashed it in and bought a filly from an old man I'd met one year at the races. He was as far down on his luck as I was, and the filly was the only thing he had left." Matt shook his head as he recalled the story. "It was the best deal I ever made. That horse gave me something to focus on, to dream about."

The story was more than Ann had bargained for. With it had come a big hunk of Matt's past life. She could see the pain hidden behind his eyes, and in the self-deprecating smile he gave. His earlier remark about trusting women zinged home.

"You have children?" Compassion for a man separated from his family rekindled the tenderness in her voice.

"They're with their mother." His tone was undercut with anger. "Monica and I strongly disagree about certain values and what constitutes an important environment for children."

Ann restrained herself from probing further. Matt's raw emotions appeared too volatile. "Blue Chip was a wise choice on your part."

"Sometimes you have no choice." The desolation in his voice hid a stronger emotion she couldn't read.

"We all gamble, Matt. All of us." She didn't add that for some, like her ex-husband, gambling had been a disease. She'd never even had an inkling of his debts until he was gone.

"I gather you, too, have been in a position to risk something?" He lounged back on the sofa, but his eyes zeroed in on her face. At last he was getting to something he needed to know.

"After my father got ill," she said, "the logical thing to do was sell the ranch. I knew he was dying, but we both decided to pretend it wasn't happening. While we were pretending Dad wasn't sick, we also pretended we had enough money. Robert and I lived here. As Jeff told you, the house has two separate wings. We were on the verge of pulling out of the hole when Robert left and a valuable horse was stolen." She shrugged to hide her emotions. "You've heard it all by now. It's ironic that Dad's death and the insurance payments from Sky Dancer's death were the very things that allowed me to keep the ranch. For a few months, though, it seemed I would lose everything."

"And you gambled and kept it all."

"So far." Ann sighed, so busy with her own thoughts she wasn't aware of his scrutiny. "If anything happened to Easy, though, it would be the end."

"Speaking of that, I want to check out that feed room in the daylight before anyone else gets in there," Matt said.

"That isn't necessary. Freddie will take care of it." Ann touched his arm. "You've really done more than enough. If you hadn't insisted on that walk, Easy might not be alive now."

"That was good fortune. If your friend Jeff hadn't put you in the position of having a guest forced on you, I wouldn't have been here. The domino effect of life." He was smiling now, all traces of pain gone from his eyes.

"Yes, thank goodness for Jeff."

Matt grasped her shoulders and gave her an impulsive squeeze. "Good night, Ann." He quickly slipped into his jacket. A blast of cold air surrounded Ann as he left the house.

Picking up their glasses, Ann made sure the fire was safely contained before she went to her own room. As she was undressing, she heard Matt return and continue down the hall to the guest room. In bed, she remained awake for a long time.

Months had passed since she'd thought of Robert, but now she went over the familiar ground of his departure. She'd suspected he was seeing someone else. The marriage had been rocky. But nothing had prepared her for the theft of Speed Dancer. Robert was selfish and a chronic gambler, but he'd never come across as a thief.

Rolling over on her hot pillow, Ann flung her arms behind her head. Robert was a ghost from the past. He'd done his damage and gone. Matt Roper was another matter and his potential for unsettling her very careful life made her heart rate increase and her mind caution her to run for cover.

Unable to remain in bed, she went to the window and looked out into the night. Without a light on in her bedroom, she had a clear view of the stallion barn, the back pasture and the woods that surrounded an old abandoned church.

As her eyes adjusted to the moonlight, a movement near the edge of the woods caught her attention. A dark, bulky figure stood by a large oak.

Ann blinked, focusing harder. The figure didn't move. At such a distance she couldn't be certain if it was a person or a small tree. But it seemed to be watching her.

Frozen with dread, Ann couldn't move away from the window. She didn't dare take her eyes off the shadow.

A gust of February wind whipped through the trees, bending branches into a lively, frantic dance. The figure turned and disappeared into the woods like a phantom.

Gripping the window ledge, Ann strained to see. She found only emptiness, dark shadows mingling and dancing in the silvery night.

Though her heart was pounding, she tried to think rationally. She couldn't swear the shadow was a person. It was too far away, too indistinct. There was only the sense that it watched *her*. Only an instinct that warned her to remember the other shadow. The one in Easy's barn.

Chapter Three

First light was streaking across the sky. Matt forced his body out from beneath the warm blankets and pulled the soft jeans on over his long legs. He plunged his arms into his shirt, hastily tucked in the tail, then donned his boots and jacket. He opened the bedroom door that led out onto a veranda. With twelve long strides he was in the pecan orchard and headed toward the barn. His investigation had taken on a more compiex nature than he'd initially intended, and he wanted the element of surprise. If Ann Tate was hiding anything, the best chance of finding it would involve good timing.

In the few scraps of paperwork the Winner's Circle had forwarded, Boswell clearly stated that Dancing Water Ranch was in a precarious position and that Ann was an inefficient and desperate woman. Because of the last-minute nature of Boswell's request, Matt hadn't been able to conduct the proper checks. He'd hoped an eyewitness investigation would be all that was necessary. Now he regretted his assignment. He'd agreed to the job knowing from his work as a broker that chance, luck and willingness to seize the moment were the most important ingredients for financial gains. Investigating the ranch for the Winner's Circle had seemed easy enough while talking to Boswell on the phone. That was before he'd met Ann Tate.

The horses greeted him with soft whinnies, but he had no time to talk to Blue Chip. He went straight to the stallion barn and into the feed room. Throwing open the doors to a burst of morning sunlight, he started his examination.

The feed sack was just as he and Ann had left it. He examined the room and found the symmetry of the carefully stacked feed disturbed so slightly that it took intense scrutiny to detect it. The errant sack had been pulled down from the others. Deliberately. Then the act had been almost completely hidden. Though he searched the area thoroughly, there was no evidence of the sharp object used to slash the sack.

As he climbed the ladder to the hayloft, he couldn't forget the look of terror on Ann's face when she saw Easy eating the feed. Matt didn't have to guess how much that stallion meant to her. Easy was the continuation of a family dream. As he well knew, dreams could be obtained, but once they'd been brutally destroyed, they were almost impossible to rebuild. The ranch was also a family dream. Was it possible that Ann Tate was a woman who might sacrifice one for the other?

He found the overhead lights and switched them on as he moved through the gloomy walls of sweet, fresh hay. Lofts were perfect places to hide. As a young boy he'd often played with his cousins when they visited his grandfather's farm in Texas. By carefully burrowing in among the bales, a full-grown person could hide, undetected and comfortable for some time.

He toured the entire loft row by row. In the far back corner he found what he was looking for—a small niche, just big enough for one person to rest in comfortably. The hay was pressed down flat.

Footsteps sounded below him—a soft, careful tread.

Matt crept to the edge of the loft. Below him a thin, nervous man was peering into Easy's stall. He finally opened the door and entered.

Gathering his strength, Matt crouched and then leaped. He landed lightly on his feet at the stall door.

"Hey!" The man threw up his hands and backed away from the door. The bucket he held in his hands sloshed water all over him. "Who are you?"

"A better question is who are you?" Matt blocked the stall doorway. With his hands clenched and ready for a fight, he was a formidable presence.

The thin man dropped the bucket and stepped back. "I'm a groom. Marshall Nicholls. I was checking Easy's water. Ms. Tate keeps extra water for him and every morning I clean the bucket." He looked past Matt, as if he wanted to make a break for it.

"What do you know about last night?" Matt had relaxed, but he still wasn't ready to let Nicholls depart.

"Nothing. I just got to work a little early today. I thought I'd get a jump on my chores, so I could leave a little early." Nicholls shifted from foot to foot. "Is something wrong with Ms. Tate?" His thin face puckered in a worried frown. "She's been under a lot of strain."

Matt's suspicions melted away completely. The man was only doing his job, and he obviously didn't know anything about the feed incident. But he did know something about Ann, and about her business.

"Yes, I've noticed Ann has been worried. I guess financial troubles are enough to make anyone upset." He knew it was a stab in the dark, but he had a job to do.

"That's right. And since her dad and the business with her husband...well, it's been touch and go." Nicholls bent to pick up the bucket. "This is a hard life for a woman on her own." He cast a worried glance at Matt, then nervously glanced into the barn. "I'd better get on with my work." As Matt stepped aside, Nicholls hurried past him and out of the barn.

MATT AND FREDDIE were sitting at the kitchen table drinking coffee when Ann walked in. She glanced at the clock. It was only seven, but it was obvious that both men had been up for a while.

"Matt found some serious evidence," Freddie said. "Someone deliberately dragged that sack out of the feed room, and worse than that, they were probably hiding in the hayloft."

His words were like a blow to her stomach. Before she could react, Matt was at her side, his hand supporting her elbow as he opened the cupboard on the pretext of looking for a cup. His real interest was getting a closer examination of her. It was impossible to tell if she was acting.

"Freddie doesn't mince words, does he?" Matt asked, trying to lighten the tension. "I was going to break it to you gently."

"Sorry, Miss Ann," Freddie said. "It's just that I'm so hopping mad I could spit nails. When I catch the bastard who tried to hurt Easy, he'll wish he'd died at birth. When he comes back, I swear..."

Matt's warning look silenced the older man. He'd deliberately mentioned a future attack to Freddie, to gauge his reaction. If Boswell was right and Ann was planning a scam, he wanted to catch her at it.

"What makes you think he'll come back?" Ann looked from one man to another. "What else did you find out?"

Matt examined his coffee cup. "I wish I could say we found some clue, but we didn't. We just found the evidence that someone was in the barn. We've no idea who, or if they'll be back."

Ann felt her heart slow a little. She took the cup from Matt and poured some coffee. "But you do think whoever it was will be back?" She swung around to face both men.

"Matt says, and I agree, that it was too deliberate. Someone wanted to hurt Easy. That someone didn't succeed. There's a good chance he'll be back." Freddie's face hardened. "And when he does, I'll be ready for him." He glanced at the clock and drained his coffee. "I left word at the barn that I wanted everyone together at seven-fifteen. I'd better get out there and let the rest of the staff know to look sharp."

As the kitchen door closed behind Freddie, Matt gave Ann a solemn look. "He's a wonderful old man. Very fierce about you and your animals." During his early-morning conversation with Freddie, his suspicions about the man had seeped away. Freddie considered Ann family. He'd do anything for her, and Matt didn't think he was capable of committing an illegal act. At least not knowingly.

"Maybe I'd better call the sheriff," she said.

"It wouldn't be a bad idea to file a report," Matt agreed. "That way it's on record—" He stopped, his eyes on her face.

"If someone kills Easy it's on record so the insurance will pay off. That's what you were going to say, wasn't it?" Anger touched her cheeks, but it wasn't anger at Matt.

"It's a practical thought, but I realized this wasn't a moment for practical thoughts. My finance background, I'm afraid." He waited, watching her closely.

An unexpected tingle of tears made it difficult for her to swallow. "It's hard to be practical when someone is trying to hurt something you care about." She picked up the phone and dialed the sheriff's office. Ten minutes later she'd completed a report to a not-very-interested deputy. She sighed and hung up the phone. "That bozo didn't believe any horse could be worth enough money to try and kill."

Evidence of a sleepless night touched her eyes like the fragile remnants of a morning mist. For a second Matt understood her despair, but he squelched the sympathy. He got up and poured them both coffee. "Any chance we can still make that ride you promised me?"

"I think we need it now more than ever. Let's have some breakfast and we'll be off."

They'd just finished eating when Cybil Matheson's large green truck pulled into the yard.

"Expecting the vet?" Matt asked as he looked out the window.

"No, not this morning." Ann went to the window and lifted it. "Cybil! We're in here!" she called loudly, motioning the vet to come into the house.

Cybil hesitated, then walked briskly toward them, entering without knocking and coming straight to the kitchen.

"Have some coffee." Ann signaled to the cupboard and the pot. "You know where everything is."

The vet cast a questioning glance at Matt, who met her look with a blank expression.

"What are you doing out this way?" Ann asked. "I didn't expect to see you until Saturday."

"I was next door at Louie's. Sick cow. I knew I could count on you for some coffee. Everything okay here?"

"By sheer luck, yes." Ann got up and removed the plates from the table and poured Matt more coffee. Her hand trembled slightly, a fact that didn't go unnoticed by Cybil.

"I sense something is afoot," she said, looking from Matt to Ann.

"Easy was afoot last night," Ann replied, sitting back down. "Someone let him out of his stall and left feed for him to get to. If Matt hadn't insisted on walking last night, Easy could have died."

Cybil held her coffee cup halfway to her mouth, halted in midair. "Someone tried to hurt Easy? Who would do such a thing?"

"Exactly what I want to know," Ann said, "and what we intend to find out!"

"Is he hurt?"

"No, he didn't get more than a couple of pounds," Matt answered. "But it was a hundred-pound sack. It could have killed him."

"Twenty pounds could have killed him," Cybil said. "Whoever did it wanted to make sure." She looked down at the table. "This is almost impossible to believe."

"I felt that way last night, but today I just want to find out who did it and convince them that it was a seriously bad idea." Ann's cheeks reddened with anger.

"Listen, I've got ten more calls this morning. Thanks for the coffee," Cybil said, rising. "I can't believe this happened. I'm going to call the other farm owners and let them know. We need to band together and find the person responsible. Last night it was this barn. Tonight it could happen somewhere else."

An icy dagger of fear traced down Ann's spine. "Cybil, you make it sound like some maniac, someone who hurts animals for the fun of it."

"Yes, I think we are talking about a psychopath on the loose. I mean, can you think of anyone who hates you enough to hurt Easy? If it isn't personal, then it's psychopathic, right?"

Her cold logic made Ann more afraid than she'd ever been. She met her old friend's eyes. "You may be right, Cybil. As much as I hate to think about it, you may be right."

Cybil turned to Matt. "I didn't realize Ann had someone to help her, but I'm glad to see you here. Are you staying long?"

"He's—"

"Yes," Matt answered. "In fact, I plan to be here for a lengthy stay. If someone has targeted Ann's place for mischief because they think she's alone, then they're sadly mistaken." He almost bit his tongue. "Besides, my horse is here," he added hastily. From the depths of his nature had come the urge to protect Ann, and simultaneously to stake some kind of claim.

"Well spoken." Cybil turned to Ann. "I like a man with a bit of chivalry in him. I'll see you two on Saturday." She pushed through the kitchen door and was gone, leaving Ann and Matt to look at each other.

"I thought you had to get back to work as a broker." Ann didn't know if she was glad or distressed. An overanxious boarder was something she didn't need. But Matt was more than that.

"I had planned on taking vacation time to hang around and learn about horse breeding, maybe keep an eye on Blue Chip. I intended to look for a place along the coast, but now, if it's okay with you, I'd like to stay on here for another night or two. Just in case." He looked down and bent to dust a fleck of mud from his boot.

Ann's heart tipped. "You really think whoever it was will be back? Tonight?"

"Tonight or very soon. Freddie agrees with me. Unless, of course, Dr. Matheson is correct and he moves on to another farm."

"Unless it's someone who wants to ruin me." Ann's voice was low and scared and she lowered her eyes.

Once again Matt found himself acting impulsively. His hand touched her cheek, a soft stroke of comfort.

"Let's take that ride," Ann said. "I need some time to sort through all of this."

Her words were stopped short by the racket of barking dogs and the arrival of a truck.

"Freddie let the dogs out," Ann explained. "Suni, Shadow and Shasta, my faithful guardians."

"But they didn't bark . . ."

"They were in the house when you came up, and they know Dr. Matheson so there's no need to bark."

"And last night? They didn't bark at us, or the intruder." His suspicions sharpened once again.

"I've thought about that," Ann said. "Freddie must have had them in his apartment. I'll tell him to leave them out tonight. They aren't bad dogs, but they'd tear someone strange to shreds."

"I'd say they were very good dogs, then. Who is it they're terrorizing now?" Indeed, the German shepherds were ferociously besieging a stranger.

Ann looked out the window at the black truck painted with a sign. "Oh, drat," she said. "It's Bill Harper."

"Someone we don't like?" Matt asked in a teasing tone that hid his acute interest. "I thought you were Pollyanna."

"Someone we heartily don't like," Ann responded. "He's a local builder with a few poor horses. He was working on part of the new racetrack just west of here, and I'm afraid he's going to be slightly upset with me."

Matt signaled for her to continue as they put on their coats.

"I rejected his bid on some work. I'm on the racing commission, and even though his bid was the lowest, his work has been shoddy in the past. I won't have stands that might collapse and kill innocent spectators." She ran her hand through her short hair. "Maybe you should stay here while I handle this guy."

"And miss all the excitement? Not a chance." He held the door for her and they walked out together.

To say Bill Harper was angry would have been an understatement. He was captive in his truck, unable to even put a foot on the ground. The three shepherds had stopped barking. They sat around his truck door waiting for one wrong move.

"Call off this pack of wolves!" Harper ordered as soon as he saw Ann. "These animals should be tied up. They're dangerous."

"Only if you come on their property," Ann said pointedly.

The dogs never gave Matt a second glance. Their intelligent brown eyes remained on Harper's tall, angry form.

"What are you doing here, Bill?" Ann asked.

"I got business with you." He threw a look at Matt. "Private business."

"I rejected your bid because the work you've done in the past was poor. I stated the reason publicly, and I'm not changing my mind. So you can leave. Now." Ann turned to walk away.

"Not so fast, Ms. Tate." His words were filled with fury. "My bid was the lowest, and I intend to take some legal action on this, you hear? You can't let a personal thing get involved in business."

"The law reads, the lowest and *best* bid, Mr. Harper. I don't consider your bid the best. In fact, based on your other work, I think it was the worst bid we received. I'm not backing down, and I invite you to take us to court. My lawyer, Jeff Stuart, is confident that he can prove I acted wisely and in the best interest of the public. Since we are building the track with public funds, I have the responsibility of the public trust, Mr. Harper."

She turned to Matt. "Now, I believe we were going for a ride?"

Without a backward glance she linked her arm through Matt's and they walked toward the barn. Behind them, they heard the angry man gun the truck's engine and spin out as he drove away.

"I thought you said no one disliked you?" Matt said softly. He was impressed with her righteous anger and ideals. "That man despises you and everything you stand for. I get the feeling he doesn't like a woman messing up his business arrangements."

"That's the problem. In the past he's had a sweetheart relationship with some of the elected officials. That was why Jeff asked me to sit on the board for the racing commission. Jeff wanted to make sure the track was built with the best materials at the least cost. Bill Harper was thinking he'd pull his usual kickback stunt. It just didn't work with me."

Matt started to say something, then changed his mind. Harper had implied some personal conflict. "Never short on convictions, are you?" he asked instead.

"Never short on opinions, Jeff would say." She shook her head. "I'm glad you're staying a few days."

"I don't think you should underestimate Harper." The realization that Ann might actually be in danger made his words forceful. Was she victim? Organizer of a scam? Or both? He couldn't decide.

"Bill Harper knew my father." Ann's brow wrinkled as she spoke. "It's difficult to make you understand, but Harper is a crook and a con man. He doesn't pose physical danger, though."

"I disagree." Matt turned her to look at him. "I got the distinct impression he doesn't like anyone or anything that interferes with his plans—and he might take whatever steps necessary to achieve his ends."

The seriousness of Matt's expression made her stop. He was truly worried. "I don't think Harper is involved, but I promise you that I'll be careful in my dealings with him."

As they entered the barn, several grooms nodded at Ann and grinned at Matt. At the tack-room door, Marshall Nicholls gave Matt a nervous smile.

"They think we've been up to something," Matt whispered in her ear. The light tone was something he desperately needed.

"They can think anything they wish, as long as they take good care of my horses," Ann responded, not the least disturbed. "I hear Blue Chip."

The mare was beckoning her master, and Matt walked faster as he neared her stall. She greeted him with a warm whinny and a push from her head.

"I know she's ready to get out of that stall, but I'd like to wait until tomorrow to turn her out. Perhaps this afternoon you might want to work her on a lunge line for ten minutes, just to take the kinks out of her from that long trailer ride," Ann suggested.

"Good idea. When we get back I'll trot her around and then let her nibble a little grass. Your pastures look terrific." Whatever else he might find at Dancing Water, he could not fault Ann on her facilities or maintenance. If she were inept and inefficient, the white fences and lush pastures said otherwise.

"For once we had enough rain in the fall and not too much in the summer." Ann shook her head, eyebrows rising. "The farm life. Who would have thought when I dreamed of being a breeder that I would know fertilizer contents, pH balance, soil tests and precipitation probabilities?"

"All much more interesting than margins, mutual funds and calls," Matt replied without a hint of sympathy.

"The least you could do is feel sorry for me," Ann teased.

"With this life? Sorry for you? Spend a week in my office in Atlanta. Then talk about feeling sorry."

They left Blue Chip and wandered down to a tack room where Ann selected saddles and bridles. She'd sent a groom into the pasture to retrieve two horses, and by the time she had grooming tools and tack ready, the young boy was back with two geldings.

"Matt, this is Skooter. He's your mount, and I'm going to ride Fool's Dream. They're both safe, dependable horses."

Matt went to work with the curry brush and a smile. "I trust you completely, Ms. Tate. At least in the selection of horses."

In twenty minutes they were mounted and walking down the long shell drive. Skooter danced, throwing his head up and down in anticipation of a run.

Ann noticed that Matt's hands were firm yet gentle as he contained the horse.

"Do you ride Blue Chip?" she asked.

"Yes, when I can. She's remarkably tolerant of me."

"You trained her?"

"Well, she isn't exactly highly trained. She accepts a rider and seems to enjoy it. We don't do anything fancy."

They left the ranch behind, crossing the road and heading west through a heavily wooded area. The path was wide enough for both horses to walk abreast.

"Not many people have the patience to teach a green horse. I'm impressed."

"Then you're easily impressed," Matt said. He looked at her perfect posture in the small English saddle. "You grew up on a horse, didn't you?"

"Yes. Jumping at the age of five, all of that. It was a wonderful way to grow up."

They nudged the horses into a long, working trot. Matt took the lead and Ann watched him rise and fall with each stride. He was a handsome, well-built man.

"Let's see if your balance holds up at the canter." She tightened her legs, and Fool's Dream shot forward. Skooter sprang after her.

The path was clear for several miles and Ann gave herself to the ride, to the feel of the horse surging over the ground. No matter how often she rode, no two horses were the same. There was always the sense of discovery, of adventure.

Matt drew up beside her, and she cast a quick look at his face, alive with pleasure. He was in perfect rhythm with Skooter, as much a part of the horse as man can be. Once again her attention was drawn to his hands. Holding the reins lightly yet with assurance, they were so sensitive that he responded to the slightest motion of the horse's mouth. Extraordinarily sensitive.

"Ann! Duck!"

Matt's warning came just in time and she flattened herself on Dream's neck to avoid a low-hanging pine limb.

"Thanks for the warning." They slowed their horses to a walk and ambled along side by side, twisting and turning through pine forest and soybean fields currently barren of crops.

The winter sun was warm on Ann's back, and she was completely at ease. Matt was the perfect companion. When they came to a grassy knoll surrounded by several oaks, Matt stopped his horse and Ann followed suit.

Their legs brushed together and Ann found herself studying the ground. The grass looked warm and inviting in the shelter of the trees. She was reminded of a place very special to her, a secluded spot surrounded by trees and warmed by the sun. There was plenty of privacy, a place she'd like to share with Matt.

"Contemplating the weather?" Matt was amused.

"I predict it's going to be a warm winter. Much warmer than expected." Ann felt the blush touch her skin, but she didn't care. Matt's company had pushed away the worries of the night before, and she was happy.

Standing beside Ann, Matt watched the expressions that crossed her face. He saw excitement, playfulness and happiness. There were no artful masks, no calculations. She was exactly as he'd first read her, a woman who met the day with spirit. Either that or an exceptional actress.

Marshall Nicholls's conversation returned to him. He'd implied that Ann was under a lot of strain. Matt tightened his legs around his mount. "Let's head back," he said. A nagging feeling about Blue Chip settled over him like a fog.

Chapter Four

Tango Dancer, Jeff's yearling, reared at the end of his line and plunged to the left. Dawn Markey dug in her heels and hauled, catching the young horse up short and pulling him around to face her. Dawn had neither Ann's height nor Cybil's wiry build. What she did have was an unerring instinct for when to insist and when to yield with a young animal, and the determination and patience to win in the long run.

From her view out the office window, Ann watched, a smile touching her lips. Matt was leaning against a fence, observing, and it had taken all of his self-restraint not to rush over and assist Dawn. Ann's smile widened. He was learning.

Ann was well aware that Dawn Markey didn't need help. Spirited yearlings were an everyday part of her life. The surprising thing about Matt was that he, too, saw and understood Dawn's abilities. Now if only he'd believe Dancing Water Ranch was completely competent to care for his mare. The fact that he was still on the ranch, despite the reasons he gave for staying, led her to believe he still had tiny reservations about Blue Chip's well-being.

As Ann watched, Dawn made several gestures to Matt, explaining as she worked. He moved forward and took the line from Dawn, assuming the position she told him. Tango Dancer began to move around Matt in a circle, giving a flashy trot and bucking slightly.

Her gaze lingered on Matt, his calm, confident handling of the colt. He had "the touch," and Tango Dancer responded. Before she could stop the thought, she remembered her own reaction to Matt, how good it felt to be in his company. She lowered her gaze to the papers before her and began checking feed inventories, vet supplies and the routine items of farm life. When she looked up again, the small pasture was empty. Matt had obviously gone on to another chore.

Picking up the phone on her desk, she dialed the number for the house and left directions with Mannie for a big dinner. Matt would be ravenous. With a flourish she signed her name to the last check and then hurried outside.

As she groomed Miss Hopper, Ann slipped back to the past and heard again her father's admonition to sell the stable's own horses. Patting the well-muscled rump of the mare, she let a grin of satisfaction touch her lips. She hadn't done it, and now she was glad.

Financially it didn't make the most sense in the world to keep horses that weren't quality breeders. But she'd had Miss Hopper and a few others since she was a teen. Though the mare would never be bred to Easy, she had taken Ann over thousands of jumps in hundreds of shows. She'd earned the right to a good life of light riding and love.

"Daydreaming?" Matt's deep voice was unmistakable.

"Visiting the past." She grinned. "I saw you working with Dawn."

"I was hoping you'd come out and join us." He was close enough to see the amber highlights in her thick hair, the clear curve of her jaw. Since they'd returned to the ranch after their ride, one thing he'd learned was that Ann had one hell of a trainer working for her in Dawn Markey. She possessed skill, sensitivity and a certain hauteur and beauty, which virtually made her the material of legends. Matt let his gaze linger on Ann's happy face. He'd stumbled into a nest of strong, compelling women, and the one before him was the most fascinating of all.

The directness of his gaze unsettled her. Hands poised in the act of grooming Miss Hopper, she paused.

"I wanted to join you but I had work to do." She resumed grooming the horse, trying to concentrate on the circular motions of the curry brush.

"Dawn said she's going to ride Easy later. Will you be there?" So far, his investigation had yielded little of value. He felt like a criminal, but he wanted a chance to look in her office without her there.

Tightening the girth of the saddle on Miss Hopper's back, Ann hesitated. Somehow, when Matt asked it, the simplest question carried many complicated possibilities.

Ann swung into the saddle. "I'm going up to the little arena behind the pecan orchard. There are a few jumps there, and I'm going to give Miss Hopper some exercise. When I finish, I'll look for you and Dawn."

Ann nudged the horse forward, away from Matt. But she could not so easily leave her thoughts behind. Up until the moment Matt Roper had arrived, Dancing Water Ranch had been a haven, an escape from romantic entanglements. She bent down to adjust her stirrup and hide her face from Matt's watchful eye. Since her divorce, she'd expended her energy in hard work and single-mindedly saving the ranch. Now, though, she had to face Matt. And her budding feelings of attraction for him.

"Mind if I watch you work?" Matt walked alongside her, his shoulder just at her thigh, almost touching. To hell with investigating, he said to himself in a rush of spontaneity.

"I thought you were going to help Dawn with the stallion?" Ann said.

"There's plenty of time, and I'd rather watch you."

Ann tried to ignore the color that crept into her cheeks. They remained silent as he opened the gate for her and she trotted Miss Hopper around, warming her up.

The mare was eager for a ride, and she circled and cantered on cue.

"I daresay she could still take a blue in any class," Matt said, watching horse and rider as they executed lead changes and turns with precision. "That is, as long as you're in the saddle."

"I've retired her," Ann called out, never taking her eyes off the course. The thought crossed her mind that it would simplify things greatly if she told Matt she had retired from the painful problems of love. But now she wasn't certain that statement was completely true.

Instead of saying anything, she took Miss Hopper over a small jump, turned, then cantered to a wooden jump painted to resemble a stone wall. The mare took it with Thoroughbred grace. After a few more jumps, Ann pulled her up and patted her neck. "That's all she needs, just enough to let her know we can still do it. Now I'll work on the flat and then we're finished."

"I think I'll wander on over to see Freddie. He promised to explain feeding ratios to me." Matt reached up and touched her knee lightly. He'd watched her closely as she rode, and he had the strangest impression she was fighting a terrible battle with herself. He could sense her profound hesitation in his presence. Though he wanted to ask her what was troubling her, he didn't. His own feelings were too uncertain, so he forced his mind to cling tightly to his reason for staying at the ranch—to learn the truth about Ann Tate and her business.

Ann still felt the trace of his touch as he walked away. Her eyes remained on his back until he disappeared among the pecan trees. He was an unsettling man with his intense stares and questions. A strange and troubling man.

FREDDIE LOOKED UP from the feed chart as Cybil Matheson's vehicle turned in at the barn.

"Used to be you couldn't get a vet, and now you can't keep her away from here," he muttered in what Matt had come to recognize as his normal grumbling manner.

"She's good with the horses," Matt pointed out. He'd successfully hidden his disappointment at finding Freddie in Ann's office. As subtly as possible, he'd attempted to draw information from the old man, but Freddie, though he was a knowledgeable source, was also very tight-lipped about Ann's business.

"Good with horses and bossy with men," Freddie allowed. "She'll come in here and start ordering the grooms around like it's her place. Where's Miss Ann?"

"Probably stabling Miss Hopper, or maybe she's already done that and gone back to the house," Matt guessed. He stood up and went to the window. There was no sign of anyone except the blond vet, her black bag swinging in her hand as she entered the barn.

"Maybe I should go out and see if I can help Dr. Matheson."

"Don't bother." Freddie shook his head. "She orders her help when she wants it and doesn't appreciate a kind word of advice. Let her call if she needs someone."

Matt recalled Ann's mentioning something about how Freddie and Cybil rubbed each other the wrong way. He restrained a chuckle and sat back down.

Not five minutes later, Cybil knocked on the office door. She didn't wait for an invitation but stuck her head inside.

"Where's Ann or Dawn?" Her voice was clipped and authoritative.

Freddie immediately bristled. "Do I look like a nanny? I don't keep up with people."

"I didn't mean to imply that you should," Cybil replied, giving Matt an exasperated look. She directed her next question to Matt. "Have you seen Ann?"

"Check the house," he suggested, feeling awkward caught in the tension between the two. "She was riding, but maybe she's inside by now. Is there something I can help you with?"

"Yes, tell Ann that I talked with other farm owners. Ben Johnson said he thought someone was sneaking around his place. In the past week he lost a good saddle and two blankets."

Even Freddie's defensiveness cooled enough to allow him to ask a question. "Anybody else got any mischief to report?"

"Not really. It's hard in a barn because things get misplaced and then show up again. Ben was reluctant to even mention the saddle, but that's a little hard to lose. Still, he pointed out that someone might have borrowed it without asking."

"Yep." Freddie nodded. "That's been known to happen."

"Do you take care of Bill Harper's horses?" Matt asked suddenly.

Cybil shot him a curious glance. "The saints take care of those animals. Bill calls me when it's time for a miracle. Then of course he can blame me for the bad result." She shrugged angrily. "Some people shouldn't be allowed to own animals."

"Then you have the same impression of him that I do," Matt responded, rubbing his chin lightly.

"When did you meet the charming Mr. Harper?"

"This morning. Just after you left."

The loud sound of a beeper interrupted the conversation.

"Damn!" Cybil muttered. "Can I use the phone?"

She didn't actually wait for Freddie's grudging nod. She dialed, asked a few directions and hung up. "Please tell Ann what I told you, and I'll be in touch later," she said. "I've got an emergency." She left without closing the door firmly.

"That woman!" Freddie threw after her, plenty loud for her to hear.

Matt laughed out loud. "She's self-possessed."

"Possessed by orneriness," Freddie contradicted. "It's women like that who make me certain we never should have given them the vote!"

He spoke with such conviction that Matt laughed even harder. "What would Ann say if she heard such a statement?"

"Miss Ann is different. She can run a farm, break a horse and still remain a lady. That Cybil Matheson, I've known her since she was a kid in pigtails, and she has a streak of meanness a mile wide."

"It's a little tough to make it in a man's world, especially a world like veterinary medicine," Matt admonished him softly. "Maybe she's just defensive."

"She's bossy," Freddie said, his jaw unyielding. "Now enough about her. That other female will be in the barn waiting to show off on Easy. You'd better hurry. Ms. Markey gets steamed if her audience keeps her waiting."

Underlying the derogatory remarks about Dawn, Matt detected a sincere note of pride. "I hear you trained Dawn Markey," he whispered in Freddie's ear. Before he turned away, he saw the older man grin. Freddie tried to be a tough nut, but he wasn't always successful.

Matt made it to the stallion barn a few moments before the trainer. He was looking at the wooden slide on the feed-room door when she walked in.

"I can't believe it, either," she said, reading his thoughts about Easy's near accident. Matt was struck again by her resemblance to an Indian princess. "I can't imagine anyone who would deliberately try to hurt Easy Dancer. He's such a dreamboat."

As she talked she took the animal's halter from the peg and opened the door. The words were almost knocked from her as the stallion charged.

"Easy!" she commanded, standing her ground. But it did no good. He reared in his stall, his front hooves aimed at her unprotected shoulders.

Matt dove toward Dawn, pushing her away just in time. Easy's right front hoof grazed his ribs, knocking him into the cement aisle as he shoved Dawn against the wall.

As Matt slammed into the floor, half in and half out of the stall, Dawn grabbed a lunge whip from the wall and rushed back into the stall.

"Easy!" Dawn brandished the whip at the horse in a warning attitude. "Easy!" She held his attention as Matt rolled out of the way.

The normally calm animal rolled his eyes and snaked his head forward, snapping at her face. Without thinking, Dawn brought the butt of the whip down across his nose, breaking his attack.

"What's gotten into him?" She was breathing hard as Matt pulled himself up and went to her side. A sharp, tearing pain buried itself in his ribs and he couldn't draw a deep breath.

Dawn shut the stall door firmly and turned to Matt. The pain etched across his forehead frightened her.

She ran to the barn door and leaned out. "Freddie! Get Ann out here quick!"

Then she was back at his side. "Let's see if we can get over to the feed and sit down," she suggested, giving her shoulder for him to lean on. An angry whinny came from Easy's stall and he threw the weight of his twelve-hundred-pound body against the door. The latch shook.

"I don't know what happened to that horse, but as soon as you're okay, I'm going to find out," Dawn said, talking to distract Matt.

The sound of running feet shot through the barn, and Ann and Freddie rushed into the feed room. Ann took one look at Matt and went to him. The air of reservation she'd worn in the pecan orchard was stripped away.

"Where are you hurt?" she asked.

"Easy caught me in the ribs, but it isn't bad." At last able to draw a breath, Matt was less shaky.

Ann's fingers probed his chest, working around to his side. Though he tried not to flinch, the pain below his left arm was excruciating.

"You might have cracked a rib," she said solemnly. "We need to drive in to the hospital and have it X-rayed. What happened?"

There was an awkward moment of silence as Dawn and Matt exchanged a look. Dawn sighed. "Easy attacked me with his front hooves. If Matt hadn't pushed me aside, I'm afraid he might have killed me."

"Not Easy!" Freddie denied it with words, but he couldn't hide the fear in his voice. "Easy's gentle as a lamb, isn't he, Ann?"

Horses didn't attack people, not without cause, Ann knew. But she also knew that neither Dawn nor Matt would provoke an animal. Something was wrong. Terribly wrong.

"We'll look into this later, when we get back from the hospital. For right now, stay away from Easy's stall. See that he has hay and water, nothing else. And call Cybil Matheson. I want her to check him out."

MATT'S FACE HAD REGAINED its natural, healthy color by the time Ann had him back in the car. She left the hospital parking lot and entered the traffic flow.

"Thank goodness it's not worse than a severe bruise," she said.

"Easy barely caught me with his hoof." Matt kept his voice even. Ann was more upset than she wanted to let on, and he had no intention of provoking her with details of the stallion's misbehavior. The attack was unexpected, but certainly nothing he could lay at Ann's door.

"Exactly what happened?" Ann steeled herself for the unvarnished facts. "That horse has never done anything like that before."

Recognizing her iron will, Matt decided the simplest thing to do was tell exactly what he remembered. "Dawn stepped into his stall and he literally attacked her. I pushed her aside and he caught me with a hoof."

"You didn't happen to see anyone in the barn before you, someone who might have teased Easy?" There wasn't much hope in her voice.

"Honestly, I don't recall anyone else, but I wasn't paying attention." He was paying attention to her now, though, noticing for the first time the small furrow of anger between her eyebrows.

"I know this is small consolation to you, but Easy has never acted like this. I've never seen him show a single aggressive trait. Yes, he's been spirited and rambunctious, but never vicious."

Matt reached across the car and touched her arm. "Ann, he could have been stung by something. There's bound to be a logical explanation for this, and I'm sure you'll find it."

"I don't understand this," she said softly. Pride kept her from revealing the true depth of her worry. Matt was a client, not a confidant. She couldn't tell him that vicious behavior in her stallion could ruin her breeding business. Easy Dancer's temperament, as well as his speed and good genes, was a big selling point.

Grimacing with discomfort, Matt forced his body up so that he was sitting erect.

The two-lane road was empty of traffic, and Ann eased onto the grassy shoulder beside a large tract of pine forest. "Matt, I'm sick about your injury. Are you in terrible pain?"

Matt's gentle fingers turned her face to his. "Don't borrow trouble, Ann. There's a simple explanation for Easy's behavior. Let Cybil find it and then we'll correct it. As for me, by tomorrow I'll be fine."

"If he'd really hurt you . . ."

"Don't talk about it. Just think how much fun I'm going to have recuperating, driving you wild with demands for hot tea and decks of cards."

Ann couldn't resist the grin he gave her. Though her worries weighed heavily, she felt her spirits rise. "You aren't hurt that bad! Dr. Zimlich said to rest at the ranch for a couple of days. That isn't exactly intensive care."

"I'm going to need constant care and attention," Matt assured her.

"You are something," she said as she pulled back onto the road. "You take a disaster and make it into a comedy."

Ann shook her head as she turned into the driveway to the ranch. There was no sign of Cybil or Dawn. Not knowing whether to be relieved or worried, she helped Matt to his room and then hurried out to Freddie's office.

The older man was pacing the floor, his head bent and his hands behind his back. Ann stood in the doorway a moment. She'd only seen Freddie this way when a serious problem threatened the farm.

"Well?" she asked.

Her presence didn't startle him, and he didn't stop pacing.

"We couldn't find anything in the stall to warrant such an outburst. I went over him, as did Dawn, and there was no sign of an injury of any kind."

Ann felt the heavy load of worry land squarely on her shoulders. "You checked inside the stall for bees or wasps, anything?"

Casting her a look that said he'd left no possibility unchecked, Freddie nodded. "I even took the shavings out of his stall, shovel by shovel. There wasn't even a sharp stick that might have jabbed him. How's Matt?"

"Bruised rib, nothing serious."

"We can be thankful for that."

"Did Cybil come?"

"She's only been gone about fifteen minutes. She did some blood tests, said to keep him off grain. She even took a sample of his feed to analyze. I told her it was pointless since I had his rations specially mixed at Dixon's Feed and Supply. She wanted to see it, anyway. Said it could have too high a ratio of protein, like I'd be stupid enough to do that to Easy." Freddie almost shook with disgust. "That woman did everything except accuse me of neglect."

"I'm sure Cybil didn't mean to sound that way." Ann automatically soothed Freddie. She'd been acting as mediator ever since Cybil had come back to the coast and become Dancing Water Ranch's permanent vet.

"She did mean it that way, Miss Ann. If she wasn't the best vet in the whole area, I'd make you choose her or me. But she is the best, and I'm a professional. I can't ask you to give up quality care for the horses just because I don't like her."

Ann sank down into the chair at the desk. "Freddie, what am I going to do?"

"Me and my big mouth." Freddie went to her and rested his hands on her shoulders. "I'm dumping my petty troubles on you when you've got your mind full. But the only thing to do is wait until the blood tests come back. Dr. Matheson said it would be a few days."

"Where's Dawn?"

"She wanted to work Easy on a line, but I told her to stay away from him, at least for today."

Ann reached up and patted Freddie's hand. "Good thinking. After today, I don't want another chance taken. Tomorrow I'll get him out and see what he's about."

She stood, a determined look on her face.

"Miss Ann, stay out of the stallion barn tonight." Freddie's voice was soft with concern.

"Why?"

"He's still in a vile mood. There's no point in your going in there. Give him a chance to calm down and come around on his own. We have no real way of knowing what might have happened to set him off. Give him the benefit. Give him tonight."

Ann paused, her hand on the doorknob. "You're right. I'm going in the house to see about Mr. Roper. I'll be there if you need me."

"Mica John is watching the barn tonight. I gave him permission to use one of the guns from the main house."

The words sent a sickening chill through Ann.

"A gun, Freddie? Do you really think that's necessary?"

Freddie's wrinkles deepened above his eyes and he met her gaze with a crystal-clear one. "Yes, I do. I've asked a man to guard against danger. I can't ask him to do that without giving him a weapon. If I didn't think there was something mighty odd going on around here, I wouldn't ask the man to lose a night's sleep."

Ann walked back around the desk and gave Freddie a hug. "That's a point well taken. I'm lucky to have you here, Freddie. I don't know what I'd do without you."

"Get on in the house and get some rest." He was embarrassed.

"Freddie?" Ann paused at the door once again. "Do you think there might possibly be some connection between last night and Easy's attack today?"

The older man resumed his pacing again. He crossed the office twice before he stopped. "I see no obvious connection. None. But deep in here—" he placed his hand across his heart "—I feel it. And I have to tell you, Miss Ann, I don't like what I feel one bit."

A TIGHT GRIN CREPT over the dry, chapped lips. The day had been long and cold, but at last, it had already started. Fear and suspicions were rife at Dancing Water Ranch. Ann Tate, with her powerful friends and meddling ways, was finally getting what she deserved. She was scared. There was great satisfaction in that knowledge. Now Ann was standing at her bedroom window, watching the darkness and waiting for disaster to strike. The grin widened, splitting the top lip. A tiny trickle of blood oozed.

The eyes, half-hidden beneath a dark, close-fitting hat, closed as a soft humming sound escaped from the partially opened mouth. A familiar fantasy appeared. The image of a large vial filled with clear liquid invaded the fevered brain. Slowly, very slowly, the liquid was drained from the vial by a syringe. As each measure disappeared, the beautiful grounds of Dancing Water Ranch crumbled into ruins.

Perfect. Everything was going perfectly though it had taken such painful planning. Three years of it. Three years of hiding in the shadows and waiting. Long, desperate years. But everything came with determination and patience. Justice was slow, but inevitable.

"It's time to pay, Ann. Time to pay for everything."

The black-clad hand reached for the telephone.

Chapter Five

Balancing the breakfast tray, set with two cups, Ann knocked on the door to the blue guest room. A few hours sleep without interruption had helped her mood, and she was eager to see Matt. He'd been in some pain the night before, though he'd tried to hide it. Dr. Zimlich had stressed the fact that his ribs would be extremely sore for a day or two. No serious effects, though, if he took care of himself.

"Come in." Matt's voice was deliberately weak and pitiful.

"Don't playact with me," Ann said as she entered. "I heard something in here that sounded like a herd of elephants moving around."

Matt was in bed, covers pulled up to his chin. "I wasn't up," he said innocently.

"I should hope not. Dr. Zimlich said a couple of days in bed, and that's exactly what you're going to do."

"What was the name of the nurse in *One Flew over the Cuckoo's Nest*? Was it Miss Raddish?"

"Don't start with me," Ann warned as he eased up and she put the tray across his lap. "I made a bacon-and-cheese omelet and coffee."

Noting the extra cup, Matt looked at her. "I'm feeling much better now that my nurse is here."

Ann's gaze was on his chest, lingering on the well-defined muscles and dark hair. The top edge of a bandage was just visible.

"Dr. Zimlich didn't put that bandage on you." Her hand went instinctively to the cover and pulled it down, revealing more of the bandage, and more of his body.

"I did it myself." Matt pulled the covers back up. "You're very bold this morning. Seen enough?"

"No," Ann said, standing and quickly moving the tray. "What I want to see—" she jerked at the covers "—is what you're up to."

From his waist down, Matt was dressed except for his boots. Ann cast a grim look at him.

"Dr. Zimlich said for you to rest in bed. Do you always sleep in your blue jeans?"

"I wanted a walk." Matt crossed his arms over his chest, wincing at the sudden pain. "I'm not an invalid, you know." All night long Easy's crazed, unexplained behavior had tugged at the corner of his mind. Something didn't wash. He was eager to get up and poke around. If Ann or Freddie, or even Dawn, had tampered with the horse in an effort to set up an insurance scam, he wanted to find out.

"No, but you're my guest, and you've been told to rest. So, I'll wait here for you to change back into something more comfortable to wear in bed." She settled into a chair beside the bed, the tray of food in her hands. "I'm waiting."

"You can't sit here all day and guard me," Matt muttered darkly. "I feel like a prisoner."

"I'll wait as long as necessary," Ann threatened.

With a shake of his head, Matt picked up a pair of pajamas and a robe and went into the adjoining bathroom. When he returned, he dropped the jeans over his suitcase and got back into bed. Ann replaced the tray in his lap, settling down beside him for her cup of coffee.

"Dawn is going to work Easy after lunch. I'll come back in and give you a full report. And Freddie stopped in this morning to say three mares will be ready to breed by Monday. That'll be our earliest February breeding. You should be feeling much better by then."

"Better or dead." Matt attacked the omelet, avoiding Ann's direct gaze. He would humor her, give her a few minutes to get busy with her own work, and then he'd do what he pleased. With any luck, he'd be able to avoid all of the ranch hands and finally get a look at her office.

Ann finished her coffee, talking about the kind of day she expected. She'd already told Matt it would be at least three or four days before the blood tests on Easy were returned from the state lab in Jackson.

"I'll be back in after lunch to check on you. Mannie is making some of her special soup for your quick recovery."

"Ann, I'm not sick enough for all of this."

"Dr. Zimlich is a better judge of that than you or me. Just to make sure you obey the doctor's orders—" Ann picked up his jeans and snapped his suitcase shut, lifting it, too "—I'll take these for today."

"Ann!" Matt's voice was outraged and amazed. "You can't walk off with my suitcase and all my clothes."

At the door, Ann turned back. "Watch me." Then she was gone.

It was nearly three before Ann returned to his room. She entered cautiously, testing the water of his temper. Her face glowed with excitement and her blue eyes were happy.

"Have you been good?" she asked, unable to resist teasing him.

"Perfectly." He indicated the horse magazines on the floor. "And I've learned a lot. I read business journals constantly. As much as I hate to admit it, this has been a nice, if enforced, change.''

"I have some good news."

"I can tell. What?"

"Dawn just finished working Easy and he was as docile as a lamb. It was as if yesterday never happened."

Reaching out, Matt captured her hands and held them. "I'm relieved, Ann. Any idea what happened yesterday?" Her excitement was contagious, and he was happy for her. No matter how he figured it, and lying in bed he'd looked at every possible angle, there was no financial gain for her in having Easy behave dangerously. In fact, there was nothing but liability. Both he and Dawn could have sued her for everything she had if they'd been seriously hurt. As a businessman, he knew that such liability was never deliberately courted, not even by a woman looking for a way out of a deep financial hole.

A frown brushed across her face but didn't stay. "No. Everyone has a theory, but no concrete reason. I still believe he was stung by something."

"Wouldn't it have left a mark?"

"Maybe it was somewhere that didn't show." She spoke as if she wanted to convince herself as much as him.

"That's probably exactly what happened. And now that your stallion is recovered, you only have to worry about me. I've been thinking of what I should do to you for taking my clothes." He pulled her closer, so that their faces were only inches apart.

Ann's heart raced. Her breasts were pressed against the hard muscles of his thighs. She, too, had spent more than a few minutes thinking about her time in the bedroom with Matt.

"You have?" She couldn't break her gaze. All day long she'd found her thoughts drifting, unbidden, to this moment. Though she had many reservations about yielding to her feelings for Matt, she couldn't summon a single one to assist her now as his hands slowly moved up her arms and drew her to him.

Matt's lips took hers gently, a tender exploration that increased as he felt her matching desire. She shifted beside him on the bed, freeing his body so that he held her with one arm as the other hand caressed her back, the curve of her hip. Beneath his hand, he felt her tension, the mixture of boldness and reservation. He found it strangely appealing.

Drawing away, he paused, his eyes locked on hers, his hand still resting on her hip. "I've thought about doing this all morning." He wasn't teasing.

"Then we've been thinking about the same thing."

Her face and voice were devoid of any pretense, and Matt felt a jolt of intense passion. In the clear blue depths of her eyes, there was nothing but honesty. There was none of the crafty games he'd come to expect from his ex-wife, none of the manipulation.

Shaken by his sudden perception, he pulled her to him for a deep kiss.

The force of his kiss shocked Ann. Matt's capacity to excite her was so intense that she had to back away, at least to get her breath. Her hands pressed against the muscles of his chest. Her slightest resistance was enough. Matt released her lips.

Feeling as if her heart might stop, Ann looked into his dark eyes. Desire, powerful and immediate, was there, as well as tenderness.

From a great distance away, the barking of the dogs penetrated her mind. She fought against hearing them, against returning to the world of tasks and responsibilities. Matt, too, heard the dogs and turned to look out the French doors that led to the veranda.

"Does this place always have so much traffic?" Matt's voice was deliberately light, teasing.

"Most of the time it's all in a day's work," Ann said, brushing her hand through her short hair. "I seldom mind, but today..." She rolled off the opposite side of the bed. "Today, I feel like hog-tying whoever it is that just drove up." She found her voice shaky and her knees rubbery. Straightening her clothes, she felt Matt's eyes burning into her, and she was torn between the need to return to the bed or tend to her business. Taking a long breath, she went to the door.

"I'll be back as soon as I can. I think we need to talk."

The promise brought a grin of anticipation to Matt's face. "This sick routine is much, much better than I ever dreamed."

She closed the door and concentrated on achieving some expression that didn't give away the pleasure she had so recently experienced. She had just arranged a smile on her face when she stepped onto the porch and saw the black truck. Bill Harper sat in his cab as her three German shepherds snarled at the door.

The smile vanished and her shoulders straightened as she walked to the truck.

"I hope I didn't disturb your nap," he said sarcastically. "I thought you might want to be at the meeting of the racing commission tonight at six. Be sure and bring your lawyer."

Before she could reply, she saw his expression change. Looking behind her, she saw Matt, in his robe and pajamas, standing on the porch.

"Well, so it wasn't exactly a nap," Bill Harper said as if he'd learned a valuable secret. "Seems to me you've forgotten how jealous Robert could be." He lifted a beer and took a long swallow. "If he should happen to come home, he wouldn't like it a bit."

Ann's pulse raced. "Robert and I are divorced, Mr. Harper. Long divorced. He won't be coming back."

"A legal technicality." He laughed, revved his engine and took off.

Ann had conquered her anger by the time she got to the porch.

"I recognized the truck, Ann. What did he want?" Matt spoke before she had a chance. "That guy worries me."

"He's somehow managed to get the other members of the racing commission to meet tonight at six. He warned me to bring my lawyer. I think he's going to try to make trouble about those bids." She tried not to be upset, but Bill Harper got under her skin. He was crooked, and he acted as if he had a right to cheat people.

"I'm going with you tonight, Ann," Matt said, putting his arm around her shoulders in an uncalculated gesture of protection. Something about Bill Harper made his nerve endings tingle with warnings of danger. "I don't like the idea that Harper thinks he can drive up here any time he pleases. He could have telephoned."

"But then he wouldn't have gotten the personal satisfaction," she replied. "Anyway, I don't suppose sitting at a board meeting would be too strenuous for you. I'd welcome your company." She didn't voice the fact that, after two attacks on Easy, it wouldn't hurt for certain people to think she had male protection, and Matt looked very capable of giving it.

They entered the house, and Ann went to the telephone to call Jeff. He'd just heard about the meeting from another board member and assured Ann he would be there.

"Harper's set for a fight, and it's going to get dirty." Jeff sounded concerned, but not panicked. "Watch him, Ann. He'll stoop to anything."

"Like slander?" Ann asked bitterly.

"He's capable of it, and defamation of character can be an effective tool in a small town."

"Well, I'm forewarned," Ann said, before replacing the receiver.

"I'd better get cleaned up," she said to Matt as soon as the phone was out of her hand. "I'm not looking forward to this fight. I have a feeling it's one that will drag on for months to come."

"With people like Bill Harper, you have to take one victory at a time, Ann. One at a time." Against his judgment he found himself lining up on her side. He wasn't at Dancing Water to get involved in her fights, but somehow, he'd done just that.

JEFF GREETED THEM at the entrance to the community center. Almost immediately Bill Harper's voice cut across the room. "How nice, Ms. Tate, you brought your...friend. Is he the artistic type?" He grinned. "I don't think we've had the pleasure." The contractor walked up to Matt and extended his hand. "I always wondered who the pristine Ms. Tate would fall into bed with. 'Course some of us local men still wonder if that Mexican divorce she rushed through is really legal. Sorta makes decent people wonder if she's the type of woman who should be on a public board."

His comments were loud enough to turn the heads of several board members. There was nothing Ann could do to stop the tide of red that climbed her neck.

"I can see you make assumptions about people as well as legal practices," Matt replied blandly. "Just remember, Mr. Harper, you can go to jail for both."

He took Ann's elbow and steered her into the meeting room.

"Well done," Ann whispered as they took their seats.

Harper didn't waste time. He told the members of the racing commission he was prepared to file individual lawsuits against each one if his bid was not accepted for work on construction of the spectator stands.

"If you have money to throw away on lawyer fees, then go to it," Ann challenged him. "I'd rather fight you in court now than be sued later by someone whose family member died in an accident caused by your criminally negligent work."

Harper rose, a stare of deadly hatred on his face. "You think you're sitting in the catbird seat now, don't you? Well, that can change. Overnight!" He pushed back his chair with such force he nearly fell, and stalked out of the room. At the doorway, he turned around and surveyed the five members of the board, as well as Matt and Jeff.

"You're letting this woman lead you around by the nose. There're opportunities here for all of us to make money."

"Is that a bribe?" Jeff asked calmly, but his eyes glittered dangerously. "Or is that just your mouth running off?"

Harper refocused on Ann. "Things around here ran smooth until you got involved. You got that fine, big ranch with that fancy stallion of yours, and you don't want anybody else to get a piece of the pie. Well, just remember. Things can change. Just like that." He snapped his fingers and slammed out of the building.

Ray Marble, one of the board members, hurried up to Jeff. "Can he sue us? Can he really take us to court?"

"Anybody can sue anybody in this country, Mr. Marble, but the ultimate answer is that he can't win. And besides,

I've already told Ann I'd represent the board at no charge. You have absolutely nothing to worry about.''

"I've worked with Bill in the past. He isn't that bad if you keep an eye on him.'' Ray Marble fidgeted nervously. "Maybe we should give him the bid and just hire someone to watch him closely.''

"You people are the board,'' Jeff said, looking around the room. "I support Ann's decision. Once we start giving in to common criminals, then the racetrack won't be ours for long. If we want an honest track, we're going to have to fight for it.''

The three other board members nodded in agreement.

"Let's go home,'' Matt whispered in Ann's ear.

Matt didn't try to force conversation as they drove back to the ranch. Ann was tense, worried, and he let her think. The meeting had been ugly, but at least it hadn't dragged on for hours. Bill Harper's threats had added a new dimension to his concerns about Ann. He found himself less interested in her ranch as a potential buy for his investment group and more interested in Ann as a woman. He gently probed his rib cage. He was healing. The thing he had to remember was that his bruised ribs would heal far more rapidly than his heart if he made a foolish step.

"I could use some brandy,'' Ann said as they turned beneath the canopy of trees that lined the drive. She wanted to feel the hot liquor in her throat, but she wanted more to delay Matt's departure for bed. He'd managed to somehow work his way into the fabric of her life. Gradually she felt herself becoming dependent on his company. His touch.

"And maybe a fire,'' Matt suggested.

"Sounds wonderful.''

"If you're nice, I might even be persuaded to rub your shoulders.''

The idea of Matt's hands on her body made her smile. "I'd like that."

She parked the car, stopping for a moment to examine the ranch. The lights were out, the horses quiet, and Suni and Shasta ran up to greet her, tails wagging madly.

"The place looks fine, doesn't it?" She couldn't help the note of worry in her voice.

"Freddie's taken care of everything. That young groom is on guard, so things should be fine. I'll check the barns later myself." He was, in fact, itching for an opportunity to get out in the barns.

Tired as she was, she felt a sudden stab of injured pride at his statement. "There's no need for that, Matt. We're capable of watching the horses." She turned away from him and walked to the house.

Anxiety lodged in the pit of her stomach and refused to leave. Her emotions were a series of tension-filled conflicts. The farm was safe, but she couldn't shake the feeling that disaster lurked just down the road. Matt's presence was comforting, and disruptively stimulating. It was a relief to finally be at home, but the safety of the ranch wasn't as tight as she'd thought.

With the door locked, she threw logs on the fire as Matt poured two brandies.

"You're wound up tight as a spring," he observed, crossing to her. "Let me rub your shoulders. It'll help you relax." He put down the drinks, and his hands started a soft kneading motion as he led her to the floor in front of the sofa. He sat above her as he worked.

His voice and the touch of his hands started to soothe the knots of tension on her shoulders. Ann felt herself beginning to relax. Matt definitely had the touch.

She closed her eyes and listened to the low, reassuring tones of Matt's voice as he pressed his strong fingers into her back. From the darkness surrounding the house there came the sound of an engine backfiring. A new stab of anxiety made her straighten her spine. Matt held his hands steady on her shoulders.

"What is it?"

"Just when I think I'm relaxing, I get an anxiety attack. Would you mind taking a walk with me around the barns? I'm positive everything is perfectly fine, but I can't seem to let it go." She was distressed with herself for behaving so ridiculously. Her actions would only confirm Matt's doubts about the safety of his mare. But Bill Harper's threats had unnerved her.

Matt eased to his feet. "A brisk walk will help you sleep."

Ann went to the closet and got their coats. As Matt snapped his jacket, she placed her palm against his face. "Thanks, Matt, you've been a tremendous help. I know your first concern is for Blue Chip. But you've been a big help to me." She turned away before she could see the look of guilt that flashed across his dark countenance.

The night was brisk and they hurried across the darkened yard to the stallion barn. Easy called a sleepy greeting, sticking his head over the door for a pat. He was the friendly, well-mannered horse that Matt had first met.

"No hard feelings, Easy," Matt said, stroking his velvety nose.

Shasta and Shadow slipped into the barn, tails wagging as they dashed around. Suni began to bark in the distance, and the other two dogs tore out after the noise.

"Rabbit?" Matt asked as he helped Ann shut the doors.

"Doubt it. The dogs don't normally chase wildlife, but it could be."

As they spoke, the horses in the west pasture began to run. The pounding hooves throbbed through the still night.

The light in Freddie's apartment snapped on and he rushed out, pulling on pants and a jacket.

"What's going on?" he called out.

"Your guess is as good as mine. Something's spooked the horses," Ann said. She wasn't too worried. In the cold weather, the horses often used any excuse for a romp.

They hurried down to the end of the pasture, and she listened, waiting for the animals to turn and come back. Instead, the hoofbeats got farther and farther away.

Both she and Matt realized simultaneously what had happened. Ann felt as if she'd stepped into a hidden room where danger lurked in every corner. Eyes wide, she looked at Matt. He wore the same fearful and disbelieving expression.

"Someone took down the fence!" Ann cried. "The horses are on the road."

Chapter Six

In the glare of the truck's headlights, Ann picked out the twenty-foot section of fence that had been destroyed. It looked at first as if a truck had run through it, only there was no sign of an accident. The boards were lying unbroken on the ground. They'd been deliberately knocked down, carefully pushed aside.

"Thank goodness this happened in the gelding pasture," Ann said, her throat tight and scratchy. She couldn't allow Matt to see how worried she actually was. Someone was striking at the core of her existence, her ability to protect the animals in her care.

Matt didn't answer, but his concern filled the cab of the truck.

"We keep the mares in stalls at night, so if you're worried about Blue Chip, you needn't be," Ann continued. Matt's silence made her defensive, as if she had to explain.

Matt sorted lead ropes as two buckets of feed rattled at his feet. It would be foolish to deny that he wasn't worried about Blue Chip. Two serious accidents had occurred in two days, not to mention the bizarre attack by Easy Dancer. He was worried about his horse, and about the woman who sat beside him.

Ann drove past the fence and continued slowly down the road, windows rolled down as she listened for the sound of the horses.

"There're ten of them?" Matt asked.

"Yes. They won't be hard to catch once we find them."

Matt put a comforting hand on her leg. "We'll get them before they get in any trouble. I'm just concerned that these acts of vandalism will continue until someone or some horse is seriously injured." Watching her face in the glow of the dash, he couldn't believe she was involved in anything underhand. More and more, he was becoming convinced that Ann was a victim in a bizarre game. Her farm wasn't for sale and, other than this rash of attacks, didn't appear to be in any distress.

"Let's worry about this one right now." Ann had to hold on. Rumors of bad luck could be just as devastating as real bad luck. Boarders wanted a safe environment for their horses. If word of the suspicious happenings at Dancing Water got out, she could be ruined. She forced her mind back to the immediate problem. "If the horses get in the road, they could cause an accident, maybe kill someone. That's what we need to be concerned about now."

As they turned a bend, the headlights picked up the floating tails and hooves of the horses. They were on the side of the road, running at a frolicking gallop in the grass.

The sight was beautiful, and dangerous.

"Maybe we could ease past them, and then head them off," Matt suggested.

It seemed the best plan, and Ann urged the farm truck slowly forward, not wanting to startle the animals into dashing in front of her. When she was about three hundred yards ahead of the herd she turned the truck to block the horses' way.

"It's a good thing Miss Hopper isn't with them. She would simply jump the truck and no doubt create a real fiasco." Ann forced a grin as she opened the door.

Aware that Ann's humor was hard won, Matt reached swiftly across the seat and caught her arm. "Everything will be fine."

Swallowing a lump in her throat, Ann nodded and stepped out into the grass. Matt took his position at the tail of the truck as they established a roadblock.

At first the pounding of hooves made a slight ground tremor, but as the herd got closer and closer the ground pulsed with their wild run. Ann scanned the night, eyes straining for a sign of the animals. It was just her luck that there wasn't a light-colored horse in the whole bunch.

"If we can stop them and catch one or two, the others will follow." Ann couldn't completely avoid the hesitation in her voice. "It isn't going to be easy," she added.

As the ground shook more violently, she tried not to think what would happen if the horses didn't see them in time.

"Betta, Duke," Ann called into the night, rattling the bucket of oats with all her might. Her voice was steely calm. Horses could easily pick up panic in a person's voice or touch. It was imperative that both she and Matt remain cool.

A large form, hurtling at full speed, came at Ann from the darkness. She caught her breath but refused to give ground. Duke came within two feet of running her down as he tried to skid to a stop. With hooves digging into the grass, he halted within arm's reach.

Ann grabbed his halter and stuck the bucket of feed in his face.

On the other side of the truck, Matt lured a young sorrel to his feed bucket. He gave a small sound of triumph as he hooked the lead line to the halter.

"Two down, eight to go," he said.

"You got ahead of them, thank goodness." Freddie's voice was puffy and exhausted as he called from fifty yards down the road. He'd cut across the pasture on foot. Mica John, Marshall Nicholls, and three helpful neighbors were at his side.

"We've got them," Ann yelled back. The loose horses were milling around, tired of the nighttime game and eager for the feed that rattled in the buckets.

Soon Freddie and his helpers were at her side. The horses, snorting and exhilarated from their long run, were settling down.

"Matt, why don't you drive the truck, and the rest of us will walk the horses back through the fence. It would be a great help if you could bring some nails. And flashlights. We'll have to mend that fence before we go to bed."

"Be glad to," Matt agreed. He looked at the men gathered around him and a terrible, sinking sensation hit the pit of his stomach.

"Ann, is anyone left at the ranch?"

His tone more than his words made her heart lurch.

"No!" The word was a strangled whisper. She'd been so intent on catching the geldings she'd never considered the fact that it could all have been a diversion, an attempt to draw everyone away so that someone could run rampant on the ranch.

"Hurry!" she urged Matt. "And take time to call the sheriff. I'm going to demand that someone look into this."

Matt drove away from the horses slowly at first, but pushed the gas pedal to the floor when he was a safe distance away. An ominous foreboding settled around him. The stabled horses were completely unprotected. His future was nakedly exposed.

The heavy truck moved laboriously around the curves, and he swung into the drive, the wheels spraying gravel and shells. An instinct for caution made him slow. The ranch appeared calm, absolutely quiet. Too quiet. Relief spread over him as the three dogs raced to the truck, tails wagging.

Whistling, he called them over. To his surprise, they surrounded the door and began to growl.

"Easy, girls," he called. The dogs had never given him a problem. Until now.

Shasta bared her teeth and stepped forward. Her deep growl meant business.

Desperately Matt thought back to the times he'd been around the dogs. Always he was with Ann, Freddie or Dawn. He'd underestimated their abilities as watchdogs. The situation was difficult now, but it also gave a measure of relief. If he couldn't wander around the barns, neither could anyone else.

Inspired with a sudden idea, he drove the truck to the window of Ann's office. There was enough room for him to open the office window and crawl through without allowing the dogs to get to him.

He was chuckling softly to himself as he pulled his legs through the window. As Ann requested, he telephoned the sheriff and filed a complaint. Then he found the hammers, nails and flashlights in the tool room next to her office. With everything gathered in a burlap sack, he traversed the short distance from the window to the truck. The three dogs were barking frantically, but Matt was just out of their reach.

"Sorry, girls," he called softly to them as he cranked the truck. "Good work, but I'm too tough to snack on."

Hurrying back down the road, Matt was strangely relieved. The three dogs were a ferocious force, something to be reckoned with. Though the dogs had prevented him from checking on the horses, he was pretty sure Blue Chip and the others were just fine.

Ann, Freddie, Nicholls, Mica and the neighbors were standing at the gap in the fence when he arrived. The horses were back in the pasture, grazing contentedly.

In a matter of minutes the boards were hammered securely back in place. Ann sat beside him, tense and silent, as he drove the neighbors home. Freddie had elected to walk the pasture, checking the rest of the fence.

Before Matt could fully stop the truck at the ranch, Ann was out and running into the barn. Lights flooded the night as she hit all the switches and methodically went from stall to stall, scrutinizing the sleepy horses as they nosed over their doors to see what the commotion was about. Relief slowed Ann's steps as she hurried to the stallion barn.

"Let her check it out." Freddie's hand stayed Matt. "She's worried and it's best to leave her alone."

Matt gave in to Freddie's gentle urging even though he wanted to be with Ann, to lend support.

The lights in the stallion barn flared to life.

"Ann's a fine woman." Freddie's voice was soft, but there was a knife's blade of protection in it. "She's been hurt once, through no fault of her own. Her friends wouldn't want to see that happen twice."

Instead of anger, Matt felt a sense of warmth. Freddie loved Ann, and he was making it plain. Freddie was telling him loud and clear not to tamper with Ann's affections.

"Freddie, why did Robert leave?"

Fixing him with a cold eye, Freddie didn't say anything. When he finally spoke his voice was tinged with sorrow. "Robert was a likable man. I think women found him charming, and there were times when I couldn't have asked for a better companion. But he lacked grit." Freddie took Matt's measure. "Things were getting rough here, what with

Mr. Tate's illness and all. Ann was worried to the bone. Robert needed more . . . attention.'' He cleared his throat.

"Did he take the horse?''

Freddie's hesitation spoke volumes. "Who else could have? Maybe he thought it was his due. Maybe it was the only way he could get Ann's interest. I've spent many a night thinking about it, wondering where that horse went. I've convinced myself a number of times that Robert lost his mind. I knew he had a woman friend—I just never knew her name. He had some big gambling debts to the wrong people. Miss Ann refused to pay them. Hell, she couldn't have even if she'd wanted to. It's possible he finally flipped completely. Like I said, he was short on grit. Anyway, it's all water under the bridge. It's Miss Ann's future that concerns me.'' His level gaze didn't falter as he examined Matt.

"She is a fine woman,'' Matt agreed. "Any fool can see that.''

"Well, now that your mare is settled, how long will you be staying in these parts? If you don't mind my asking.'' Freddie shifted uncomfortably as he talked.

A small grin pulled at the corners of Matt's mouth, but he fought it down. Freddie had assumed the role of parent, and it was an awkward situation with a grown woman. "As long as—''

The enraged scream of a horse split the night, followed by Ann's harsh command. "Get back!'' The words were a steel blade. "Get back!''

Galvanized, Matt and Freddie ran to the stallion barn.

"Easy!'' Ann refused to show any fear of the horse. She was trapped against one side of his stall where she'd gone in to pick up a lead line.

"Miss Ann!'' Freddie's frightened voice sent Matt forward. Easy stood at the open door of his paddock, ears pinned back and eyes rolling. His long, elegant neck snaked forward and his bared teeth went for Ann's shoulder. She dodged away, stifling the scream that rose in her throat.

"Back, Easy!" she commanded as she turned to face the horse.

Matt stopped at the stall door, assessing the situation. Ann was to his right, ten feet from the door. The horse formed the third pinnacle of a triangle, and Easy eyed Ann and then Matt with malicious intent.

"I'm going to charge him, and you make a break for the door," Matt ordered Ann.

"Wait!" Freddie's voice sounded ill. "Let me get the gun."

"No time!" Matt replied, grabbing a wooden-handled switch from the side of the stall. Wielding the switch like a club, he ran directly at Easy's face. His attack was so sudden and forceful that the horse turned and fled into his paddock. With lightning speed, Matt swung the door shut, confining the horse in the paddock.

"Miss Ann!" Freddie rushed forward, drawing Ann from the stall. "Whatever happened?"

Breathless and scared, Ann turned distressed eyes to Matt. "Thanks."

"Miss Ann, what happened?" Freddie pressed. "What made Easy Dancer attack you? For a minute, until Mr. Roper went in for you, I was afraid I was going to have to..."

The horrible image slammed into Ann like a torpedo. Her knees turned to jelly, her world spun, and it was only Matt's arms that kept her from falling in a dead faint to the cement. This couldn't be happening. Not to Easy. Not the horse she'd raised from a foal. They had an understanding. He was mischievous, but never dangerous.

Scooping her up, Matt looked at Freddie. "Let's get her inside."

"Go on, man, take her to the house. I'm going to see about Easy."

"No, Freddie!" Ann roused herself. "Don't go near him alone. Call Cybil. We'll sedate him and then check him. He came at me like he wanted to kill me. For no reason!" Her voice started to shake and she stopped talking. "He must be sick," she managed weakly. She couldn't believe anything else. The bond between them was too strong.

Without another word, Matt strode toward the house. When they were halfway across the pecan orchard, Ann insisted she could walk.

"Your ribs," she reminded him as he set her on her feet. "You were supposed to rest."

"We Ropers have a family tradition of healing fast." He kept his hand under her elbow and propelled her up the steps. "My mother always said we made up in toughness what we lacked in brains."

"I'll bet," Ann said, finally able to smile. "You don't seem to lack either. That was quick thinking back in the barn. But how did you know you could force him off me?"

"He isn't a vicious horse, Ann. Something's happening with Easy, but he isn't a killer. He isn't a rogue."

At the door she stopped and faced Matt. "Rogue." The word was a death sentence. "I've never seen a real rogue. I've heard stories." Tears clouded her eyes. "They always destroy rogues, don't they?"

"Ann, no one can manage over a thousand pounds of horse that's determined to kill. You know that. It's better for the animal, and all the people around him." Matt opened the door and gently pushed her inside. "But Easy isn't a rogue, so don't go borrowing trouble."

"I saw the lead line in his stall, and I walked in to get it before it got buried in the shavings. Then he came in from the paddock and reared. His feet hit the wall and I got away. But he almost hurt me.''

They were standing in the den. Ann's expression was dazed and filled with disbelief. "He could have killed me, but he didn't. He could have and he didn't," she repeated. Matt helped her out of her jacket, removed his own and then put both hands on her shoulders.

"I'm going to run a hot bath for you, and then I want you to soak. Now sit right here while I get everything ready."

"Matt," she called after him as he started down the hallway.

"Yes?"

"I've never come close to fainting before in my whole life."

He grinned at her mischievously. "A virgin faint? Remarkable."

Ann felt her mouth lift at his impudence. "Thanks," she said softly as he disappeared down the hall.

Moments later she was soaking in a tub full of deliciously hot water. She stared at her toes, the bright pink polish poking out of the water. The horrible incident with Easy couldn't have happened. It was impossible. She'd dreamed it.

A rapping at the door brought her back to the moment.

"Everything all right in there?" Matt was concerned.

"Fine. I'm coming out." She rose from the water and quickly dried. From an antique chiffonier in a corner of the large bathroom she took a pair of fuchsia silk pajamas and matching robe.

"I've got a nice fire going in the den. I thought maybe you'd want to talk for a while."

Ann smiled as she opened the door. "Maybe for a while."

"I went out to the barn and reopened Easy's paddock door so he could get back in the stall." Matt stood in her bedroom, his broad masculine shoulders seeming to fill the room.

Ann stopped dead still and looked at him. "And how was Easy?" she finally asked, almost dreading the answer.

"He kept his distance, but he wasn't very nice. He made a few nasty sounds in my direction, but he didn't come at me. Anyway, let's get you in front of that fire. You still look pale and cold. Though I have to admit those pajamas are very nice."

"Are you taking flattery lessons from Jeff Stuart?" Ann forced humor into her voice. She led the way down the hall and settled into her favorite chair. "Matt, I want to apologize for my almost passing out earlier tonight. We've kidded about it, but I'm not prone to attacks of fainting. I was so shocked at Easy's behavior. It was so awful, so unexpected."

He handed her a cup of fresh coffee. "I took the liberty of your kitchen. And forget the apologies. I've never considered you a weak or foolish woman." As he looked at her, he almost added that his adjectives included smart, warm and irresistibly sexy. He brushed her cheek with his fingers.

Passion tingled through Ann, coded in her skin at his softest touch. She reached up and touched the flat plane of his cheek, tracing the high cheekbone that gave his dark eyes such a strong setting.

Unable to resist the softness of her skin, Matt stroked her face, his fingers trailing down the tanned column of her neck to the collar of her silk pajamas.

Ann could feel her heart pounding. They were drawn to each other, as surely and strongly as if some physical force compelled them. The attraction was so intense, so overwhelming that they both drew a long breath. Firelight danced in their eyes.

"I'm not going to lie to you." Matt spoke, his voice husky and ragged. "I haven't been able to trust any woman since my wife. Maybe I haven't really tried."

Ann's breath came in shallow gasps. She, too, had her difficulties with trust. But it wasn't men she didn't trust; it was her own judgment.

"Matt, I—"

He touched her lips lightly. "I've been concerned about Blue Chip. I won't deny that. But I'm also worried about you. I'm even worried about that stallion of yours. Anyone can see how much you care for him."

A log in the fireplace crackled, sending a plume of small sparks up the chimney.

"Miss Ann! Miss Ann!" Freddie's excited voice preceded him up the steps. "You've gotta hear this!"

Matt was standing discreetly by the fire when Freddie burst through the door. The old man stood indecisively for a moment at the edge of the rug as he took in her attire. "I'm sorry if I interrupted..." He looked from one to the other.

"Not at all." Ann signaled him to the sofa. "Matt will even get you some coffee." She was flushed, and when she caught Matt's eye he raised his eyebrows suggestively. Her flush deepened.

"I did interrupt." Freddie stood up. "This can wait until tomorrow. I don't know what got into me. I'll just leave."

Matt stopped him with a cup of coffee. "Sit down, Freddie. Ann and I were just talking about Easy. I gather you've come up with something."

"I have!" He sat down and his eyes widened with delight. "Someone's been into Easy's feed. I went and looked myself. After that last incident, I made up a trap. And sure enough, it was sprung!"

"Freddie!" Ann leaned forward, her face alive and excited. "Tell us."

"Well, like in all the movies on television, I took some hair from one of the horses' tails and every night after I fed, I put the hair across the bin where we keep Easy's feed." He looked from one to the other. "Horse hair is very strong, and I wedged it into the wood so it wouldn't blow away. Sure enough, the hair was all knocked away when I checked. Someone had been in his feed."

"They could have given him something to make him act so terrible." Ann turned to Matt. "I knew there was a reason. He's wild one minute and calm the next. Someone's been putting some kind of drug in Easy's feed!"

"Right!" Freddie exclaimed, almost jumping up from the sofa. "Just as soon as Dr. Matheson gets here in the morning, I'm going to have her run a sample of that feed."

"Have you checked the feed for the rest of the horses?" Doubt tinged Matt's voice. "I knew I should have moved Blue Chip."

Freddie shook his head. "That's not necessary, Mr. Roper. The other horses are acting normal and fine. There's not a problem. It's Easy that's been acting odd."

"Tomorrow, check all of the feed." Ann's voice was cool. "We don't want Mr. Roper concerned over the health of his mare. In fact, we can't afford to have any of our boarders worried that we aren't giving the finest care possible."

Freddie's mouth opened and then shut as he looked from one to the other. There was an emotional current in the room he could feel.

"When I called Dr. Matheson, like I told Mr. Roper, she said she'd be here first thing in the morning. There was some emergency over in Covington, Louisiana, and she couldn't get back before dawn. But she'll be here bright and early, and I'll have feed samples from all of the horses ready for her."

"I knew I could count on you." Ann rose. "Both of you finish your coffee. I've got a terrible headache, and if you'll excuse me, I think I'd better go to bed."

An awkward silence fell between the two men after Ann left. Freddie hurriedly drank his coffee, his gaze at last shifting to Matt.

"I'm sorry if I interrupted anything."

Matt shook his head. "No, you didn't."

"Is Miss Ann sick then?"

"I think the fact that I'm worried about Blue Chip upsets her."

"There's been some strange things happening here," Freddie said, nodding. "There's no denying that. But there's no place that gives better care than Dancing Water. I've seen Miss Ann call out the vet for a horse when she knew the owner wouldn't pay for it. She'd rather pay the bill than see the animal suffer."

"I can readily believe that," Matt agreed, "but you have to put yourself in my position. If there's any chance that something might happen to Blue Chip, I'd have to take her home."

"You mean you're thinking about driving away with the mare before she's even bred?" Freddie's horror showed in his face.

"I have thought of that," Matt admitted. It was a new thought, though, one he hadn't fully explored. It would mean leaving a job unfinished and his mare unbred. But above all, Blue Chip's safety was his concern. Or it had been until his feelings for Ann Tate began to develop. He hadn't come to a clean decision.

"If word got out that Miss Ann's clients were leaving, it could ruin her business."

"No one need know," Matt said. "It isn't that I don't trust Ann, or you, or the care that the horses get. It's just that I can't risk Blue Chip because some character is trying to get even with Ann."

"And what about Miss Ann, then?" Freddie demanded, rising angrily. He stalked to the door and turned back. "One last thing, Mr. Roper. Has it occurred to you that none of these bad things started to happen at Dancing Water until you arrived?" He slammed the door with such force that the house shook.

THE LONG COARSE HAIR slid through the gloved hand. Black hair, from a bay or brown animal. A sly and clever little trap set up by one of the useless minions at Dancing Water. Well, they'd soon be looking for work elsewhere. That would be a big part of the satisfaction. A very big part.

Once Ann was ruined and the ranch put on the block, a lot of things would change. The payoff would be the look on her face. Everything she loved would disappear in a gust of righteous wind.

The figure stood and paced the confines of a darkened room. With a flourish, the gloved hand dropped the horse hair into a trash can lined with heavy plastic.

They would suspect the feed. That was good. They'd want tests and more tests, all giving time for more little incidents. More accidents. More suspicions.

The only troubling thing was the man. Matt Roper. How inconvenient that he should have fallen victim to Ann's charms. He was supposed to help negotiate the sale. Well, if he valued his mare, and his life, he'd soon take the hint and clear out.

No one could save Ann. No one. Other good men had suffered trying. She used and destroyed those who loved her best. No one could really care for her because she cared only for her ranch. Her ranch. It was the only thing that had ever mattered to her. But that had always been her way, the little princess. Luck smiled on her, and she thought it was because she worked for it.

A bitter grimace stretched the chapped lips into a frightening imitation of a smile. Working outdoors all day had dried and cracked the tissue into a painful web. But pain didn't matter, not when justice was so close at hand.

The next lesson involved money. Everyone had his price, and Ann was going to soon find out that money and fear were powerful motivators. It was going to be a lesson she'd never forget, because it might well cost her the life of her stallion—or someone she cared about.

Chapter Seven

Her third cup of coffee in her hand, Ann watched the pastel shades of sunrise creep over the eastern horizon. Through the lace curtains of her kitchen she noted the rapid transition of the sky from gray to pink to gold. The promise of morning failed to bring the hope that usually marked her beginnings. She was tired from a sleepless night, and restless with the thoughts and emotions that bedeviled her.

It wasn't enough that her most prized horse was being threatened by some, as yet, unnamed person. The worry about Easy would be enough to drive a normal person up the wall. But on top of that, she had Matt Roper to contend with. As the sun moved higher, Ann admitted to herself that Matt was not just an ordinary boarder. In the short span of time since he'd driven his rig onto her property, she'd become involved. His doubts about her professional abilities were just that much more devastating.

Sighing, she got up and put her cup in the sink. She went out the back door, eager for action and the crisp winter air.

Although she'd expressly forbidden anyone to approach Easy Dancer without someone else in attendance, she went into the stallion barn alone. The beautiful sorrel swung his head over the door and called a friendly greeting. Nosing out to invite her over, he waited expectantly. It was a long established routine between them. She drew a carrot from her pocket and held it as he took neat, careful bites. When he was finished he thanked her with a nuzzle from his soft nose.

"Easy," Ann whispered, feeling a rush of tears that at last slid down her face. "I hope to goodness that feed sample shows some drug, 'cause if it doesn't you're in a whole lot of trouble."

His soft whinny was another invitation to come closer.

Ann walked up to his stall and he nosed against her stomach, pushing as he gently nuzzled into her jacket pockets looking for more treats.

With her nerves keyed so tight, she heard the sound of a vehicle in the drive. She knew without looking that Cybil Matheson had arrived, as early as she'd promised. She smiled, thinking of the many nights Cybil had spent at the ranch as a teenager. She'd always been such a hard worker, always sacrificing even her smallest pleasure to study or work. Ann recalled the morning she'd asked Cybil to be her maid of honor. Crushed, Cybil had to refuse because she had a veterinary exam the day of the wedding. Ann, too, had been let down, but she understood her friend's single-minded pursuit of her dream.

"Morning," Ann greeted the blurry-eyed Cybil as the woman walked into the barn.

"Is it morning?" the vet asked. "I hadn't noticed. The interstate looks the same, night or day, when you're as tired as I am. What happened out here last night? Freddie was upset when the office patched him through to me."

"Easy attacked me last night. If Matt hadn't been here, he might have killed me."

"So the handsome Mr. Roper isn't just a pretty play-thing?"

"Cybil!" Ann was shocked and irritated by her friend's manner. There was sometimes an edge of harshness to Cybil, which Ann attributed to her hard childhood. Her teasing went a little too far.

"Sorry. I'm just too tired. I thought a little levity might make you feel better. You know, they say laughter is the best medicine."

"Easy and Matt are two subjects I don't feel much like joking about." Ann tried to smooth out her voice. "I've been worried sick about this business with Easy, but at least we have a lead."

"Oh, yeah?" Cybil's dark blue eyes widened.

"Freddie set a trap for the culprit, and he found that someone has been tampering with Easy's feed." There was a small note of triumph in Ann's voice. "When he told me last night, I felt much better. Until I began to consider the possibilities. If someone has been playing in Easy's feed, then someone has had free access to this barn, to the other horses. Some kook could really injure some of the animals."

"Or you." Cybil showed no trace of humor. "This is beginning to scare me, Ann. A vandal on the loose is one thing. A person with the intention of harming you deliberately is something else. Have you called the sheriff?"

"Of course, but that's like shouting into a hurricane. They aren't interested until a serious crime occurs." Ann shook her head. "It's up to me to solve this mess and put the person responsible behind bars."

"Any clues?"

"The majority consensus is that Bill Harper is somehow behind the trouble." She went on to tell Cybil about the pasture fence being knocked down.

"Well, let's take a look at Easy and see what we can find," Cybil suggested. "Although I didn't locate any type of sting or bite, there is always that chance."

Ann brought the big stallion out of the stall and hooked him in the cross ties. He stood as calmly and gently as an ancient gelding. She automatically began to stroke his glistening hide. "Look at him, Cybil. He looks a little depressed. Have you tested that first feed sample?"

Backing off a few steps, Cybil took in the horse's attitude. He was too calm. His normal sparkle was missing. "You're right. This may give me something else to go on. And, yes, the first feed sample was exactly what Freddie said it was. Nothing out of the ordinary."

A worried frown touched Ann's face. "I hope this one shows something. Since Freddie sprang his trap, he's certain the problem is with the feed. I can only pray he's right."

"My faith is with Freddie." Matt's deep voice startled both women. Ann's reaction to him was instant and alarming. Her heartbeat quickened and a now-familiar warmth flushed over her body.

"He looks deceptively human," Cybil said to Ann in a deliberately loud aside, then turned to Matt, "but I hear you're making quite a reputation as a rescuer of damsels in distress."

"You know how Ann exaggerates," Matt said smoothly, walking into the barn. "It looks as if the horse has returned to his normal, easygoing self. Any clues, doctor, as to what's ailing your most valued patient?" He pointedly ignored Ann. He'd watched her leave the house at daybreak, heading straight for the barn and a rendezvous with Cybil Matheson. All of his suspicions were alerted.

"All of the last tests were negative, but we'll run them again. I'm sorry I wasn't here last night to get a blood sample."

Thinking of the stallion's wild and dangerous behavior, Ann was almost glad that Cybil wasn't around. Twelve hours before, Easy Dancer was an animal capable of killing. Though Cybil was a close personal friend, she was also a member of a medical community with rules and responsibilities involving animals considered dangerous to human life.

"What's your educated guess?" Matt persisted as he walked up to Cybil. "We all have our own theories, but I'm sure your training indicates some possibilities." His concentration was focused wholly on the vet.

Cybil's gaze flicked to Ann and then fell to the floor. "I hope we find the feed tampered with." She returned to her work, drawing a blood sample from Easy's neck. The stallion didn't even flinch as the needle stuck his vein.

"And if it isn't the feed?"

"Let's not probe distressing possibilities, Mr. Roper."

Matt shot a glance at Ann. "Let me ask one additional question. Is there a possibility that there's something wrong with the stallion, something that might be transmitted genetically?"

The question was like a physical slap. Ann reached behind her to the wall for support, as she raised disbelieving eyes to Matt.

The shock didn't last long. Before Cybil could reply, Ann straightened. "Wait just a minute, Matt Roper. I don't know what you're trying to do, but I won't have you implying that I would breed anyone's mare to an unstable stud. That's insulting!" With each word her temper rose.

"Ann," Cybil interrupted, rushing over and grasping both of Ann's hands in hers. "Calm down." She squeezed hard. "Ann!"

White-hot anger dimmed Cybil's protests as Ann gazed at Matt. The betrayal was too great. How could he even consider such a thing? He knew how much she cared about the animals in her charge, her own and her boarders'. And he was standing there as if he had every right to say such things.

"I didn't imply anything," Matt said softly. "I was merely asking a question I consider very legitimate. It's the same question you would ask if the roles were reversed," he pointed out.

"Ann!" Cybil grabbed her by the shoulders and shook her hard. "Matt's right. You'd want to know the same thing. Think about it."

The lightning streak of anger was passing, but Ann only felt the sense of betrayal more acutely. She looked directly at Matt. "Of course. It's exactly the question I'd ask of a woman I didn't trust, a woman who might not be able to do a job properly. A woman who would do anything to get what she wanted." She turned on her heel and strode out of the barn, long legs swinging in hurt and anger. Suddenly she turned back.

"Cybil, let me know what the test results show as soon as possible. And Freddie has all the feed samples ready for you. I want the supplies for the whole barn tested."

"Ann, that will take forever and cost a fortune!" Cybil protested.

"Cost is not a factor. After all, we wouldn't want people like Mr. Roper to think we'd cut corners." She flung the words at Matt and went to her office.

When her tall figure had disappeared, Cybil turned to Matt. "That wasn't a very bright move if you plan on staying around here for long."

There was remorse in Matt's eyes, but his jaw was firm. "It was a legitimate question."

"Perhaps. But what was the motivation? Were you trying to get under Ann's skin, or are you playing some other game?" Cybil's eyes were as bright and alert as a cat's.

Matt didn't answer. He walked out of the barn and into the sunshine. He had no intention of telling Cybil or anyone else that his actions were based on his own feelings, a mixture of suspicion and rejection he'd felt as he watched Ann, so supremely confident and self-possessed, walking across the yard as the sun came up. He, too, had been unable to sleep and was waiting for daylight, waiting to see her. At his first glimpse of her, his heart had stirred in a dangerous way. At that moment, he'd resolved to look after Blue Chip. And himself.

Once he was clear of the stallion barn, he didn't know exactly what to do. He could almost feel Ann's disapproving and pained eyes on him and he walked quickly into the main barn, hoping to find Freddie. At that moment, he felt certain the old man had a wonderful theory about all women.

Still burning with anger and hurt, Ann sat down at her desk and forced herself to look calmly over the inventories Freddie had left on her desk. She couldn't think about Matt. Not yet. She was too angry.

For thirty minutes she concentrated only on work. Still, Matt didn't completely leave her mind. At last she tossed the pen on the desk and looked out the window. She could always ask him to pack up his mare and leave. That was surely the most sensible thing. She started to rise, and then settled back in her chair. Or was it sensible? Blue Chip and Easy Dancer were the perfect pair. Of all the mares Ann had ever seen, Blue Chip was the most ideally suited to Easy. If she lost this chance, she might never again have such an opportunity. Wasn't that worth putting up with a distrustful, irritating man?

Yes. But not one who made her tremble with desire, who slipped into her dreams and daydreams with kisses and touches that made her blush in the light of day.

She had to send him home.

She rose and made it all the way to the door before she turned around. If she sent Blue Chip away because she couldn't control her own emotions, she'd be the biggest fool that ever put a penny on a pony at the gate.

Drawing a deep sigh, she went to the window. It was still early morning and the horses were grazing in the pastures. The barn had a stable, protected rhythm that made her taut nerves relax. There was no instant answer to Matt. She leaned her forehead against the cool glass of the window and then firmed her shoulders. Matt would have to wait. At the moment she had another showdown to contend with— Sheriff Martin Welford was going to come and personally hear her complaints.

"BY THE LOOKS OF IT, I'd say female troubles," Freddie diagnosed as Matt sat morosely across the small kitchen table in Freddie's apartment.

"A little of that and a lot of my own overreaction," Matt said, rising to walk over to the kitchen sink and scan the grounds once again for a sign of Ann. He was standing there when the brown patrol car of the sheriff pulled into the drive.

"I see Ann called the law," he commented.

"Ann said you insisted on dragging the sheriff in." Freddie didn't bother to hide his lack of enthusiasm. "I told her that no one in these parts took crimes against an animal seriously. But like she said, it's a good matter to have on the record." Freddie rose and went to get his jacket. "Want to go help Ann?"

"You go on." Matt hesitated. "I don't think Ann would really welcome my interference now."

"Interference, is it?" Freddie grinned. "Like most women, Ann can take only so much pullin' and tuggin'. It appears you might have gotten your rope a little too tight on her."

Matt couldn't help but smile at Freddie's analogy. It sounded so simple, but with Ann it wasn't that clear-cut.

"Listen, man." Freddie went to Matt and put a callused hand on his shoulder. "Miss Ann can be a very giving woman." His face drew together in a frown. "I've seen her give to the point of using herself up. She can take, too. But I watched her last night when you seemed to doubt her abilities to care for your horse. You should know that Ann would never endanger an animal. Not hers. Not yours, not some stray down the road. To question that is to question the essence of her."

Freddie withdrew his hand and waited for his words to sink in.

"If Blue Chip's foal is a winner, I might be able to convince my ex-wife to let me have my children back," Matt said without looking at Freddie. A bitter grin touched his mouth. "With enough money, she might be willing to part with her maternal responsibilities." He ceased trying to contain his anger and struck the table with his fist. "All it takes is enough money."

"Does Miss Ann know this?" Freddie asked. Matt's reasons for being so cautious with his horse put a different frame on the issue.

"No, and don't tell her," Matt said.

"But it might make your doubts—"

"No." Matt's voice was firm. He'd conveniently explained his concern about Blue Chip, but he had other doubts about his presence at Dancing Water that he could not so easily justify to Ann's most loyal coworker. He squirmed and stood up, feeling slimy and traitorous because he'd gained Freddie's sympathy so easily. "I have to learn to trust Ann. That's true. But she has to learn to trust me, too. And herself. Just the same as I do."

"But of all the reasons in the world, Miss Ann would understand about children. That conniving Robert. Why, that was what she wanted most—" Freddie broke off, shaking his head. "And that, too, is none of my business. That's for Miss Ann to be telling if she chooses."

Matt wanted to push the issue, but he knew it was pointless. Freddie's loyalty to Ann was deep. He'd never divulge anything he thought she might prefer to keep to herself. Matt also felt like a heel for prying so shamelessly into Ann's personal secrets.

"Well," said Freddie. "I'd better be going to see what Sheriff Welford can make of our troubles. It'll be a few lines scratched on an official report and tucked in a drawer, but at least I can make certain he takes down the information correctly."

"If you don't mind, I'll stay here awhile and then go work Blue Chip."

"That'll do you and her some good," Freddie agreed as he left. "As the philosophers say, the outside of a horse is good for the inside of a man."

Matt was still standing at the window fifteen minutes later when the sheriff drove away. He watched as Ann and Freddie crossed the yard and entered the house. When the telephone in Freddie's apartment rang, he answered it, hoping to hear Ann's voice. It was Freddie. The farm manager was calling him up to the house for lunch.

Desire to see Ann flashed through Matt, and his step was long and eager as he hurried across the yard and into the gracious old house. To his disappointment, Ann was taking her lunch in her room.

"Headache," Freddie said without meeting Matt's gaze.

Matt wasn't hungry, but Mannie's hot roast beef "po' boy" sandwiches and steaming gumbo were irresistible. He and Freddie were just finishing when he noticed Dawn Markey running across the yard. Her scarf was flying out behind her and her black riding boots were churning at a frantic pace. Matt knew instantly that there was trouble in the barn.

He jumped up and raised the window.

"Help!" Dawn yelled. "Come help me!" Then she turned and ran back the way she'd come.

Matt and Freddie were only twenty yards behind her when they heard the door slam and Ann raced after them. Panic and fear etched deep lines in all of their faces. Matt was running as hard as he could, but he had time to notice Ann's pallor. A twist of protectiveness wrenched at him, and he slowed to wait for her.

"What?" she panted.

"I don't know. Dawn called for help." Matt's stomach twisted as he saw Dawn enter the main barn. He'd anticipated trouble with Easy again, not one of the other animals.

"Dear God," Ann murmured as she spurred herself forward.

When Ann and Matt entered the barn, Blue Chip's door was open. Freddie and Dawn were in the stall, urging the mare to her feet. Mica was hanging at the edge of the stall, and from the west pasture a worried Marshall Nicholls puffed into the barn.

"What's wrong with her?" Nicholls asked in a soft voice.

"We have to get her up," Freddie said. "It's the colic."

"Colic." Matt didn't have to be told the gastrointestinal upset was the number-one killer of horses. Blue Chip had to be gotten to her feet and forced to move around.

"I'll get some banamine," Ann said, rushing to her office.

Matt grabbed Blue Chip's halter and gently tugged. "Come on, girl, let's get up." She struggled a moment to rise to her feet and then dropped back on her side in the shavings.

"Get her up!" Freddie ordered, taking a position with Dawn on the lead rope. "It's her life, man. Get her up!"

As the three of them prodded the sick horse, Blue Chip found a surge of energy and struggled to her feet. She turned to bite at her stomach, and then the pain made her throw herself against the stall.

Ann arrived with the banamine and sent the needle home with steady surety. "Cybil's on her way." She saw the horror in Matt's eyes. "She doesn't look that bad, Matt. She's going to be fine."

Dawn took the lead rope from Matt's hand and walked the mare out to the yard. With firm commands she started Blue Chip walking in a circle around her.

Occasionally the mare tried to stop and lie down, but Dawn adamantly refused to yield to her. "If she gets down, she could twist a gut," Dawn pointed out. "Keep her moving, let the banamine take effect and pray that Cybil gets here soon."

Ann's earlier anger at Matt had evaporated as she looked at his stricken face. It was clearly written there that Blue Chip was very special. If he was obnoxious about her handling, it was because she mattered so much.

"She doesn't appear to be in terrible pain, Matt. In all probability, it's a light colic brought on by the trip here and the strange surroundings. We've checked her water closely, and she's backed off a bit, but she was drinking." Ann recited the facts in an effort to calm him.

Matt finally looked at Ann. "Will she make it?"

"I can't promise anything, Matt, but my trained opinion is that this isn't a severe case." His look, so naked with fear, was as intimate as a touch. Ann maintained the contact, wanting to give him the comfort he needed without false promises.

"Thanks, Ann. I've been lucky with her. She's never colicked before with me. I know it happens for a number of reasons, or for no reason at all. Thank God Dawn found her in time."

"We patrol the barns on a regular basis, checking on all the horses, Matt. We do our best here." Ann softened her words further with a gentle touch on his arm. "I'm sorry this happened."

Matt could no longer resist. He cupped her chin in his hand and raised her gaze to meet his. "I owe you an apology. My words today were harsher than my thoughts."

"Accepted," Ann replied, her heart thudding with wild joy.

"She's coming 'round," Dawn called out, letting Blue Chip pause for a moment. She made no effort to lie down and bent her head to inspect the grass.

"If she's interested in nibbling, that's a very good sign," Freddie said as he came to Matt's side. "I've sat up many a night with a colicky horse. Seeing 'em go for the grass is like a gift from heaven."

With the atmosphere around Blue Chip lightening, Matt felt his own anxiety easing off. "I'll take her now," he told Dawn. "I know you've got plenty of other things to do."

"That's right enough," the trainer said. "I just happened to be in the barn. Mica would have been around in another ten minutes, but now I'll get back to my schedule.'' Black hair bouncing on her back, she hurried away.

"I'll be getting back to my own chores," Freddie said, taking his leave before anyone could stop him.

"Go on and finish your work," Matt urged Ann. "Blue Chip and I are perfectly fine."

"I'll wait for Cybil," Ann said, taking a seat on a fence rail twenty feet away. "I'm sure Blue Chip is better, but I want Cybil to put some oil down her and make a thorough check."

When Dr. Matheson arrived, the strain of her long night and busy day were evident in the slump of her shoulders and the redness in her eyes. "If you call me one more time I'm going to insist that you build me my own place attached to the barn, like Freddie has," she warned Ann.

She went straight to work on Blue Chip, listening to the rumblings of the mare's stomach with a stethoscope, checking her pulse and temperature. "She appears to be over the worst of it," Cybil said. "You must have caught it early."

"Dawn found her," Ann said quietly, aware of Matt's intense scrutiny.

With great skill, Cybil ran a tube down Blue Chip's nose and finished the treatment.

"You're a very lucky man, Mr. Roper," she said to Matt as she packed her instruments. "There is something I want to check, though." Without an explanation she left Matt and Ann holding the mare and went into the barn. When she returned, her face was coldly disbelieving.

Staring at Ann she lifted her right hand, a fistful of hay clutched in it. "What's going on, Ann? This hay is moldy. I've never seen such carelessness here before."

Chapter Eight

Another bale of hay toppled to the cement aisle of the stallion barn. Jaw clenched, Ann pulled the bale to her and ruthlessly inspected it. When she was satisfied that it wasn't moldy, she nodded to a groom and he stacked it to one side where more than two hundred other bales had been placed. As soon as Ann was certain Blue Chip was out of danger and resting comfortably in her stall, she'd gone to the barn and begun an immediate investigation of the hay.

"How many more are up there?" she called to Freddie, who was in the loft with a spotlight.

"I can get the rest up here," he said. "It'll take some work restacking, but it's better than having to lift it up again from the floor. Miss Ann, there's not a sign of a spoiled bale here." Frustration and worry made his words fast and harsh.

"I never expected to find bad hay in my barn," Ann said, at last looking at Matt and Cybil, who stood in the shadows. "Whoever gave Blue Chip that hay didn't get it from my loft. Someone brought that hay in here and deliberately gave it to her."

"Ann," Cybil said softly, at last going up to her and putting a sympathetic hand on her shoulder, "accidents happen." Leaning down she whispered fiercely, "Don't make this worse than it is already. Bad hay is damaging, but a horse killer on the loose will destroy your business. Let this thing settle down. No damage has been done.''

Ann swallowed her denial. She felt Matt watching her, and after the incident with the hay, she couldn't meet the challenge of his gaze. Bad hay was the type of carelessness rank amateurs committed. All of her grooms were trained to recognize it, and they knew to call it to her attention at once. And every other bale of hay in the loft, nearly three hundred, was clean and sweet and of the highest quality.

"Ann, I'd like to talk to you this afternoon," Matt said.

Though his tone was soft and unaccusing, Ann bristled. "Of course. If you want to take your mare and leave, there'll be no charges at all, Mr. Roper. After this accident, I would understand any doubt you expressed." She bit her lip and turned away. "I'm going to make some coffee. I'll bring some out."

"I'll help," Matt said so forcefully that Ann didn't dare disagree.

She wanted to wait to talk with him, to give herself a moment to get over her bitter disappointment. If he insisted, then the least she could do was get it over with and let him get on his way before it got much later. There was a fine Arabian farm in Montgomery that she could recommend for a stopover if he didn't want to drive at night.

Though she tried to think calmly and rationally, she was acutely aware of the man who walked beside her. He lacked the anger she'd expected. Daring a sideways glance at him, she saw that he was deep in his own thoughts. A frown drew his dark eyebrows together in a fierce slant, but she knew he was puzzled, not angry. She studied him until they reached the steps to the house.

In the kitchen, she put coffee on and confronted him. "Matt, whenever you're ready to leave, I'll get one of the grooms to help you gather your things."

"Don't you find it suspicious that out of hundreds of bales of hay, there was only one tiny segment, one flake, that was bad? And that one flake was given to my horse?" His dark eyes were brilliant with some idea. He went to Ann, eagerly taking her shoulders in his hands. "Why Blue Chip? Of all the horses here, why her?"

"I've asked myself that same question." Ann's body tensed at his touch. No matter how hard she tried, she couldn't erase the feelings he created. She wanted to draw away, and she also wanted to share her fears with him. "The only reply I've been able to come up with is that it's my rotten luck."

Matt was not immune to Ann, but as he'd watched the process of checking the hay, a new and terrible suspicion had dawned on him. Ann had to be made aware of it.

"There are other horses here whose owners might accuse you of neglect and try to damage your reputation if their animals were injured, aren't there?"

Uncertain where his line of questioning was going, Ann hesitated. "Many horse owners don't realize how delicate their animals are. When something goes wrong, they invariably blame someone. Me, the vet, the person who sold them a 'defective' animal."

"And you have those types of boarders?" Matt pressed, his hands tightening.

"Yes. Every barn does."

"So bad hay, if it was given deliberately to ruin you, could have been given to any number of horses here?"

Eagerness made his eyes dance with excitement. His hands caressed her shoulders in a steady movement.

"Yes," Ann said, finally catching onto his line of thought. Her eyes began to glitter. "You're saying Blue Chip was deliberately selected, out of thirty other potential candidates?"

"Right!"

"Because you're here and would have known what happened?" Ann asked.

"No," Matt said, pausing dramatically. "Because whoever did this wants me to leave. If Blue Chip had died, my reason for staying would be gone. If she lived, then surely I'd pack her up and clear out. Either way I'd be gone. Don't you see? In some small way, I'm a cog in the plans of this person who's trying to hurt you."

She looked up at him. She did not allow the sudden fear to show in her eyes. "Are you leaving?"

"Not on your life," he said, "unless you'd prefer that I go." For the first time since his talk with Freddie he was beginning to feel better about himself. He'd come to breed his mare and scope out her farm. Now someone was trying to run him off, force him to leave Ann alone and unprotected. His doubts about her were growing steadily smaller. He'd have to give Chrissy, his assistant at the brokerage firm, a call and tell her to contact the members of the Winner's Circle and tell them the deal was off. The way things stood, he didn't feel right about representing anyone's interests except Ann's.

Watching the swift changes in his face, Ann forced her chin to steady, her voice to calm. "Earlier today, I was going to ask you to leave. As much as I wanted to see Blue Chip and Easy produce a foal together, I thought it would be best for you, the mare and for me if you left. Now, though, I don't know. Matt, someone could injure or kill your mare. They almost did it today in broad daylight. The possibility frightens me."

The urge to hold her was so strong that Matt could no longer resist. He drew her gently to his chest, circling her with his arms and holding her tightly. "Ann, we've got to get to the bottom of this. Together. I can't leave you alone to face this." It was as close to a commitment as he'd come in the long years since his divorce.

For a moment Ann relaxed in his arms, savoring his strength, the help and support he offered. The world she'd worked night and day to create was turning upside down. Safety, care, all of the attributes she'd fought to instill at her farm were being routed out by some unknown person.

"Matt, we have to figure out who's behind this and put a stop to it. Right now," Ann said, her cheek still resting against his neck.

"I agree, and if you accept my help, I have a few ideas."

"Tell me." She drew away from him and motioned to the table. "Let's go over everything. Maybe we should call Freddie and Cybil in?"

"No!" Matt spoke more harshly than he'd intended. "Ann, whoever is tormenting you is on the inside here."

"No, Matt!" Her response was automatic. "Most of the employees have been here for years, except the grooms. But I know all of them personally. They're local men and they're devoted to the horses, and to Freddie. They'd never do anything wrong."

Matt reached across the table and took her hand. "The person who's been in Easy's feed, the person who planted the moldy hay, this person has had free run of your barn area."

"What are you saying?" She heard him, every syllable, but what he implied was preposterous, unthinkable.

"Ann, the night I came to get the hammer and nails for the pasture fence, your dogs tried to eat me alive. I had to slip through your office window. Those dogs knew me, but they wouldn't let me put a foot on the ground. Each time an incident has happened here, the dogs have given no warning." He squeezed her hand gently. "It has to be someone on the inside. Someone the dogs accept."

"And you think it's Freddie?" Ann asked, horrified eyes meeting his. "Don't you?"

A twinge of doubt touched Matt's face. "I'm not sure, Ann. But let's say I'm not willing to rule anyone out. Freddie doesn't seem to have motive or desire, but he has had opportunity. I—we—have to suspect anyone who's had the chance. I read some statistics somewhere that showed most violent acts are committed by family members."

"Not Freddie." Ann shook her head.

"I'm not saying it is Freddie," Matt insisted. He had more than a little difficulty with that idea himself. "I'm just saying we have to be careful. We can't rule out anybody who has opportunity."

"Why would someone who works here do something so terrible?"

"Because they're being paid to do it."

Matt's words were a series of shocks. "I pay a better wage than any other ranch. I'm a fair employer. My workers respect me."

"I haven't any proof, but I suspect that the person behind this was paid a great deal of money. A lump sum, let's say."

Ann shook her head as if to deny it, then covered her eyes with one hand. "I've fought against accepting this, but I'm afraid you're right."

"Exactly. And we have to find out who's behind this. Any ideas?"

"Just suspicions, Matt, no facts. We can hardly convict someone on suspicions."

"No, but it's the best place I know to start, and I'll bet you're thinking of the same person I'm thinking of. He made a direct threat against you, and bribery is a favorite mode of his."

"Bill Harper." Ann looked out the kitchen window at the horses grazing in the pasture, the sparkling white fences.

"I'm going to do a little sleuthing. I need a list of all of your employees, and their addresses, as much family information about each as you can get." He stood up.

"What kind of information?" Ann rose also, pouring the coffee into a large thermos to take to the barn.

"If they're buying a house, how many children they have, things like that."

"Whatever for?" Ann paused as she reached into the shelf for cups.

"A little debit and credit balance sheet. Facts and figures are the way I make a living, Ann. I think I'll be able to tell if someone's life-style doesn't match his salary."

"You're looking for the Judas."

"Right. And though I won't be able to prove anything conclusively without verification from the bank, I can narrow the field. Then we'll call Jeff in to help us."

Excitement tingled through Ann. "Once we find the person on the ranch—if there is one," she added hastily, "then we can make them tell us who's behind the scene."

Matt nodded. "It's the logical, businesslike approach to the problem." He grinned as he finished. "Let's get cracking."

Carrying the thermos and cups, they returned to the barn. To Ann's surprise, Cybil Matheson was still there.

"Lost in my barn?" asked Ann. "The way your schedule's been going I thought you'd be long gone." Ann poured coffee for the vet. "I can't thank you enough for dropping everything to come out here. I know it makes it impossible for you."

"I just wanted to caution Mr. Roper about trailering his mare. He should wait until tomorrow." Cybil sipped her coffee.

"Matt's going to—"

"Thank you, Cybil," Matt interjected. "That's good advice. I didn't like the idea of pulling out in the dark anyway. Ann and I discussed it, and I'm going to wait until the morning and get an early start."

Cybil nodded, eyeing Matt, then Ann. "I'm glad to see that you both settled this in a sensible manner. These accidents are unfortunate, Mr. Roper, and you shouldn't hold Ann at fault. But I'm sure she understands your desire to leave."

"Yes, I do," Ann said. She was completely baffled by Matt's sudden turn, but she played along.

"You're leaving?" Freddie asked as he came down the ladder. "You're making a mistake. For your horse and for yourself."

"I've made my decision," Matt said firmly. "Now, Ann, if you'll be kind enough to show me that list of farms?" His tone was domineering and irritable.

"Of course, but let me ask Cybil one more question. What about the tests on Easy and the feed?"

"The blood-test results aren't back yet, but the feed samples I've run show negative. I'm going to run the sample from Easy's feed today. You have to admit, what with running out here every two hours, I haven't had much chance to conduct tests."

"I know," Ann soothed her. "We've kept you hopping. But let me know as soon as you hear anything."

Cybil held up a hand to signify a promise.

"Ann?" Matt was growing impatient, and he let it show in his stance.

She hurried to his side and they started for her office.

"What was that all about?" she hissed.

"I want everyone to think we're at odds with each other. That way it looks as if the plan to run me off worked. It's safer."

In the office, Ann gave Matt access to her books, the ledgers and the computer. She watched in fascination as he drew columns of comparisons and then printed out a list of names and addresses.

"I'm going to need your help," he said. Though he was no longer interested in examining her ranch as a potential investment for the members of the Winner's Circle, he couldn't avoid noticing the neat, orderly accounts. Dancing Water Ranch wasn't a gold mine, but neither was it a dry shaft. Ann was earning a respectable living, one that would increase tremendously once the racetrack was in place. He could see why the Winner's Circle might want to buy the ranch, but the information they'd sent him didn't jibe with Ann's ledgers. It appeared to be a curious case of overeager investors wanting to believe bad reports on a piece of property for their own profit. It happened every day in the business world.

"*You're* going to need *my* help? Isn't that slightly reversed?" Ann was standing over him.

"We need to visit every one of these addresses. This afternoon, while your employees are at work. By examining the home area, we'll find clues of recent affluence."

"Let's go," Ann said with resolve.

The first five stops showed average homes with average cars. There was nothing elaborate or suspicious.

"That doesn't mean these people are innocent," Matt cautioned her. "It just means they aren't flamboyant. I was hoping for something obvious."

The next three addresses also appeared to check out. Ann felt her hopes falling, but there was also a sense of relief. It was horrible not to trust her employees. She'd always thought of every one of them as above suspicion.

They turned down a dirt road. "Who's this?" Matt asked.

"Marshall Nicholls."

Matt examined his printout. "He's been with you two years. Three children on his insurance policy, a wife with cancer." Matt felt his heart begin to quicken. He knew that medical bills often put people in precarious financial situations.

As they drove nearer the small frame house, they noticed the neatness of the yard, a few bicycles scattered around. And behind the house a new satellite dish.

Ann slowed until Matt reminded her to speed up. "A dish doesn't prove anything, Ann," Matt reminded her.

"He just borrowed a thousand dollars against his salary to pay for another medical problem," Ann said in a flat voice. "Let's go back to the ranch."

"I want to talk with Jeff and see if he can help me with some confidential information."

"Like bank deposits?"

Matt touched Ann's arm. "We want to be positive before we accuse anyone of anything."

Ann was still pale and drawn when they returned to the ranch. She went straight into the house, leaving Matt to work in her office. She wanted desperately to call Freddie in and advise him of their findings, but she didn't.

She wandered around the den, undecided whether to start a fire or not. When the phone rang she nearly jumped out of her skin.

"Ann, I spoke with Jeff and he's going to try to help us. He also wants to talk with you immediately," Matt said. Calling from the telephone in her office at the barn, he sounded as if he were in the next room. "It seems Ray Marble and another member of the racing commission want to reconsider hiring Bill Harper as the contractor. They're changing their vote."

"Apparently I'm not the only one who's suffering from Mr. Harper's criminal tactics," Ann said through gritted teeth. "Well, he's not going to get that bid. Let me talk to Jeff."

Her hand was steady as she dialed Jeff's number. "Who's been threatened?" she asked him point-blank.

"Marble wouldn't say outright, but it seems he may have some past affairs he doesn't want aired in public. And there's another board member whose car tires were slashed. Viciously slashed. He's taken it as a warning, though there was no note."

"Can we prove it's Harper?"

"No," Jeff admitted. "That's the effectiveness of intimidation. The threat is implied, but never concrete."

"I'm learning that firsthand."

"Is something wrong, Ann? Have you been threatened?"

"Not in so many words, but I'll tell you later. I've got to get ready."

Within ten minutes she was changing her clothes for a trip into Biloxi. An emergency board meeting had been called at Jeff's estate, Magnolia Point. Ann calculated she was outnumbered, and that knowledge infuriated her. Harper was winning with strong-arm tactics.

As she started down the drive, she was suddenly conscious of Matt's absence. They'd agreed that he would stay on the ranch to guard the horses. Now she sharply felt the lack of his support. The understanding of how much she'd come to rely on him made her drive faster than usual.

THE SECOND HAND OF THE WATCH swept around the wide, round face with a pleasant, calming effect. It was an old, inexpensive watch. An anniversary present from Ann. She was always so pushy about time. Well, she was right. Split-second timing was essential in carrying out a plan.

The figure, clothed in a worn leather jacket and jeans, stood and extended both arms in a long, catlike stretch. Life was wonderful when an ingenious plan was in place and working.

The business with the mare had gone as planned, or almost. Blue Chip had been discovered before she died. Some might consider that a small setback, but it did have some positive elements. To compensate for the mare, the plan had changed, too.

That was so essential in planning the future, maintaining flexibility.

Blue Chip was a lovely creature. If that meant Matt Roper died, then so be it. He was already half-lost anyway, mooning around like a lovesick calf after Ann. It was sickening. Ann needed a man who wouldn't yield to her every whim. It might have saved her life if someone had taught her not to be so self-centered, showed her how life was meant to be. Instead she had Prince Valiant trying to rescue her from her fate. Too bad for him.

Boiling with anger at the thought of Matt and Ann together, the heavily clothed figure stood and paced the small office. The only light came from a multiline telephone dial, as if an important call was expected.

"Soon we'll count the sheep. They're already turning on you, Ann. The board members are gone. You can't look to them for help. They're gone, gone. Matt Roper will take his mare and leave, if he's smart. Then who's left to help you?"

A burst of deep laughter rang through the small room. "There's no one left to trust, Ann. No one. When the black night settles around you, you'll be all alone. But for now, my little princess has to learn about the dangers of dark roads at night."

THE SCENE AT MAGNOLIA POINT was worse than she'd imagined. Not even the fairy-tale quality of the setting could dispel the ugliness behind the board's action.

Ann openly accused the board of yielding to illegal pressure, but not a single man would admit he was being blackmailed or threatened. Ray Marble made the motion to give Bill Harper the contract.

"When someone dies because of this decision," Ann said coldly, "remember that it's your responsibility." She gathered her coat and purse and started to leave.

"Ann, wait." George Williams stood up. "Ann's right. Let's not be bullied by Harper. I vote against him."

One by one, the men voted. The count was two for and two against when Ann cast the deciding ballot against Harper. She was completely exhausted by the time she shook Williams's hand and left.

Jeff walked her to her car. "They're scared, Ann," he said. "Some peculiar forms of bad luck have struck all of them."

"*I* haven't gone unscathed!" Ann replied, hot anger whipping her cheeks. She told Jeff the series of incidents that had occurred at the ranch.

"This man has to be stopped," Jeff said tersely. "Tell Matt I'll do everything I can to help." He hesitated a moment. "Will you be okay? I mean, I may be out of town for a day or so."

"Sure, and thanks, Jeff." Ann leaned over and kissed his cheek. "Maybe things will cool off around the ranch now that Harper sees he can't frighten us. That'll give us some time to work on solving this."

"When are you scheduled to begin your breeding season?" Jeff asked.

Ann cocked her head. "Tomorrow. I'd forgotten about it. We may have to delay until Cybil gets the feed samples checked, but I don't know. Easy's been a perfect doll lately, strange as that sounds. His erratic behavior makes me believe he has an allergic reaction to something we haven't found yet."

"I have complete confidence in you and Easy Dancer. Go ahead and breed Tango to him again. That'll get your breeding season started with a proven mare, and it'll give Tango another chance to produce the next grand champion."

"You don't need another horse," Ann pointed out. She was moved by Jeff's gesture.

"I didn't need the first two, but I wanted them. Now I want another. Think how valuable those animals will be." Jeff put his arm around her and gave a hug. "Where's Matt? He hasn't gone back to Georgia yet, has he?"

"He's watching the ranch." She tried to keep any emotion from her voice. "We can't breed Blue Chip just yet. She hasn't come into season."

"It appears that his visit has gotten rather extended." Jeff was teasing her.

"The accidents have prevented him from leaving," Ann said quickly. "He's been very helpful."

"Ann?" Jeff turned her to face him, the light from the porch touching both of their faces. "Is it just the horses he's staying for? I thought I saw the possibility of something between the two of you. That's why I worked so hard to get him invited to stay.''

"He's also staying to help me." Ann didn't waver. She'd never lied to Jeff Stuart, and they'd been friends since high school. "I like him a lot, Jeff. Maybe too much."

Jeff pulled her to him and held her in a warm embrace. "It's a scary business, isn't it? I know how you've avoided caring about anyone else romantically, how much you were hurt in your marriage. Sometimes, though, you've got to take a risk. Maybe this is it."

"Maybe," Ann said, drawing away. "I'd better get back. There's no telling what might have happened while I was gone."

Kissing the top of her head, Jeff released her. "Ronnie will be sorry she missed you."

Ann pulled out of the drive, aware as always of the majestic beauty of Jeff's home. The oak-lined driveway was magnificent even in winter. She turned right on Highway 90, catching sight of the three-quarter moon on the Mississippi Sound. Slowing, she pulled over to a rest area and killed the engine.

The light danced on the water. At a small boat yard in front of her, several small sailboats rocked peacefully. Rolling down her window, she heard the sounds of tie lines complaining, of hulls gently bumping the rubber protectors on the dock.

The romantic setting made her think of Matt. If he were beside her now... A delicious shudder ran through her. In the rearview mirror she saw another car pull into the little parking space. A couple out for a little spooning in the moonlight, she thought, though she could only make out one person. Smiling to herself, she started the car. Rest areas were for lovers.

Once she crossed the bridge over Biloxi Bay and made it through the small town of Ocean Springs, there was little traffic. A long stretch of untouched land, a preserve for the sandhill crane, was between town and her ranch. It was a lovely drive through tall-pine forest, and she slowed, allowing her thoughts to wander to Matt. She forced her mind off Bill Harper and the racing commission. She'd won this battle, but the war was hardly over. She was going to have to regroup and find new defenses.

A single pair of taillights had been following her some distance behind ever since the Ocean Springs turnoff. But now the car was coming up on her at an impressive speed. Plenty of teenagers used the deserted road as a place to race, and every year several deer and hundreds of raccoons, opossums, armadillos, dogs and cats were killed by drivers going too fast.

Tightening her grip on the wheel, she kept looking into her rearview mirror. The car behind was moving at breakneck speed. A chill of fear made Ann press down hard on the gas pedal. Whoever was driving wasn't going to slow down or stop.

Ann's car began to pick up speed, but not enough to escape the approaching car. Without warning a pair of headlights came at her from the front. She had only a moment to realize that the vehicle must have been on the road with the headlights off. It was only fifty yards away and directly in front of her. Jerking her wheel, Ann hit the shoulder of the road, flew into the ditch and crashed into the dense shrubbery on the side of the road.

Chapter Nine

Condensation beaded on the glass of bourbon and rolled onto Matt's fingers. He automatically took a sip, not tasting the watery drink. His eyes, unfocused, gazed blankly at the dying fire. When the clock struck eleven, he went determinedly to the phone. He'd memorized Jeff's number but had forestalled calling. He had no desire to interrupt a meeting of the racing commission, but his worry over Ann's lengthy absence had become too great.

He dialed and counted the rings. Eleven. Twelve. Thirteen. No answer. He discounted the possibility that the meeting was so intense no one would answer the phone. Obviously everyone had left Magnolia Point. Maybe hours before. Something terrible had happened and the only thing Matt could do was retrace Ann's route.

Since his horse trailer was hooked to his truck, he took the farm truck. Dim lights issuing from the windows of Freddie's apartment let Matt know the farm manager was still awake, but he didn't stop. Driving fast, he turned onto the main road.

The night was brightly lit by a three-quarter moon, and he inspected the sides of the road as he drove. He couldn't shake the feeling that Ann needed him. And he wanted to be there for her. It was exhilarating, and frightening. She was a courageous woman, but not even her courage could completely protect her.

The road was fairly straight with only a few dangerous curves. When his headlights first picked up what appeared to be a large object half-thrust into the woods, he thought it was a trick of his imagination. In a matter of seconds he recognized Ann's car.

Whipping the truck to the side of the road, he cursed his foolishness for not bringing Freddie. If Ann was hurt, he'd need help. If Ann was hurt ... He ran, his feet sliding in the cold pine needles as he jumped the ditch. The front of the car was wrapped around a big pine. His harsh breathing was the only sound in the darkness. There was no movement in the car nor any sign of Ann.

The driver's door was jammed shut, and he couldn't see into the interior. Racing around to the passenger side, he pulled the door open.

Ann was sprawled across the front seat, blood covering her face and hands. Beside her, thrust viciously into the seat, was a hunting knife. For one nightmarish second, he thought she was dead. The thought was almost paralyzing. He forced back his emotions and fought for a clear head.

"Ann." Matt touched her wrist, finding a steady pulse. She was alive, but he had no way of judging her injuries.

Torn between getting help or taking her to the hospital himself, Matt tightly gripped her hand. When she responded with a moan and an attempt to sit up, he held her steady.

"Don't move," he urged her, his voice soothing. In the circle of light from the flashlight, he found a large gash on her head. A cursory examination revealed no other serious injuries. He expelled his breath in relief. There were no stab wounds. Her breathing was regular and slow, a fact that calmed his worst fears.

As he examined her, he was aware of her trembling. He had no way of determining how long she'd been unconscious in the freezing night. Her jacket was unzipped, her hands and face icy.

"Ann," he whispered, making a decision. He pocketed the knife, but not before he noticed the intricately carved ebony handle. An image of the slashed feed sack entered his mind, and he realized that the knife could easily have been the instrument used. Taking great care, he slid Ann across the seat and into his arms. "Hang on, everything's going to be fine." He kept telling her that, wanting to believe it himself.

He felt her stiffen slightly, then her arms and legs began to flail. "No!" she cried, struggling with all her might.

"Ann, it's me, Matt." He held her tightly, hoping to prevent further injuries as he hurried back to the truck. "It's Matt."

Her struggles slowed. "Matt?" she murmured as if she were half-asleep. "The headlights were coming." She took a deep breath and then started to struggle again. "It's so cold and I couldn't get out. I couldn't see."

Opening the truck door with one hand, he eased her into the passenger seat, pushing in beside her and closing the door. Very gently he wrapped her in his arms and drew her close.

"We need to get you into the hospital," he said softly. "I don't think you're badly hurt, but it would be better to check it all out."

The raw fear was subsiding, and Ann found herself taking comfort in the nearness and warmth of Matt's body. His soothing voice was a line that held her moored against her fears. Those headlights had come at her out of the night deliberately, intending to cause her to swerve off the road.

"They tried to kill me." She spoke in a flat, emotionless tone. "They set a trap and tried to kill me, and it almost worked." She burrowed closer to him, conscious of the aches and pains on every inch of her body. Her head was throbbing as if it were being struck with a hammer, and each breath sent a spark of pain across her chest.

"You can tell me everything that happened on the way to the hospital."

"No." Ann's voice was still flat, but it was steely with iron determination. She sat up straighter, forcing her teeth to stop chattering, fighting the dizziness that momentarily threatened. Matt's body was secure, steadying. "I'm not really hurt badly, just a few cuts and bruises. Thank goodness I had my seat belt on. Those headlights..."

"Let me crank the truck and get some heat going." He slipped out and hurried around to the driver's side. Several minutes later the blast of the heater filled the cab with warmth. "Did you see anyone?" The knife in his pocket was a potent threat against her.

Ann gingerly explored her forehead. The cut ran into her hairline. It was ugly, but not dangerous. "No, just the headlights and then I was knocked out. Matt, I'm not going to the hospital. I can't." The vibrancy was back in her voice. She continued before he could interrupt. "Rumors are already circulating about the 'accidents' we've had at Dancing Water. I can't afford to let another one happen. Take me home."

"I think you should see a doctor." Matt turned on the flashlight and shone it on her head. "I'm no doctor, but I think you need to be looked at, Ann." He started to show her the knife, but stopped. How much could she take in one night?

"The cut isn't deep." She took the light from him and turned it off. "I promise you, I'm fine."

Recognizing the futility of arguing with her, Matt relented. "If I do that, and it seems as if you need a doctor, will you let me take you to one?" He drew her against his side. "You scared the life out of me when I saw you sprawled on that car seat."

In the darkness of the truck she smiled. "I promise."

"Okay," Matt reluctantly agreed, making a U-turn in the middle of the road and heading back toward the ranch. He wasn't satisfied with Ann's decision, but his immediate concern was getting her to a warm place.

"What happened?" he asked.

She cleared her throat, gradually relaxing in the warmth of the cab, in the nearness of Matt's masculine strength.

"I was coming home when I noticed some headlights behind me. They'd been behind me the whole way, but way behind me. Then they sped up and got really close—too close." The increase in her heartbeat as she relived the terrifying moment made her pause to fight for control. In a shaky voice she continued.

"I stepped on the gas and was trying to get away from them when another pair of headlights snapped on in front of me. I had no choice but to go into the ditch."

Anger made Matt clutch the wheel so tightly his hands felt frozen. This was no longer an attempt to ruin Ann's business; it was attempted murder. And the attacker had left a knife, an explicit calling card that served notice that he would return.

"I thought Bill Harper would have been put off after tonight," Ann said softly, her hand gingerly exploring her forehead and crown. "He didn't get the bid, and he won't ever."

Watching her from the corner of his eye, Matt shook his head. "That isn't a very pretty gash. I'll look closer when we get home." His brushed the backs of his fingers along her cheek. "So the board held together."

"Just barely. Marble is gone and the others are hanging by the skin of their teeth." Ann spoke bitterly. "Everything I worked for, everything Jeff sacrificed to accomplish, is jeopardized now. First it will be Harper with his shoddy work, then it'll be some trainer with a long needle or a jockey who knows a few illegal tricks." Tears threatened so she stopped talking.

Matt tightened his arm, pulling her against him. "Mr. Harper hasn't won yet," he said with conviction, as he turned down the driveway to the ranch.

He drove the truck right up to the steps and insisted on carrying her inside. His hands were as gentle as his soothing words as he took her into the bathroom and carefully examined her head.

She bit her lip but didn't cry as he cleaned the wound with peroxide. The cut ran from her hairline two inches toward her crown. Once the blood was removed, it didn't look too serious, but Matt still wanted a doctor's view.

"Put some of those adhesives on it and leave it alone," Ann argued. "If I called a doctor every time there was a cut or bruise at this place I'd have to build an entire wing of a hospital."

As Matt applied the bandages, he noticed the color back in her cheeks, the spirit in her voice and eyes. With the bandage placed rakishly on her forehead, she was incredibly appealing.

"You look like a patient who's just taken control of the hospital," he said. "What's going on in that mind?" She obviously wasn't aware that her attacker had been in the cab of the truck with her.

"I want Harper's head," she replied. "He's frightened a bunch of old men and tried to ruin my business. We need a plan, and I think it will be very interesting to see what happens when they begin looking for me tomorrow.''

Matt had been so concerned with her health that he'd given no thought to the future. Now all of his instincts told him Ann was a smart woman.

"You're right," he said. "Tomorrow morning I think I'll learn some valuable things."

"The staff comes in at six, and several of the men will pass my car." Ann grew excited. "Nicholls will be one of those men. If he's involved in this, then he might have been involved last night. Unless he's a very good actor, he'll make a slip." Her gaze locked with Matt's.

When his strong hands reached down and drew her to her feet, another touch of dizziness threatened.

At the sign of her unsteadiness, Matt's arm slipped beneath her legs and he lifted her against his chest. "If you won't see a doctor, the least you can do is go to bed."

He followed his words with direct action, swinging her gently onto the bed. He undressed her as if she were a child, then tucked her snugly beneath the warm comforter.

As he took a seat in a chair he pulled to the bedside, he gave her a crooked grin. "I'll make you a promise, Ann, if you'll make me one."

Something in the tilt of his mouth warned her to tread with caution. "That depends," she said.

"Promise me that if you have any dizziness, any twinge of pain, you'll see a doctor tomorrow?"

"That's easy enough," she agreed, still wary of the strange light that danced in the depths of his eyes. "And your promise?"

He leaned closer. "The next time I take your clothes off, I won't leave you alone in bed."

Something in her stomach tightened fiercely, but before she could respond, Matt brushed his lips across her cheek and stood up. He left the room without looking back.

"DO YOU KNOW WHERE Miss Ann might be?" Freddie asked with a pinched face the following morning. He stood at the door, shifting from foot to foot, obviously reluctant to even enter the den.

"She went to Jeff's house last night," Matt responded, just as Ann had instructed him. It was almost criminal to keep Freddie in the dark, but Ann was right when she insisted that he'd never be able to contain his anger if he knew Ann had almost been killed. "I went to bed before she came back."

"I heard the farm truck go out last night, before midnight," Freddie insisted, unwilling to leave. "I thought you might have gone to meet her."

"I went out for a pack of cigarettes, down to Bugle's." He deliberately lied, giving the name of the small country store in the opposite direction of Ann's car. He only hoped that Freddie didn't remember he'd never seen him smoke.

"I thought you turned the other way." A red splotch of anger burned in each of Freddie's wrinkled cheeks.

Matt assessed the older man. Freddie was no fool, and he wasn't a man to be played with. Hating that he had to continue to lie, Matt adopted an angry tone.

"I went to Bugle's. I didn't see Miss Tate, and I resent your questions. I'm leaving here this morning as soon as I speak with her." He started to close the door.

"That's what I'm trying to tell you, man," Freddie shot back. "Miss Ann's car isn't here. She never came in last night."

The fear and worry on the older man's face were almost more than Matt could bear. He opened the door wide and drew the farm manager into the warm den.

"She didn't come home?" he asked, assuming a shocked tone. "Does she do this often?"

"Never!" Freddie exploded. "I'm telling you something's happened. Miss Ann would never stay away all night. Now if you'll give me the keys to the farm truck, I'm going looking for her."

"Have you called Jeff Stuart?"

"I did, and his housekeeper says he left last night around eight to go to New Orleans. Miss Ann's been missing for nearly twelve hours."

Matt couldn't help himself. He put a reassuring hand on Freddie's shoulder. "Take it easy. I'm sure Ann's going to be just fine."

Freddie tensed. "You're sure, are you? What have you done with her?" He tightened his fists. "Things have gone wrong ever since you put foot on this place, and now Ann is missing. What's going on?"

Before Matt could answer, a small red truck tore down the driveway, its horn honking furiously.

Freddie stepped back into the cold. The red truck cut across the pecan orchard, crushing through a bed of flowers and continuing to the porch. A small, thin man jumped from the cab.

"There's been an accident. Miss Ann! Her car's in a grove of trees and she's gone!"

Freddie staggered, then caught himself on the porch rail. Before he could protest, Matt helped him into the house, signaling the other man to enter also. Watching the anguish on the old man's face, Matt decided he would tell him the truth as soon as possible. Freddie's love for Ann was etched in his drawn features. Matt could no longer deceive him.

Supporting Freddie's sagging weight, Matt helped the older man to the sofa. "Ann's fine, Freddie. I promise you," he whispered fiercely.

When Nicholls entered, Freddie shrugged away from Matt. He nodded to the thin man and assumed control of the situation. "Tell me what you found, Nicholls."

Throughout the worker's agitated recital, Matt kept a blank face. He intensified his scrutiny of the thin man, noticing his flushed face, strained eyes and shaking hands. Nicholls knew something, and he was making no effort to hide it.

"I was driving in, and I saw the car slammed into the woods. I went to see, and there was blood all over the seat, but Miss Ann was gone." His voice cracked. "She wasn't supposed to be hurt!"

He started toward the door, but Matt's harsh voice stopped him.

"I think perhaps you should tell us what you were doing last night about eight o'clock, Mr. Nicholls." Matt hid the anger that bubbled just beneath the surface. Ann could have died in the accident, and it was hard for him to forget that fact.

"What is this?" Freddie asked, swiveling from Matt to the other man. "Does Nicholls know what happened to Ann?"

"I think he does," Matt said. "Freddie, would you mind going to the kitchen and calling the sheriff? I want to have a word alone with Mr. Nicholls."

Hesitating only a second, Freddie left the room.

"Were you in the car behind her, or the one in front?" Matt's voice was as vicious as a whip.

"We only meant to frighten her!" Nicholls strained forward, grasping Matt's hand. "We never meant for her to wreck. We only wanted to scare her a little, so she'd understand what would be best for her.''

"Best for her?'' Matt snapped. "Like it was in her best interest to scare off her customers, to make her horses sick?'' Matt's hands closed on the lapel of Nicholls's jacket. "I should beat the life out of you.''

"It's not that way.'' Nicholls twisted but couldn't break free of Matt's grip. "The man said that Miss Ann had to realize how much she needed him.''

"Who paid you to hurt Ann?'' Matt asked, tightening his hold.

"I . . . don't know,'' Nicholls said.

"Murder is a serious charge,'' Matt threatened.

"Murder?'' Nicholls collapsed. "Miss Ann isn't dead? She couldn't be. He said she was alive, just knocked out. He said it would teach her to stay home where she belonged. He said she'd wake up knowing how much she needed him and that she'd honor her commitment to him.''

Disbelief hardened the corners of Matt's mouth, and he loosened his hold. Nicholls dropped to the floor.

"Tell me she isn't dead,'' Nicholls begged, unaware of the change in Matt's face. "She was good to me and my family. The bills were so high. He gave me some money last Christmas for the kids. A big hunk of money. Told me to think of it as a loan until my wife got better. Then he started asking me to do things. Bad things. He promised me twenty thousand dollars to put the amphetamine in the feed and another five to put out the spoiled hay. I wouldn't help him with the fence. I was afraid one of the horses would really get hurt. That's why I was hanging around the barn that night.'' His voice broke. "All he wanted was for her to take him back.''

"Who?'' Matt thundered.

"Robert, her husband." Nicholls struggled to his feet. "That's the God's honest truth. Here!" He fumbled in his coat pocket and withdrew a note.

Matt quickly scanned the boldly written message that gave exact instructions for Nicholls to flash his headlights when Ann was twenty-five yards away. The note concluded, "Remember, this is the woman I love. And she loves me. Don't hurt her. Just scare her."

"Where is he?" Matt's voice cut through the room.

Nicholls blanched, but he shook his head. "I swear I don't know. I honestly never saw the man. I swear. My wife has been so sick, and the children—"

"How long has Tisdale been back?" Matt's dark eyes were black with anger. "The truth!"

"A few weeks." Nicholls looked around the room as if he hoped to disappear. "I don't know. Harper told some of the guys at the dirt track that Robert was back and that he was going to remarry her." Nicholls dropped his head. "That's why I agreed to help. I didn't mean to harm anyone, and it seemed like he really loved her. Harper told me that Miss Ann had tricked Robert into leaving, then charged him with stealing the horse. He didn't want to go away. He didn't have a choice. She wanted the insurance money so the ranch wouldn't go under."

Matt's face registered contempt. "Can you identify Tisdale as the man who paid you to sabotage Ms. Tate?"

"I assumed it was him, but I'm telling the truth when I say I never saw him. Never. The man said he only wanted to frighten Miss Ann into realizing she loved him. I needed the money. I had to have it. My children..." He started to sob.

Freddie pushed through the kitchen door, signaling Matt with his eyes. They went into the kitchen, carefully closing the door and leaving Nicholls huddled on the sofa.

"Where's Ann?" Freddie's tone was demanding. "If she was really hurt, you wouldn't be so cool. I've seen the way you look at her. I should have known this morning that you knew where she was."

Matt's face was grim. "She's in my room. It was her idea to hide, hoping that someone would panic and confess, and Nicholls did exactly that. Perhaps a little more."

Relief swept the worry from Freddie's eyes, and he was unaware of the anger in Matt's quiet stance.

"Then everything has worked out fine. You won't have to leave. We've found the man who tried to hurt Easy and Blue Chip. Now the horses are safe and we can get on with the breeding season."

"Almost." Matt practically bit the word in half.

"Something wrong?" Freddie asked.

Matt withdrew the knife from his pocket and handed it to Freddie.

"That's Robert's knife." Freddie held the blade as if it would poison him, quickly giving it back. "Where'd it come from?"

"It was sticking in Ann's car seat. A warning. You heard what Nicholls said?"

"Some of it." Freddie nodded, never taking his gaze from the knife.

"Her ex-husband's back in town. And he wants her back." Matt waited for Freddie to say something, but the old man clamped his mouth shut. "Well, what do you think?"

"I've dreaded this day." Freddie started toward the den and then turned back to face Matt. "Robert gave her no choice."

"Don't tell her about the knife." Matt put it back in his pocket.

"I'd rather die than give her that news." Freddie pushed through the door and left Matt alone in the kitchen.

Freddie's haunting words were still echoing in Matt's head when the sheriff arrived, Freddie behind him. Nicholls, bowed by guilt, was led away, his hands cuffed behind his back.

As soon as the sheriff left, Ann entered the den. She was freshly bathed and dressed, and the white bandage on her forehead immediately caught Freddie's attention. He went to her, clucking and demanding that he look at the cut.

Though she tried to resist, Freddie had his way.

"You needed stitches," he scolded her. "If you don't you'll have a jagged scar there."

"In my hairline, Freddie." Ann sighed, casting a surreptitious glance at Matt, who was staring out the window in stony silence. "This is nothing compared to what I want to do to Bill Harper and whoever else is involved with him."

"Would you care to be more specific?" Matt asked, a tinge of sarcasm in his voice. No matter how he tried, he couldn't erase Nicholls's words about Tisdale. Had Ann played her husband for a fool, somehow forced him to leave and take the stallion? She'd admitted herself that it was the insurance money that had saved her farm. Now she was ready to sacrifice Easy. When he thought of the way the horse adored her, trusted her, he felt sick.

Freddie cast a startled glance at him.

"I think it's time for a plan," Matt said, the corners of his mouth bitter. "If Ann can act frightened enough, then she can convince Harper she's not going to give him any more trouble. He has to be convinced that Ann has fallen prey to the greed bug, too. Which means that you—" he placed his palms gently on Ann's face but his eyes were hard and dangerous "—are going to have to ask Mr. Harper for a cut of his contract."

"What?" Ann said. Matt's eyes frightened her. He looked completely hard, ruthless.

"Convince the man that you'll help him get additional contracts—for a price. Tell him you want a cut of his action. To be his partner." He ground out the last word. She looked so damned innocent. Nothing had really changed. He was still the fool, the dreamer. And Ann was still a woman. She'd manipulated him as successfully as Monica ever had.

"He'll never believe that." Ann shook her head.

"You can make him believe it." Matt turned away. "I have all the confidence in the world that a woman can make a man believe anything she wants."

Ann drew her breath in sharply. She started to respond, but she didn't know how. Matt was acting like a stranger.

"Deception doesn't come with gender," Freddie said softly, walking to the door. "Neither does trust, Matt." He closed the door with an emphatic slam as he left.

"We're going to breed Tango Dancer this morning," Ann said, her voice even as she sought for common footing with Matt. She could see the rigidity of his back, sense the anger flowing through him. His actions, so unexpected after his tenderness the night before, cut into her. She forced herself to speak calmly, pleasantly. "What are your plans?"

"I'm going to make some calls." He walked across the den and entered the hallway.

She called him back. "Matt, you're free to leave here. This isn't your fight, you know."

"I know that." His face was a mask hiding all emotions. "Maybe I'm odd in some ways—I don't like being lied to. When I learn the truth, I'll be gone." But he wasn't leaving until he was certain Easy Dancer was safe.

MIDDAY SUNLIGHT STREAMED through the expensive curtains, striking the elegant walnut desk.

A capable-looking hand toyed with a telephone cord, straightening each coil, willing the phone to ring. When it did, the hand clutched it eagerly.

After listening for a moment, worn leather boots were placed on top of the expensive desk. "I told you I wouldn't kill her." The voice snapped with impatience. "This is no time for cold feet. That contract is still at stake."

During a pause the fingers tightened around the telephone until the knuckles were white and dangerous looking. "Don't threaten me!"

The phone was replaced and a smile touched the cold features, highlighting the determined jaw.

The plan was still in effect, working perfectly. Nicholls had planted the perfect seeds of doubt. Plant, harvest and sow. That was the plan. With careful tending, the harvest would be bountiful and the season of sowing would be total justice.

The important thing was not to lose sight of Ann. That was the key. Very soon she would be without her prince. She would be alone—and completely vulnerable.

Chapter Ten

The day finally ended. Ann walked toward the house, her heart feeling as fragile as the pecan leaves beneath her boots. All day long Matt had passed her without a glance or a word. He worked with Blue Chip, deliberately ignoring her when she took Tango in for breeding. He watched Dawn handle Easy Dancer while she was busy with Madcap, another mare in for breeding. Though she'd expected him to take an interest in the breeding, and in Easy's perfect behavior, Matt had maintained a physical distance. There had been no opportunity to question him about his disconcerting change of attitude. He made certain of that.

As far as she could tell, and she had gone over every minute of their time together, there was no basis for his sudden attitude change. She was sorely tempted to confide in Freddie, but her pride wouldn't allow it. What could Freddie tell her that she didn't already know? There was no rationale for emotions, no guarantees in the word love. That was a lesson she'd learned in her marriage. Or at least she'd thought she learned it until Matt Roper almost made her believe otherwise.

Grim and hurting, she kicked a pile of leaves and hurried up the steps and into the house.

ANGER DROVE THE BREATH out in short, shallow gasps as the figure in black leather crouched in a corner of the feed room, one eye on the door. So Matt Roper had decided to play the fool and stay. The attack on his horse and a blade of jealousy hadn't been enough to drive him away. He was getting in the way too often. With Matt's support, Ann wasn't alone. There were other meddlers, too. Busybodies like Jefferson Stuart who would have to be dealt with. They were a simple, expendable matter. A settlement long due for years. But Matt . . . too bad.

The figure crouched, muscular legs flexing with annoyance at the close quarters. It would be a long, long night. In the darkness, though, many things would be accomplished. Ann would learn what it meant to suffer loss, to be pushed out alone. Her father had died, but the old man had left her money, which was a balm for the pain. Yes, it was going to be a night well worth planning and waiting for.

The strong hands slipped into the black leather gloves and flexed. Then the fingers curled around a thick iron bar wrapped in leather. The bar lifted and fell, lifted and fell. Each time it smacked solidly into a leather-clad palm.

ANN QUICKLY PREPARED a tray of food and a thermos of coffee and started down the hallway to her room. A confrontation with Matt was the last thing she wanted. She was tired, confused and angry. She didn't understand Matt's evasive behavior, but she had decided he was right about the plan to trick Bill Harper. The man had to be stopped, and she was the key to trapping him.

To her dismay, she turned into the hallway and almost ran Matt down.

"Dining alone?" he asked. It was impossible to miss the sarcasm in his voice.

"I thought I'd eat in my room. I want to think about the idea of luring Bill Harper into a trap." Her voice shook but there was nothing she could do about it. She forced her gaze up from the tray and met his. The coldness mixed with the heat of anger was like a physical blow. She stepped back.

"If your husband hadn't run out on you, you wouldn't be alone, would you?" Once again the sarcasm was impossible to ignore.

"No. Maybe, I don't know." Ann gripped the tray tighter. What was he getting at?

"Yes, I believe you've mentioned your solitary life-style was because your husband simply vanished, right? Of course, you knew nothing about it. How much was the stolen horse insured for?"

"Where are you going with these questions, Matt?" Her own anger surfaced with a wave of heat and fury. "Are you getting some joy out of badgering me, or is there a good reason?"

"Probing the depths, Ann. That's all. Somewhere beneath all of that subterfuge I'm sure I'll find at least one honest answer."

He stalked past her, slamming the door to the den with such force that the coffee cup on her tray rattled.

Ann put the tray on the floor and raced after him. Her cheeks were burning with fury, and her blue eyes were cobalt. Damn him! He couldn't talk to her like that and walk away. She slammed through the den and into the empty kitchen.

Hurrying outside, she saw him disappearing into the barn. Though the wind was cold, she didn't stop for a coat.

The pink light of dusk was evaporating from the sky as she raced through the pecan orchard. In another ten minutes it would be dark, and colder. But she had her anger to warm her, and it surged through her as she hurried after Matt's tall figure.

When she got to the barn, the aisle was hauntingly empty. The horses, busy with their hay, gave her only a cursory glance as she hurried down the cement corridor, her footsteps echoing sadly.

"Matt." Something about the emptiness of the barn made her hesitate. Unseen eyes seemed to watch her. Her spine tingled at the idea that someone hidden mapped her every move. Not Matt. Angry or not, he never made her feel as if the point of a knife was at her throat. But where was he? She'd seen him only a moment before. Where had he gone?

"Matt?" She started forward again, and this time her steps were slower, cautious. The main switch for the barn lights was by the entrance, and she was tempted to go back and turn it on. As soon as that thought entered her mind she stopped. Matt should have turned on the light. Unless he didn't want to be seen.

Her heart squeezed. The same fear she'd felt on the road the night before slammed into her. She felt the sides of a trap closing around her.

At the end of the barn was Freddie's apartment and safety. If she could only make it that far. The horses shuffled in their stalls, nosing the sweet hay. There were twenty stalls on each side, and all but two were occupied. She ran through the boarding pattern in her head. It was unlikely someone would be hiding in a stall with a horse. The empty stalls were another story. Her skin tightened and crawled, warning of impending danger.

An unfamiliar noise halfway down the barn caught her attention. The sound was ghostlike, an eerie moan emanating from the darkness.

In the pasture several horses whinnied, then broke into a gallop. Sudden panic swept through the barn as the stalled horses neighed and danced, answering the horses in the pasture.

Concern for the animals prompted Ann to turn and rush back outside. The horses in the west pasture were streaking away from her, sleek Thoroughbred bodies stretched out in powerful, ground-covering strides. As familiar as the sight had become, it never lost its power or majesty. But for Ann now, the beauty was dimmed by fear and worry.

She watched as the horses ran to the back pasture fence, then turned and came back toward her. Several bucked without breaking stride, rising up and twisting only to touch ground once again in a dead gallop.

"Just a game," she murmured to herself, relief settling in the pit of her stomach. After her last scare with the pasture fence, she was overly anxious. Whenever the horses made a sound, she couldn't help but worry that someone was trying to cause trouble.

She started back to the barn but stopped. For the first time since she'd been a young girl, the dark, massive structure scared her. The sensation that someone evil was waiting for her was very strong, even as she stood by the pasture. She had to force her feet to move back to the doorway, to enter the darkness. She paused, her fingers on the light switch, trying to decide if she should check the barn or call Freddie. And Matt. Where was he?

The leather-gloved hand that grasped her mouth was strong. She struggled, fighting the blackness that swept over her and became total when something heavy struck her above her right ear.

THE COLD DAMP seeped through her thin cotton shirt and she drew her knees to her chest in an effort to find warmth. Her face was pressed into the wet grass and she shifted, seeking a more comfortable position.

A low whine and a wet tongue made her jerk away, and the motion gave her a piercing attack of nausea. As awareness began to return, Ann knew she was hurt. The low throb of her head accelerated into a full-blown hurricane of an ache. Her body, shaking spasmodically from the cold, was bruised and sore. Whenever she tried to sit up, her head pounded so hard it made her stomach flip.

Taking several deep breaths she forced herself up on one elbow and took in her surroundings. She was outside the main barn, about halfway to the stallion barn. Shasta sat a few feet away, whining worriedly. When Ann moved, the shepherd rushed over to her, licking her face and nosing her.

"Easy, girl," Ann whispered, surprised to find that her voice was one part of her that worked without pain. Resisting the temptation to lie back down and go to sleep, Ann forced her knees under her and finally stood. Though she was wobbly, she made it to the wall of the stallion barn and rested there, sucking in great gulps of air.

From the shadows of the barn, Suni joined Shasta, and both dogs jumped about and whined, eager for Ann's attention but careful not to get too close to her.

"What's wrong, girls?" she asked, trying to understand the dogs' erratic behavior. They were normally calm animals, not given to jumping and whining.

When Shadow's low howl split the night, Ann thought she would faint. The baying of the dog came from somewhere in the stallion barn, and it was as eerie and sad as a dirge.

A bright moon was climbing the horizon, not yet high enough to give good light. Distracted by the dogs, Ann hadn't been able to piece together how she'd arrived on the ground in the middle of the barn area. As she leaned against the barn, she remembered the strong grip of the hand around her mouth, her fear, and then the viciousness of the blow to her head.

Instinctively she pressed herself closer to the barn. The old wood was rough against her chilled skin, and it was strangely comforting as she faced the knowledge that someone was on the grounds, someone capable of violence.

Matt! The picture of him disappearing into the darkened barn stabbed her brain. Had he struck her? Based on his own rules, he'd had opportunity. Or was he in danger, a victim, too?

Shadow's mournful voice soared into the night once again. It was so filled with sadness that Ann felt a deep, unexplainable sense of loss. Gritting her teeth, she pushed away from the wall and eased toward the house. She had to get inside, get warm and call Freddie. And where was the groom who was supposed to be standing watch at night?

"Ann!"

Matt's frantic voice stopped her in her tracks. Instead of answering him she slinked into a hedge of redtops that grew beside the barn.

She wanted Matt, wanted to fly into his arms and let him hold her. Only the night before he'd held her in his arms and protected her. Dizzy and scared, she wanted him beside her. The physical need almost made her ill. But a tiny voice in the back of her brain warned her against such a move. Matt's behavior had sprouted the seed of distrust. Dropping to her hands and knees, she crawled between the hedge and the wall of the barn. The fact that she was hiding from Matt only intensified her fear. Her only hope was that the moonlight wouldn't strengthen enough to give her away.

Her breath was harsh and ragged in her own ears as she moved. Shasta and Suni were at her heels, still whining lightly.

"Ann!"

Matt's voice held an edge of something raw, and Ann responded with a new surge of strength. Cold, and still dizzy from the blow to her head, she crouched lower. It took more of her will not to answer.

When she heard his footsteps hurrying in her direction she pressed against the barn, swallowing the fear that threatened to turn into a sob.

Matt! her mind called to him, but she didn't allow her voice to utter a sound.

He went past her toward the house, an unsteady, limping quality in his gait.

When he was gone she rose, then slipped around the corner of the stallion barn and into the open door. She nearly fell over Shadow. The dog was lying in front of Easy's stall, her pointed ears trained at it, her eyes unwavering as she watched it. Harsh breathing came from within the stall.

An extraordinary sense of fear numbed Ann. Silently she walked to the door of Easy's stall and looked in. The huge stallion was in the back corner, his ears pinned back, his eyes rolling. Sweat was lathered on his shoulders and chest, and foam dripped from his mouth.

"Easy," she pleaded softly, knowing it was futile. The animal in the stall bore no resemblance to her stallion. This was the other stallion, the murderous half ton of muscle and meanness.

"No," Ann whispered, "this can't be." Looking at Easy, she fought to put together the pieces of a puzzle that didn't fit. Marshall Nicholls had been under arrest all day. He couldn't have returned and given Easy more drugs. None of it made sense anymore.

Outside the barn footsteps approached. Ducking into the feed room, Ann carefully worked the slide on the door. She couldn't help but remember the night, almost a year before, when someone had knocked Ronnie Stuart unconscious and tried to burn her to death in the barn.

Those men were behind bars. Jeff had seen to that. But now someone else was trying to wreak havoc on her ranch.

The smell of feed and hay, usually so comforting, was all around Ann as she nestled into a cranny near the feed sacks. She had to face the issue. Was it possible Matt was somehow involved? Freddie had told her once before that it was a striking coincidence that so much trouble arrived at her farm the same day Matt Roper did.

She closed her eyes, trying to calm her whirling thoughts. The sound of the feed-room door opening startled her. In the darkness she could barely make out the figure who cautiously entered the feed room. Blood pounding in her ears, Ann held her breath, straining to see. The figure moved lithely, quietly.

Crouched in her tiny niche between the feed sacks, Ann bit her knees to keep from screaming. As the bulky figure shuffled closer and closer, Ann thought she would die of fear. She could see only the vague outline of motion in the near-total darkness of the feed room. Suddenly the figure paused, shifted directions and hurriedly left. In a single shaft of moonlight, Ann discerned the leathery texture of the jacket. The feed-room door was carefully closed, and then there was the sound of footsteps pounding the ground, running rapidly away.

Count to twenty, Ann ordered herself, striving for calm. She was a victim, prey for some unknown predator. Backed into a corner of the feed room, she could find no way to alleviate the fear. Someone wanted to hurt her, possibly kill her. That was all she knew.

But suddenly that wasn't all. A new, icy tentacle of fear wrapped around her heart as she realized that the person who had just entered the feed room had passed unobstructed by Shadow, Shasta and Suni. Whoever it was wasn't a stranger, and it wasn't Bill Harper....

She had to get to a telephone. She steadied herself with the picture of Freddie picking up the receiver in his warm little apartment and calming her fears. Then she'd call the sheriff and Jeff. In her mind, she surrounded herself with the people she knew she could trust. First, though, she had to get to a telephone.

She eased the latch of the feed-room door open and stepped into the aisle. To her surprise Shadow still alertly guarded the door to Easy's stall. Suni and Shasta had joined her, and all three dogs were whining deep in their throats. Inching across the aisle, Ann made her way to the stallion's stall.

Out of the darkness Easy neighed shrilly and lunged at her. The stout wooden door of his stall held the charge. Easy's teeth snapped in the air, making Ann draw back. Out of the corner of her eye she saw something on the floor in the corner of the stall. She rushed to the door. Against the far wall, twisted and broken, was Freddie.

Shadow's renewed, dismal howl mingled with Ann's scream.

THE LARGE LUMP on Matt's head pounded with the intensity of a sledgehammer. Blood soaked the front of his shirt and jacket. In his search for Ann, he'd forgotten about his own injuries. The last thing he remembered was walking into the darkened barn, a carrot in his hand for Blue Chip. He'd intended to give the mare a treat and then go down to Freddie's for a chat. If he couldn't face Ann with his questions, he'd have to put his pride away and ask Freddie about Ann's relationship with her ex-husband. Harper had mentioned Robert's jealousy. Then there was the knife. It was possible Ann's divorce was just as she had so succinctly portrayed it.

With the passage of each minute, he felt more and more like a fool.

Since his conversation with Marshall Nicholls, he'd done a lot of thinking. About Ann, and about himself. He'd come to the conclusion that he'd reacted solely in an emotional way, without thought. He'd tried and convicted Ann based on his past, not hers. He'd never even given her a chance to explain.

When he'd run into her in the hallway, instead of asking her about her ex-husband, he'd adopted a sarcastic, bitter attitude to disguise his own pain. He'd wanted to hear her answer, but he had been afraid that Nicholls's accusations were true. If she had played Robert for a fool, using him in an insurance scam, then a lot of what was happening at Dancing Water made sense. Revenge was emotional, after all. But if that was the case then Ann wasn't the woman Matt thought she was—wanted her to be.

Those things had been on his mind as he walked through the darkened barn. He didn't see the hand that clubbed him. He was out cold before he even struck the cement, and so had no idea who pulled him into a stall and left him there, where a nervous horse might step on him.

Now Ann was missing. Her jacket was in the closet, and her tray of food was on the hallway floor where she'd left it at least an hour earlier. Concerned, he'd gone to Freddie's apartment to ask the farm manager for help. But the apartment was empty, the place ransacked and trashed. He'd just been reaching for the telephone to call the sheriff when he heard Ann's scream.

As he entered the stallion barn he stopped. Ann clung to the door of Easy's stall, her face stripped of everything except horror. He rushed to her side and saw Freddie. The old man was trampled, his body obviously broken. Easy had backed off into a corner, his eyes rolling and his teeth snapping at the air in Ann's direction.

"He's dead, isn't he?" Ann said softly.

Matt had to pry her fingers from the door as he physically moved her away from the sight. Ann's assessment appeared to be correct, but he wanted to make certain.

"Ann." He spoke calmly, trying to reach through her shock. "We're going to have to get Easy Dancer into his paddock. We're going to have to get Freddie out of here. What I want you to do is call an ambulance right away."

"Of course." She stood without moving.

"Ann!" Matt grabbed her shoulders and shook her hard. "We've got to act!"

A faint moan from the old man in the corner of the stall caught their attention. Ann's spine stiffened and she braced herself against Matt's touch.

Matt gave her a slight shove in the direction of her office. As soon as she was gone, he took a whip and a pitchfork from the wall and slowly entered the stall. He didn't want to hurt Easy Dancer, but he had to get to Freddie.

The stallion, as if sensing Matt's cold determination, backed slowly away toward the paddock door.

Matt continued his cautious advance. When Easy was fully out of the stall, he hurried forward and closed the door to the paddock. Then he turned his attention to Freddie.

Blood covered the old man's jacket, and there was a terrible gash on his head. One arm was twisted at an odd angle. Matt felt for Freddie's pulse. It was weak, but it was there.

He found horse blankets in the tack room and gently covered the old man. When Ann returned, she knelt beside him, rubbing the hand of his uninjured arm between her own. Her tears fell unchecked, coursing down her cheeks and dripping onto the soft shavings.

She remained there until the ambulance attendants moved her out of the way and began their examination. They exchanged medical terms, each one sounding more ominous than the last.

When Ann asked to ride in the ambulance, one attendant took Matt aside.

"It would be better if she didn't. I doubt the old man's going to make it to the hospital. We'll do the best we can for him, and we can work better without a hysterical family member in the way." The young man eyed Ann as if he expected her to fall apart at any minute.

"We'll follow."

"Take your time. If we make it to the hospital we'll be in emergency for quite some time."

The ambulance pulled away with a loud shriek and flashing red lights casting eerie patterns down the driveway.

Ann stood at the barn, her arms dangling helplessly at her side and sobs tearing through her. Matt turned her to face him and put his arms around her tightly.

She was shaking in his arms, and her skin was cold. With as much speed as he could manage, Matt led her through the pecan orchard, up the steps and into the house.

As they entered the den, Ann surrendered to Matt, shock and pain finally canceling her fear. Freddie might die. Freddie, her mainstay on the farm, her friend. The image of his body, trampled by her horse, made her double over with grief.

"Go ahead and cry," Matt told her softly. "Go ahead." He held her to him while she sobbed.

Pulling herself together, Ann drew a ragged breath. "Someone tried to murder Freddie." She stepped back from Matt. For the first time she saw the blood on his shirt, the gash on his forehead, and she remembered her own encounter with a club. Her fear. And her suspicions.

"Call the sheriff, please." She tried to hide the tremble in her voice. She'd read somewhere that the safest thing to do was never let an enemy see your fear. She couldn't take her eyes off the blood and cut on Matt. Had he been fighting with Freddie?

"Where have you been?" Matt said. "I've been hunting everywhere for you."

"Where have *you* been, Matt?" Ann's question was tinged with anger. "The last time I saw you, you were going into the barn. Then someone struck me from behind and knocked me out."

"You were hit?"

"With something that felt like the peen of a hammer." She spoke as her fingers touched the sore spot on the back of her head.

"You were knocked out?" He reached out to her, but she backed away. The fear in her face stung him. He let his hand fall to his side. "I went out to see Blue Chip, and that's the last thing I remember. Someone hit me, too."

"What was Freddie doing in Easy's stall?" she asked, trying not to cry.

"I have no idea, but I do have a question." Matt found a comforter and wrapped it around her. "When I first came here and the trouble started, I asked you if there was anyone who hated you enough to try to hurt you, remember?"

Ann nodded, too drained to talk.

"You lied to me, Ann."

His accusation made her look up, tear-filled eyes ready to burn with anger. "I didn't lie. I never suspected Bill Harper would do anything so treacherous. Business disagreements don't usually lead to criminal acts."

"I'm not talking about Harper, I'm talking about Robert Tisdale. Marshall Nicholls more or less said you'd double-crossed him and forced him out."

"Get out." Ann spoke clearly and distinctly. "Pack your things and leave. My best friend is almost dead, and you're spouting nonsense about a man who walked out of here three years ago without even a goodbye!" She struggled to her feet, the comforter falling to the floor.

"Nicholls said today that the man who hired him to sabotage you was acting out of spurned love and revenge." Matt held his ground, determined to finish what he'd started. "Nicholls said the man was Robert Tisdale, and he said you'd set Robert up to steal the horse so you could collect the insurance money. Then Nicholls said you charged your husband with horse theft."

"Nicholls can go to hell," Ann said. "Robert, too! If he's around telling lies and making accusations about me, why doesn't he show up out here? Why doesn't he press charges against me?" She threw the question at him like a challenge. "He would never come back. He was never any good at facing the consequences of his actions. But while you're so busy doubting me, consider the fact that tonight while I was hiding in the barn, it occurred to me that it was you who was stalking me."

Reaching slowly into his pocket, Matt withdrew the ebony-handled hunting knife. Ann's eyes widened in fear, and her hand flew to her throat. The same hand reached for the knife, then dropped back to her side. "Where did you get that? It was Robert's. He took it with him when he disappeared."

"I found this in your car the night of your accident. It was stabbed into the seat, right beside your head."

"Robert." Ann could barely speak. "He's really back."

Chapter Eleven

"I'm very sorry," Cybil Matheson said the next day, as her hand touched Ann's shoulder. "I ran every test. There wasn't enough amphetamine in the feed to account for Easy's behavior. In fact, there was hardly enough to say that the possibility of tampering exists." She put a sympathetic hand on Ann's tense shoulder. "To stretch the point I let the report read trace elements of an undefinable amphetamine. That's going to be the official version. My personal opinion is that Marshall Nicholls didn't know enough about doping a horse to have any effect on Easy. Whatever's wrong with the stallion doesn't involve feed. I'm afraid it's a lot more serious." She turned a sympathetic glance at Matt, who stood silently against the wall of the barn.

Cybil's words were ringing in Ann's ears as she stared out over the pasture. Freddie was hovering near death and her stallion was the cause. And Robert was back. The idea was still so shocking she couldn't even mention it to her best friend. If Matt's accusations were correct, then the Robert who had returned was a very sick man. She just couldn't put the thought into words. Not even to Cybil.

"Ann, are you okay?" Cybil examined Ann's face. "That's a nasty-looking bump on your head." She cast a glance at Matt's bruised face but said nothing. "What's the word on Freddie?"

"He's in a coma." Ann's voice was lifeless. "It's amazing he's alive at all. The severe blow to his head may have caused some permanent damage. They can't be certain until he wakes up, if he wakes up." She was weary and sick. She'd waited at the hospital while Freddie had undergone surgery, and now she was home. The ranch, though, wasn't the familiar haven she'd come to love. It was now a place with danger and pain. It was also a place where she had to make a decision about Easy Dancer.

As if reading her thoughts, Cybil sighed. "For the moment forget about Easy. There's nothing you can do for him, Ann. If he's dangerous we'll worry about that later. I'm just terribly sorry that it wasn't something in the feed, as we all hoped."

Matt exchanged a penetrating look with Dr. Matheson. By the expression on her face, he knew what she was getting at. Easy Dancer was now classified as a rogue, a killer horse. Freddie's battered body, found in the stallion's stall, was as good as a death sentence for the animal.

"I need to go inside," Ann said, suddenly aware that she was on the verge of tears. She hadn't had a moment alone since finding Freddie. She needed time to think about Robert's return and what it might mean.

"Several reporters have called me asking about the... accident," Cybil added hastily. "Would you like me to take care of them?"

"Please." Ann choked and started running toward the house. Casting a backward glance at the vet, Matt followed her.

Cybil watched as Matt caught Ann in the pecan orchard. She saw Ann's hand reach out and then fall to her side. Matt put an arm around her and they went into the house. Cybil picked up her bag and went to her truck.

Inside the house, Ann rallied. "I'm not having Easy put down on the basis of one series of tests." No one had mentioned destroying Easy, but she knew that when word of the stallion's behavior got around there would be pressure to destroy him.

"Let's wait until Freddie gets better before we jump to any conclusions," Matt said calmly.

"I'm not jumping to conclusions. You know as well as I what will happen," Ann exclaimed. "And I don't care what anyone else believes, Easy didn't maliciously attack Freddie." All night long she'd thought through the sequence of events. "Freddie would have come to get me if he thought something was wrong with Easy. He would never have entered the stall, unless he had a reason more important than his life."

As she talked, Ann grew more and more convinced. Freddie had seen something in Easy's stall. A clue. There could be no other reason for him to enter the stall. Though the stallion had been perfectly behaved for the past few days, Ann had given strict orders that no one was to be with him alone. Freddie, after fifty years in the business, had agreed with her on that decision.

"Easy Dancer isn't a killer. He's charged at me and Dawn, and at you, but he didn't kill. He could have. I believe that wholeheartedly. But he didn't!" Exhaustion and jittery nerves propelled her feet across the floor. "The thing we're forgetting is that someone knocked both of us out."

Hope touched her blue eyes, deepening the color. "We're all like pawns in a chess game that someone else is playing. We have to prove that one incident is linked to another. After all, Easy didn't sneak out of his stall and clobber both of us just for the opportunity to stomp Freddie." She took a deep breath, wondering for the hundredth time if the dangerous intruder was her ex-husband.

Matt touched the lump on his head. "Whoever hit me meant business. I got the distinct impression that permanent damage wasn't a concern. Then I was rolled into a stall. Thank goodness the mare was even tempered."

A chill swept across Ann as if someone had opened the door on a cold, dark, evil cellar. She shuddered and quickly threw together kindling to start a fire. The dark figure that had entered the feed room haunted her. Had it been a dream? There was something that didn't match in the sequence of events, the stealthy figure.

"What is it?" Matt's sharp eyes caught her involuntary shudder.

"When you said you thought the person who hit you didn't care about the results, I had the oddest feeling. I think that, when I was hit, it was very calculated—just enough to knock me out but not enough to hurt me seriously. It was as if the person was taking great pains not to kill me." Another shudder coursed through her.

"Could it be that the person who struck you has feelings for you?" Matt decided to broach the subject of her ex-husband. Since he'd shocked Ann with Robert's hunting knife, she hadn't spoken his name.

"Feelings?" Ann puzzled over the idea. "What kind of feelings could someone have when they bash you over the head, not to mention clobbering your houseguest. That's a pretty sick way of showing your feelings for someone, I'd say."

"Remember the first day I was here and Cybil mentioned the possibility of a psychopath?" Matt leaned forward. "People do strange things for...emotional reasons."

"None of this makes sense." Ann paced the floor, her long, slender hands tightened into fists at her sides. Every accident that had occurred she'd accepted as a business-related threat. Now Matt was digging up an uglier, scarier motive. Her stomach tightened painfully at the veiled implication. "You think it's Robert, don't you?"

Matt was at her side, his hands gripping her arms. "Since you didn't double-cross him, was there another reason your husband might have left? Were you involved with someone else?"

Emotions played across her face. Confusion gave way to disbelief, and then anger tightened the corners of her mouth. The blue depths of her eyes burned.

"Are you implying that my ex-husband has returned to ruin my business and kill Freddie because of some past dalliance I committed?"

"That's not exactly what I meant to imply, but the possibility did cross my mind." Matt shifted from foot to foot, his hands releasing her shoulders. "I think Harper's involved somehow. It was odd how he happened to mention Robert that second time he drove over here, as if he knew that Robert had a reason to be jealous."

"Jealous! That's absurd. Robert owed him money. Robert was a compulsive gambler." Irony spiced her cold smile. "He never bet on a horse in his life, though. He said they were too unpredictable. Cards were his game." She didn't bother to tell Matt that if anyone had a right to jealousy, it had been her.

"How deep was he in?"

"Deep enough. I never knew the exact figure, but Harper told me once he would own me lock, stock and barrel."

An idea was forming in Matt's mind. "Could Harper and Robert be in this together? With Nicholls on the inside, they'd have a sure lock on most of your business transactions." A sudden revelation made him start. Nicholls had access to Ann's office, and a list of all potential breeders. He realized the call from "Gordon Boswell" was not just a funny coincidence. It was calculated.

"What's wrong?" Ann was watching him.

"I'm not certain." Now that he'd made the link, he was sure he could take it further. Boswell's voice had been hoarse, but there was something in it that reminded him of the contractor's. The hoarseness could easily have been a disguise. Watching Ann's troubled face, he started to tell her but held back. Now wasn't the time to explain about his involvement with the Winner's Circle.

Ann considered the possibility of a partnership between Harper and Robert. The idea had merit. They might be in league, though she couldn't imagine what they intended to accomplish. "What purpose could it possibly serve? Robert comes back, frightens me with threats and accidents, then what?"

"They could both benefit. If Robert could get you to take him back, he could take the insurance money from Easy Dancer's death and pay his debts. Or maybe influence you on the racing commission." Pieces of the puzzle dropped into place.

"I don't know." Ann couldn't meet his gaze. "I don't want to believe Robert would do this."

"Even after he abandoned you and very likely stole a valuable horse?"

She kept her gaze on the floor. "I just find it hard to picture Robert doing all of this. He might try to frighten me. But attempted murder...there's no motive."

"Unless Robert has somehow come to believe you tricked him. That you deceived him."

The idea pierced Ann's anger; if Robert was that warped, he might easily try to hurt her. "But Robert would never voluntarily commit such a violent act." She spoke to convince herself, as well as Matt.

"Could he be blackmailed? If he owed Harper a great deal of money?"

"I don't know." She was miserable at the idea. "Harper is rash and arrogant and mean, but he isn't stupid enough to think he could get away with something like that. That would be crazy."

"Crazy," Matt echoed the word, his own sense of foreboding almost making him stagger. "Whoever is doing this, Harper or not, is unbalanced, Ann. At first, I thought it was just strong-arm methods, a way to make you give in on that bid. As awful as it was, it was logical. Now, though, things have gone beyond that stage. There's no logic in what's happened lately, only malice."

A million things flew through Ann's mind, but the one that stayed with her was the feel of a leather-clad hand clamping over her mouth and another closing around her throat. There was the sensation of suffocation, of falling into darkness, then the blow. But there was something else, something she had to remember but couldn't. Something that terrified her so much her subconscious wouldn't let it come to the fore.

"Ann!" Matt caught her and helped her into a chair. "You look like you've seen a ghost."

"I was thinking about last night, a split second before I was hit." She turned wide, fearful eyes to Matt. "You're right, Matt, there's an element of something terrible in this. I know who struck me. I know who it was and I can't remember!"

Kneeling beside her, Matt was all too aware of her fear. He could see it in her eyes, feel it in the cold touch of her silky skin beneath his hands. "Relax," he soothed. "If you know, then you'll remember soon. Are you sure you knew the person?"

"Positive. There's one thing about them, one distinctive thing I can't pinpoint now. Before I blacked out, I recognized it, and now I just can't recall it."

"What kind of thing? A smell, a voice, what?"

Ann shook her head. "I don't know. I just know that something triggered in my head, and I was thinking of who it was when I was hit. Then I forgot everything until now."

Matt took her hands. They were deathly cold and he pressed them to his chest. "Was it someone you know well, do you think?"

Ann's heart pumped painfully. "It was someone I care about a great deal."

"Is it . . . could it be . . . Ann, was it Robert?"

She wanted to cry. Her feelings were caught like a cement block in her throat. Swallowing, she tried to push the painful lump of emotion down.

Watching the delicate muscles of her throat, Matt disregarded her earlier anger at him. He stood, bringing her to her feet with him. His arms wrapped around her and he held her without comment for a long time.

Ann gave herself to the security of his embrace. It didn't make sense. None of it did. At one point in her life, she'd loved Robert. That was what she couldn't explain to Matt. Even when Robert left and Speed Dancer disappeared, she'd found it hard to pin the theft on Robert. Freddie and Cybil had urged her to make the charge against him, as protection for herself. Now Matt was asking her to consider the possibility that Robert might have attempted to murder Freddie.

Had it been Robert's hand in the glove? The hand whose touch at one time made her laugh and cry? Was that what she'd recognized in the split second before blackness claimed her? Was that the terrible revelation she was hiding from herself?

She clung to Matt as she silently fought the battle with herself.

Had it been Robert's worn leather jacket that triggered her recognition? His voice or breathing?

Maybe. She had to accept that answer, because she couldn't remember. It could have been any number of things, any slight nudge of her senses that rang the bell of recognition. It could have been anyone, even Matt.

"What do you suppose Freddie was doing in Easy's stall?" Ann's voice was remarkably strong and composed.

Matt held her tightly, wanting to shield her from some of the pain and knowing there was nothing he could do. "If I could have one question answered tonight, that would be it. Freddie was too smart to get trapped in a horse's stall. Unless it was deliberate. Ann, the stall door was latched from the outside."

"What are you saying?" Ann lifted her head and examined the distant, unreadable expression on Matt's face.

"I'm not really certain, but there's something about all of this that isn't right. As you said earlier, we've overlooked the most obvious clue. So many things have happened that we can't be certain what relates to what. I mean, did what happened between Freddie and Easy have anything to do with the fact that we were both knocked out? Does that connect with your car accident, the fences torn down in the pasture and Easy's strange behavior? The only thing I can say for certain is that someone else was on this property, too. Someone who threw that latch behind Freddie."

"What about Freddie finding the feed tampered with? I've got to ask Cybil about that. Someone could be slipping Easy something in a handful of feed. Someone like Nicholls who had access to the barns. That would account for Easy's Jekyll-and-Hyde behavior."

"Unless Freddie was wrong." Matt tightened his hold on her, thinking she would respond in anger. Instead, she made no move of any kind.

"If Freddie was wrong, then I've been wrong about everything my entire life," she whispered softly. "Everything." She stepped out of Matt's arms and walked distractedly to the fire.

There was nothing Matt could do to ease her pain. Silently he left the room and went into the kitchen. A cup of coffee wouldn't cure anything, but then again it wouldn't hurt.

When he returned, Ann was sitting calmly in her chair, her eyes wide and unfocused. He stood in the doorway, letting his gaze rove over her. He was struck again by her lack of pretense, the bare revealing of herself. In her face there was weariness and pain, a touch of defeat. But that was tempered by the determination of her jaw and the angle of her head. She held it high, undefeated. Wrapped around those qualities was skin as soft and delicate as the petals of a rose. A curvaceous rose. He smiled at the thought. He'd been a gentleman the night he'd put her to bed, but he hadn't been blind. The memory of her body, pressed into the sheets, had goaded and fired his jealousy about her ex-husband. He wanted no other man to touch her, to lay any claim on her. A remarkable turn of events for a man who'd vowed his strongest behavior around women would be avoidance, he thought wryly as he brought her a cup of coffee.

"Thanks." Her eyes cleared and she turned her full attention to him. "Maybe I should go back to the hospital. If Freddie regains consciousness, he could solve a lot of mysteries."

"That isn't a good idea." Matt had to dissuade her from setting up house at the hospital. The doctors had taken Matt aside, explaining that the prognosis for Freddie was poor. He was elderly, and he'd been badly trampled. There was a broken arm, broken ribs and a crashing blow to the skull, his most severe injury. The doctors had been horrified at the force of the blow. Matt had seen it clearly imprinted on their faces, though they'd tried to show Ann a calmer demeanor.

"Freddie will need me when he comes to," Ann insisted softly.

"The best thing you can do for Freddie would be to rest here, take care of things. The hospital will call if his condition changes." The words almost lodged in his throat, but he forced them out, knowing that above all else, Ann needed hope to hang on to.

"How's Blue Chip?" Ann asked abruptly.

"She's fine. Dawn told me yesterday she's ready..." He looked down into his coffee cup, furious with his own careless tongue.

"She's ready to breed," Ann finished for him. "What irony. We've already bred half the barn. If Easy's convicted of his crime, I wonder what will happen to the foals." An edge of bitterness colored her voice. "If you don't mind, I think I'll take a walk. Alone. Then I'm coming in to take a nap and get ready to go to the hospital."

Matt recognized the iron in her voice. There was no changing her mind now. It was a trait he loved and despaired in her, that unyielding stubbornness. He could only concede gracefully and move along with his own plans. He wasn't Sherlock Holmes, but he could see that life had become too rife with coincidences. Accidents, Robert's return, Easy's behavior... and the Winner's Circle.

"After dinner we'll drive back into town," he offered, eager for her to leave the house so that he could use the telephone.

Ann caught his too-easy agreement with her plan, but she let it pass. Rather than fight with Matt, she had something else to attend to. She faced him as she zipped her jacket. "You asked me what I felt for Robert. I'm very confused. I don't know what I think or feel anymore. All I know is that if Robert is back, I need to see him." She walked away without waiting for him to respond.

Watching Ann walk away, Matt had to exert his will to control his worry. For her safety, he didn't want Ann to see Robert. Realistically he knew there was nothing he could do to stop her. Unless he caught Robert first.

He forced his mind to the Winner's Circle. He didn't know the men. The tight time frame hadn't allowed him to meet any of them, including Boswell, personally, but with the opportunities available for the purchase of farms, it didn't make sense that investors would attempt to kill a reluctant owner. But if he was right about Boswell's actually being Harper, he had a lead to follow. And, as Freddie had so pointedly remarked, Ann's troubles didn't begin until he came to Dancing Water as Boswell's representative.

ANN'S MIND KEPT SEEING Matt's face. His concern was a double-edged sword. That he cared enough to show jealousy was an exhilarating feeling. That he doubted her motives and conduct was troubling.

Her long strides took her in and around the farm buildings, from the office down the aisle of the main barn. She stopped at Freddie's ransacked apartment. Law-enforcement officers had been unable to make any sense of the wanton destruction. Clothes had been torn from the closet and tossed onto the floor. Dishes were broken indiscriminately. It looked like the scene of a domestic fight, not a criminal act. The person who trashed Freddie's apartment must have done it for the pleasure of destroying the old man's things. As she scrubbed at a large smudge on the wall, she decided the destruction was simply more malicious scare tactics.

She busied herself cleaning everything, and finally, when his apartment had been returned to some semblance of order, she started to the destination she'd sought and avoided all afternoon—Easy Dancer's stall.

The big stallion crested his neck at her approach, his soft brown eyes liquid with welcome. He rumbled a greeting, low and deep.

"Come here, boy," Ann whispered, calling him to the stall door. As he extended his head, she rubbed his ears and let him nuzzle her chest. "Such a big old boy. Such a nice fellow." She talked to soothe herself as much as the horse.

Once again, Ann ran her eyes over his glistening body. He was flawless. If there was a problem at all, it was that he seemed slightly depressed, a little melancholy, as if he knew what had happened and that his fate was in jeopardy.

"If you could only talk," Ann whispered, trying to recall the events of the night before. Resting against the horse, she thought it would be easier for her to remember who had struck her. She put herself in the main barn, her hand on the light switch, waiting for that one jolt of recognition that would allow her to remember. But the only thing that came was the cruel memory of the blow to her head.

"I've got to do better than this," she said, tickling Easy's neck as she closed her eyes and tried to concentrate. But to her bitter disappointment, she could not connect with that elusive portion of her memory.

Mica John entered the barn and cleared his throat. "Excuse me, Ms. Tate. We were wondering about Freddie?"

Ann gave the details, watching the groom eye her, then turn a speculative glance at Easy. She knew he was wondering if the horse would be destroyed.

"Mica, who was supposed to be guarding the barn last night?" It was a tiny detail, but one that had worried her.

"I was, ma'am, but Freddie gave me the night off. He said he was restless and couldn't sleep, and that he'd take my night if I would trade with him. Since it didn't matter to me, I went on home. I wish I'd stayed now."

A smile of gratitude touched Ann's pallid face. Mica was a good boy, a devoted worker who loved the horses and Freddie.

"Freddie is an old man, but he's smart, Mica. I don't know if anything would have happened differently if you'd been here. Please don't blame yourself."

"Ms. Tate, who could it have been?" He stepped toward her, his young face drawn in worry and anger. "Who's been doing these things. And Freddie? What was he doing in the stall?"

"Those are the same questions I'm fighting to answer. Mica, are you afraid of Easy?" A wild plan sprang in her head.

"Not a bit, Ms. Tate. Whatever happened to Freddie, it wasn't this boy. I know he's attacked you and Dawn, and Mr. Roper, but it isn't his nature. Look at him. He's as gentle as a lamb." Mica stepped forward and stroked the stallion's neck. "I've never been around a better animal."

"I want to breed Easy today. To Blue Chip. Would you help me?"

"Are you going to have to put him down?" Mica's doubt showed.

"I'm going to fight that, but I can't make any promises. That's why I want that mare bred."

Mica grinned. "Let's do it right now."

Ann's heart was pumping rapidly as she hurried into the barn and prepared Blue Chip. It was a rash, crazy thing she was doing. Something that might well bring down Matt's complete wrath on her head. But she knew Easy wasn't a rogue horse. Something bad was happening to him, and if she didn't breed Blue Chip now, it might be too late in another day or two. The mare would be out of season, and Easy might be dead.

When she met with Mica in the breeding pen, she carefully went over the procedure. "She's a green mare," she warned him twice. "Easy's always well mannered, but you're to make sure that he is."

Mica nodded, and they let the animals get acquainted. To her relief, Easy played his role perfectly.

When Easy had been returned to his stall, and Blue Chip out to pasture, Ann stopped Mica with a hand on his shoulder. "This must be our secret, Mica. No one must know that Blue Chip was bred."

"Not even Mr. Roper?"

"Especially not Mr. Roper," Ann replied.

"Especially not Mr. Roper what?"

Matt stood behind her, hands on his lean hips.

Chapter Twelve

"Mica, please bring the mares in from pasture," Ann said calmly, though her heart was pounding. She needed a few moments to gather her wits. Her first impulse was to tell Matt the truth about what she'd done and face the consequences immediately. Only one thing stopped her. Matt could react by having the mare aborted. In a few days, though, once she'd proven Easy's innocence, then Matt would be delighted that his mare was bred.

"It's nothing, Matt," she said, her lips tight and uncomfortable around the lie.

"It sounded like a solemn pledge to me," Matt responded. Ann was guilty as sin about something, but he had no idea what she could be conspiring about with a groom. He took in the flush on her cheeks, the discomfort in her eyes. Ann Tate wasn't a very good liar.

"I was enlisting Mica's aid in a plan." She held to the truth, feeling some relief.

"What kind of plan?" Matt pressed. He had a sudden idea that whatever Ann was up to, it wasn't safe.

"I'll tell you later," she replied, trying to walk past him. "It's chilly out here. Let's go back in the house. Maybe Jeff and Ronnie are back from their trip. I'm going to need Jeff's help. I can't believe those two decided to take off for a second honeymoon on some remote island. Can you imagine? And they didn't bother to tell anyone." She babbled, knowing that her verbal barrage revealed her intense nervousness.

Matt's hand was a gentle but effective silencer.

"What went on out here in this barn while I wasn't watching you?" His dark eyes were riveted on hers. Ann found it impossible to look away, and staring straight into his eyes she couldn't consider subterfuge.

"Matt, I..." She couldn't tell him the truth. He'd be furious. The foal that was the perfect union of Easy Dancer and Blue Chip hung in the balance.

"Ann." The tension between them was so powerful that he forgot where they were, forgot everything but her blazing eyes staring into his.

Recalling Matt's earlier concern, Ann summoned a last surge of will. "Mica was helping me plan something. A meeting with Robert. I'm going to meet him. Alone." If she could make Matt angry enough, he'd leave her alone.

It was the worst possible tactic. Matt tensed.

"I realize I've behaved badly, but that's no excuse to put your life on the line by meeting a man who could be dangerous." Matt had the feeling he was talking to a wall. With her jaw squared, she seemed oblivious to the danger that meeting her ex-husband might bring. "You act as if you really want to see him." He couldn't completely hide the jealousy in his tone.

He'd moved no closer, but Ann was overwhelmed by his presence. Matt intended to force her hand, and she was locked motionless in his tempestuous gaze. If she'd wanted to run, her legs would have betrayed her. So she simply stood, heart pounding as she waited for him to touch her.

His fingers grazed her cheek, lingering on the pulse that beat at her throat. "Are you still in love with him?" he forced himself to ask, to give her a chance to explain. Once before he'd jumped to the wrong conclusion.

Ann refused to answer. She couldn't.

"There's only one way for me to convince myself that you aren't still in love with him." His fingers slid to the back of her neck, tightening ever so lightly. He took his time, finally claiming her lips in a kiss that was powerful yet tender.

The hazy afternoon light shifted through the hayloft and fell about them in golden shafts. Ann was intoxicated by Matt's touch, the clean masculine scent of his skin mixed with the smell of sweet hay.

With a half step he pressed her against the wall, the old wooden boards, the only tactile familiarity in the wild passions that Matt aroused with his touch. His hands held her, caressed her, excited her, as she returned his kiss with frightening hunger.

He captured her face between his palms and held it as he drew back. "Do you still love him?"

Ann's breath came in short gasps. Her arms clung to his neck, and she realized her legs were weak. "No."

"You're sure?"

She couldn't take her gaze from his. "I'm sure."

"You aren't planning to meet him, and you only said it to provoke me," Matt said, his thumbs sliding along her jaw to lightly touch her neck.

"I only said it to provoke you," she repeated, swallowing hard. She was mesmerized by the controlled desire in his eyes, the seductiveness of his touch.

"The thought that you might still care for him disturbs me."

His vulnerability showed for only a second, but it was enough to break the spell. Ann's own strong feelings rushed to the surface and she lifted her hands to Matt's shoulders.

"It was a miserable thing to say. I care for you, Matt, a lot more than I'm comfortable with." Her gaze faltered. "I never thought I would trust myself enough to love again. You've changed that."

His hand took hers and he led her into the feed room.

"On that tour you gave me the first day, I think we missed the loft," he said, a mischievous glint in his eyes.

"The hayloft?" Ann was amused but hesitant.

"How long has it been since you've lain in the hay watching the sun slant across the bales?"

He took the first step up the ladder and then reached for her hand, drawing her up with him as he slowly ascended.

The loft was golden with sunlight, the bales soft shadows. From behind several bales Matt withdrew a colorful blanket, a bottle of wine and glasses.

"You planned this," Ann said.

"My background in business has done me some good. I do plan for the future." He spread the blanket and settled down on it, motioning for her to follow. "I have to plead guilty to premeditation. The first time I saw this loft, I knew it was meant for a long afternoon of wine and... conversation."

Ann sank onto the blanket, accepting the glass that Matt offered. The wine was light and delicate. She watched him over the rim of her glass. She could picture him in a business suit, telephone at his ear, portfolio spread before him. She could see him working in a busy office. But if she reached out her hand to him now, she would touch the faded jeans, the soft chambray shirt, the clean line of his jaw. He was completely at home in her hayloft, a devilish smile on his face and seduction on his mind.

"Is it always this peaceful?" Matt leaned back against a bale. He was perfectly content to watch her. The shafts of sunlight set off red alarms in her dark hair and gave an ad-

ditional bronze to her healthy skin. She sat with her legs
curled under her, slender and graceful as a child.

"The winter light is always solemn. When I was younger, I did spend many afternoons here. Alone," she added
with a grin.

"If I'd lived in the neighborhood you wouldn't have been
alone." He leaned forward and grasped her, easing her back
into the hay with him. "If I have my way, you won't ever be
alone again." And with that he put his mouth to hers.

The kiss lengthened and intensified. Gently Matt eased
her down on the soft blanket, his lips never leaving hers. His
fingers worked the buttons of her shirt, and his warm mouth
followed the trail he'd opened down to the waistband of her
jeans. His palm slid beneath the flap of her shirt to cup her
breast as he raised his head and met her gaze.

Hands trembling, Ann slowly began to remove his shirt.
Drawn to the dark curls of his chest, her fingers roamed
across his skin, at last moving to his back to tug his shirt free
and slip it over his arms.

"Is it too cool?" he asked, warming her with his mouth.

"No." Later it would be cold, but at that moment she felt
nothing except delicious passion.

They undressed each other slowly and completely, cling-
ing and touching until articles of clothing were scattered all
around them. Kneeling beside her, Matt pressed her back
into the blanket. His hands slowly traced the outline of her
body, lingering at the curve of her hip, the silken length of
her thigh.

Above her, Matt's body caught the afternoon sun.
Shadow and light played across the muscles of his chest, his
flat stomach and lean hips. Ann's hand touched his stomach and then slid around to the small of his back, pulling
him down beside her for a kiss that spun them into a world
where only their feelings for each other existed.

When they were spent, Matt held her tightly against him and flipped the sides of the blanket around them. Snuggling down in the dying afternoon light, they were silent. The pleasure of their lovemaking still warmed them and held them in a bond of intimacy.

Wrapped in the double cocoon of blanket and Matt's arms, Ann had never been so content. Reality was at bay, at least for a little longer.

"Ann, I haven't been completely honest with you." Matt's sudden declaration seemed to hang in the air like dust motes.

"About what?" She couldn't keep her body from tensing. All of her guards were down and she was completely vulnerable. And very guilty.

"Blue Chip."

"She isn't your horse?" Ann almost sat up but Matt gently held her.

"No, she's mine. Everything I told you about Blue Chip is true. There's more, though. A lot more." He tightened his hold on her and took a deep breath. He'd decided on a tactic. He'd tell her the personal part first, and then the business about the Winner's Circle.

"If I can produce the foal I think I can with Blue Chip, I'll be able to pay off my ex-wife and get my children back with me. My whole future depends on that mare and getting her bred this year to the best stallion around."

"I see." Dread numbed Ann. She did see, and what she saw was the worst mistake of her life. She'd violated a boarder's trust, and after the afternoon she'd spent with Matt, she'd betrayed his love. His voice continued, piercing her private pain.

"That's why I wanted to stay here at first, at least partly. I was a little overanxious about her. But then I saw the place and the way you handled the horses. I was satisfied it was the best place and Easy the best stallion. Now, though, I may have to find a different route."

"Yes." She stared at the ceiling, seeing nothing. Her mind was too busy remembering the act she'd committed that very afternoon.

"I know this isn't the best time to talk about this, but I feel so close to you, so completely trusting, that I wanted to tell you that I'm considering taking her to another farm. I have to get her bred this cycle if I'm going to make it work."

Ann's head pounded with a sickening crash and her stomach was on the verge of revolt.

"When were you planning on taking her?"

"Tomorrow or the next day. She's ready to be bred. Another month could make a difference. Can you possibly understand? I didn't want to tell you, but lying here with you, I felt dishonest." He sat up on an elbow so he could look at her. "I never want a trace of dishonesty to come between us, Ann. It's the one thing I can't stand. That's why I have to tell you the rest of how I came to stay at your ranch."

Throwing aside the blanket, Ann sat up and began fumbling for her clothes. "We'd better go. Mica will be in here soon for some hay for tonight."

"My timing isn't great, Ann, but I have to tell you."

"I understand." She pulled on her jeans. In the midst of her hurried dressing, she looked at him. "I do understand, and I'm not upset. With you."

Before he could ask any further questions, she stood up. "I have to go to the hospital. Maybe Freddie is better." Her voice was hoarse, unsteady.

"I'll go with you. I want to tell you about my idea, how I came to Dancing Water Ranch."

"No!" She backed several steps toward the ladder. "I mean I'd prefer it if you stayed here. To watch the horses. I'll be fine."

"Maybe we could call Dawn to stay at the ranch," Matt suggested, folding the blanket. "I want to be with you. In case you need me."

"We'll talk about it in a few minutes. Let me go to the office for some papers." She hurried down the ladder and walked briskly out of the stallion barn, too afraid to turn back and face Matt for fear he'd see her panic. How was she going to tell him that she'd taken his fate, and the fate of his mare, into her own hands? She fled across the yard as if a troop of banshees were on her tail.

Matt bit back the frustration that threatened to erupt as he folded the blanket and retrieved the wine and glasses. His timing hadn't been bad, it had been atrocious. He'd been so concerned with clearing his own conscience that he hadn't considered what he might be doing to Ann. She had begun to explore her feelings for him, to trust her instincts, and then he slapped her with what surely appeared to be a form of abandonment. From all he could tell, it was a repeat action of what her ex-husband had done.

"Good work, Roper," he mumbled to himself.

And that wasn't the half of it, either. He hadn't even gotten around to telling her the full truth about his interest in Dancing Water Ranch.

He took the blanket and glasses into the house and morosely watched the pecan orchard for a sign of Ann's return to the house. He was going to finish what he'd started. Bad timing and all, it was a matter of clearing the air forever.

He watched the grooms bring in the mares from pasture. Blue Chip fairly danced in, along with the others, her mahogany coat thick and lustrous in the dying sunlight. She was a beautiful mare, and he could easily picture the foal she

would have had with Easy Dancer. On first meeting the
stallion, he could never have guessed the horse was capable
of such violence.

He sighed. Since Cybil had tests that showed no foreign
substances in his bloodstream or urine, Matt could only assume that the horse had a mental defect. He was calm for
days and then freaked out and became dangerous. If it was
a person, he knew the diagnosis would closely resemble
psychosis or schizophrenia. No one would ever want a foal
with such a sire. There was no way to tell when such an animal would explode and become violent.

Though his thinking was rational, he couldn't stop the
regret he felt. Easy was a magnificent animal. It would be
heartbreaking to have to destroy him. It would kill Ann. He
shook his head at the idea. Maybe it wouldn't come to that,
but he held little hope. The horse had already injured one
human critically, and in the past he'd come very close to
hurting others. If only Cybil believed someone was tampering with the horse. But the vet didn't give any credence to
the idea, and she was Ann's best friend.

The day faded on the western horizon, and Matt spied the
first star. Ann would wish for her horse to be healthy, so
Matt made the wish for her, smiling at his foolishness. He'd
never been one to wish on stars. At least not until he met
Ann.

When darkness settled thickly around the house, Matt
grew impatient. Ann had seemed in a rush to get to the hospital, and now she'd been in her office for more than an
hour. He hurried across the orchard to the barn. The lights
were on in her office, but there was no sign of her.

As awareness dawned, Matt uttered an oath. Ann had
taken a vehicle and gone. Without a word, she'd driven
away.

Mingled with his anger was a new, sharper stab of fear. Ann was out on the roads alone, and someone was trying to hurt her. She was out there by herself because he'd been a fool.

He didn't wait to phone the hospital. He simply unhitched his trailer and drove as fast as he could down the narrow, dark roads. His hands gripped the wheel and he bore down on the accelerator with relentless pressure. He had to get to the hospital before she left. She wasn't safe. Not by a long shot.

The lights of the hospital were like an oasis to a dying man. Matt whipped into the parking lot. The key was barely out of the ignition by the time his feet struck the asphalt in a wide-open run.

Nurses and visitors gave him looks of consternation as he ran down the white, tiled halls. His heart pounded in his ears as he rushed past carts and wheelchairs, medics and aides.

"Hey, mister," a young man called out in an angry voice, "you can't run in a hospital."

Not bothering to answer, Matt kept going.

The intensive-care unit was on the ground floor through a series of waiting rooms. When he pushed through the double doors he finally slowed. His hopes were dashed when he scanned the empty room.

The second waiting room, for family members only, contained a brunette with shoulder-length hair.

"Matt, what's wrong?" It was Ronnie Stuart, clutching her purse, her dark eyebrows drawn together in worry.

"Ann. Where is she?" Matt searched the small, bare room again, as if he couldn't believe Ann wasn't there. In his single-minded search for Ann he'd failed to recognize Ronnie.

"She went home," Ronnie said. "I told her I'd wait here with Freddie. She looked exhausted so I sent her home."

"But she didn't come home." Matt's hands clenched at his sides.

Ronnie looked at her watch. "She's had time to get home. Maybe you passed her on the way."

Matt shook his head. "I didn't pass a single car."

"She could have come in another way." Ronnie didn't even believe what she was saying, but Matt was so distraught she felt it was necessary to calm him.

"She didn't say she might go anywhere else?"

Ronnie took his hands. "Sit down." She maneuvered him toward a hard chair and sat beside him. "Let's think this over. I'm sure Ann is fine. Maybe she's at the grocery store or running an errand."

"Thanks for trying to make me feel better, but it isn't going to work. I have to find Ann, before something else happens to her."

Matt's words were chilling. Ronnie brushed a strand of hair from her face. "Let me think. I'm sure we can figure out where she went."

It took all of Matt's restraint not to jump from the chair and run, but he had no idea where to go. Ronnie was his only hope.

"Ann was tired, very edgy. We were waiting for the doctor to talk with us about Freddie, so I didn't pry. Then Dr. Zimlich came out." She put a hand on Matt's arm. "The prognosis for Freddie has improved. His functions are holding steady and the CAT scan showed no internal bleeding in his brain. Ann was elated, even though she was still upset."

"She left after the doctor spoke with her?" Matt probed.

"No. We talked a few moments, and then she got a phone call."

"From who?"

"She never said. She came back in and checked on Freddie and then said she was going home." Ronnie shook her head. "She looked so tired, so frazzled that I said I'd wait here a while longer and make sure nothing happened with Freddie."

"You don't have any idea who called?"

"I thought it might have been you. She said you'd volunteered to guard the ranch for her."

"I didn't volunteer, I was left behind." Matt had a pang about the horses. He'd left them unguarded, but his major concern had been for Ann.

"I wonder who called." Ronnie tried to hide her worry. Ann had seemed awfully pale when she came back into the waiting room. Ronnie's first assumption had been that she was tired, but now she wasn't so sure. Her background as a journalist had trained her to look for detail. There had been something odd about the look in Ann's eyes.

"How long did she talk?"

"Only a few minutes, then she came back here for about two minutes. She seemed anxious to leave."

"As if someone might be waiting for her?" Matt asked, standing up abruptly.

"I don't want to alarm you, but looking back, that is the way it seemed."

"Did she say anything at all?"

Ronnie went over the scene with Ann. "She said she had to go. She checked on Freddie." Ronnie's eyes opened wide. "She said something about the racetrack."

Matt's jaw tightened. "What?"

"It was odd, something disconnected from everything else. Like if the track ever got built it would be a miracle. I can't remember exactly, but it was something to that effect. I just thought it was strange that she said it because we hadn't been talking about the track at all."

"Thanks." Matt wheeled to leave the room. "Call Jeff and tell him to meet me at the racetrack," he called over his shoulder.

"Matt!" Ronnie ran after him. "What's going on?"

"Tell Jeff to meet me as soon as he can." He didn't pause to explain.

Running back down the corridors, he was met with more hostile stares, but he didn't stop. Lucky for him he knew where the track was. It was a long shot, but if Ann was meeting someone at the track site, it could only be Bill Harper. Or Robert.

He gunned the truck down the highway, weaving in and out of the slower coastal traffic. The shoreline was beautiful, but he had no time to admire the scenery. Crossing into Harrison County, he turned north, circling a portion of Biloxi Bay.

The city gave way to rural roads only a few miles from the beach, and Matt knew he was nearing the track.

When he came to the turnoff, he coasted to a stop. He killed the lights and reached under the seat for the flashlight. From the glove compartment he took out a .38. The gun had been a gift from his father years before. Hefting the deadly weight in his hand, he realized that he'd never considered using it against another person. Until tonight. He was ready to use it to protect Ann.

Sliding out of the seat he ran silently down the muddy path that led into the construction site. The place was enormous, with huge piles of rocks, sand and gravel everywhere. Construction materials from steel girders to huge cement culverts were scattered around.

Matt eased behind a pile of cement blocks and his heart dropped to his stomach when he saw Ann's truck near a pile of sand. Parked beside it was Bill Harper's small black truck. Both vehicles were empty, and the night was as still as a cemetery.

Chapter Thirteen

Harper's truck was parked just where the voice on the phone said it would be. Ann climbed out of the truck, instinctively keeping low so that her head was protected. The caution was reactionary. There had been no threat in the phone call. Not exactly a threat, just the promise of seeing Robert. She thought about Matt, his strength and security. She wanted him beside her, but she didn't deserve him. Because of her own dream, she'd betrayed him. He might forgive her. Eventually. But she didn't know if she could forgive herself. She could no longer involve him in her life, her problems. Her first order of business was to find Harper and make contact with Robert. It was still hard to believe that he was back, that he could be involved in violence. Matt would have been furious with her for taking such a risk.

Her shoes digging in the soft dirt of the construction site, she pushed Matt to the back of her mind. She had to concentrate on the job at hand.

The voice, indistinct and sounding slurred with drink, had told her to meet Bill Harper here. Ann hadn't been able to clearly identify it as Harper's voice. Her instincts told her, though, that he was the caller.

Triumph had been mixed with the alcohol, in the caller's reference to the "accidents" that had been happening at the farm. The voice had been sneakily friendly, but also cautious. It had warned her to come alone if she wanted to see Robert and find out what had really happened to Speed Dancer.

That was the part that frightened Ann. She wasn't afraid of dark places, or of Bill Harper. She was afraid of the past, of learning that her judgment of Robert was even further askew than she had imagined. Facing Robert would be the hardest thing she'd ever done in her life, but she had to get to the bottom of what was happening. Easy Dancer's life depended on it, and in a large measure, so did her future with Matt.

The construction site looked like a moonscape. Were there large craters where heavy equipment paused on the brink of shimmering pools? The moonlight, bright outside of the city, reflected back to her from standing water in some of the craters. Lumber, cement pipes and mountains of dirt, sand and gravel were scattered all around. Because she knew the plan by heart, she could tell she was standing in the center of the track. To the west would be the stands, just to the right of the stable area.

It was an enormous track with facilities for quarter horse, Thoroughbred and, in the future, Arabian racing. The concept of such a multipurpose track was relatively unique.

Looking around, she felt a thrill of accomplishment. So much work and sacrifice had gone into the track. Soon opening day would be a reality.

The skin along her neck prickled. She could feel eyes on her back, and with the feeling a sudden awareness of danger. They were the same eyes that had watched her at the barn before she was knocked unconscious, the eyes of someone she knew. Robert? She held herself in check, turning slowly to survey the area. There was not a sound or movement to indicate the presence of another living creature. That didn't matter. She knew she was being watched, and closely.

She started to call out to Bill Harper but stopped. The stillness was too eerie. If Harper was around, and he had to be since his truck was there, she'd prefer to find him.

Leaving the protection of the pile of sand, she felt vulnerable and exposed. Several large pieces of equipment loomed like sleeping dinosaurs, casting shadows darker than the night.

She skirted them, her feet crunching softly in the gravelly dirt. Frequently she paused, listening for the sound of other steps. There was nothing, not even the hum and buzz of insects. Foreboding stole up her spine, but she kept walking away from her car. Harper had to be in the area. He had to be.

Dodging around culverts large enough to hide a small band of thieves, she made her way to the place where the spectator stand would be built. There were to be open stands, and then the more expensive, private-club seats. This was the section Harper had bid on and lost. Ann eyed the skeletal structure that was already erected. Staring up at the bones of the building she heard someone clear his throat. Whirling around, she saw only the black night.

"Bill?" The word slipped from her, showing her nervousness. She cursed silently.

"So, you did come alone." There was a grudging touch of admiration in his voice. "Where's that boyfriend you moved in with you?"

It was Harper, and he sounded drunk. It was the same voice that called her at the hospital, and Ann searched the darkness, but she couldn't be certain where his voice was coming from.

"Matt's at the ranch, watching the horses. We've had a little trouble lately. I'm sure you don't know anything about it." She issued the challenge, hoping to ascertain Harper's attitude. He had a vile temper, and she could only imagine that it was worse when he drank. She didn't want to push him, but she wanted to show she wasn't afraid of him or his tricks.

"Oh, Mr. Roper's the broker from Georgia, right?" Harper shifted the focus suddenly.

"That's right." Ann searched the darkness to no avail. Wherever Harper was, he was well hidden. She wanted to ask about Robert, but she was afraid to push too hard.

"Mighty interesting business, brokering. I bet you can make some fascinating friends." Harper laughed softly. There was the sound of liquid sloshing in a bottle.

"I'm sure Matt has a lot of nice friends, but I don't understand what that has to do with us or why we're here tonight."

"We're here tonight—" he paused for a moment as the liquid sloshed in the bottle once again "—because I always liked your ranch. Hell, I always liked you. Thought maybe if you'd get your nose out of the air we might give it a try."

"You thought..." Ann could feel the anger burning her cheeks.

"Now don't go getting all superior." There was an edge of warning in Harper's tone. "I thought some friendly conversation wouldn't hurt." He swallowed again. "I don't think we've ever had a friendly conversation, have we, Ann?" He said her name with a nauseating intimacy. "Now that Robert is back, though, I guess that changes things. Robert and me, we were friends."

Real, cold fear raced through Ann like poison. She'd been a complete fool to step into this trap. Harper was drunk and more dangerous than she'd ever seen him. She was alone, and no one even knew where she was. She had to think of a way to defuse him.

"No, Bill," she said, stressing his first name also, "we've never had a friendly chat. Maybe we could go somewhere and sit down, have a drink. Maybe Robert would join us."

"What would your houseguest think?"

"I don't understand why you want to discuss Mr. Roper."

"I thought you'd be fascinated." He laughed, his hand slapping some part of his body in his amusement. "If you knew, you'd be fascinated." His laughter gurgled.

"I'm always interested in my boarders, but now I'm much more interested in what you have to say."

"I'll bet Mr. Roper hasn't told you why he came to your ranch, has he?"

"He brought his mare for breeding." Ann felt her impatience rising, but she tried to hide it. She would listen to Harper's absurd rantings and then find a way out of there, pronto.

"A mare, and a pair of eyes."

"What are you getting at?"

"He's the front man for a syndicate that wants to buy your place out from under you. They sent him down to inspect the ranch, put a price on it and report back. With the financial problems you've had the past five years, you're like a wounded quail. Easy to kill." Harper's voice dripped smugness.

At first Ann didn't believe him. Matt wasn't that type of person. He wouldn't worm his way into staying at the ranch just so he could inspect the property for investors.

"You don't believe me?" Harper guessed.

The sudden glare of a flashlight in her face was blinding. She threw her hands up to deflect the beam, but it was useless. She couldn't see a thing.

"You'll learn." Harper had adopted a superior tone. Rising from his perch in a dark corner near the bleacher stands he kept the light in her eyes. "Call Mr. Matt Roper about his secret mission for the Winner's Circle. Ask him if he's familiar with a Gordon Boswell." He laughed again. "He can't deny it, 'cause I'm the one who called him. Could be those accidents you've had have a lot to do with the man who'd like to drive the price of your farm down. Now that's something for you to mull over on those long nights when you can't sleep. See ya." He switched off the light and Ann heard his shoes on the gravel.

"Wait!" She was still blinded, but her eyes were readjusting quickly. "How'd you find out about all of this? You said Robert would be here."

"Oh, a mutual friend. That's all I can say. As for your ex-husband, well, he's around. He asked me to give you his regards."

"Why are you doing this?" Ann struggled to think coherently, to ask questions.

"You sit out there at your place like the Queen of Sheba." Harper suddenly turned angry. He snarled and stepped back toward her, his body a dim silhouette in the night. "You think you've got it all, people eating out of your hand, Miss Importance, better than anyone else who's trying to make it. You tried to mess it all up for me, and I've had to work for everything I've ever gotten. You needed to be taught a lesson, and it was a good opportunity for me. I wanted to see your face when you found out your lover was only using you. And I thought what you did to Robert was rotten."

The force of his animosity was overwhelming. Ann had to grit her teeth not to back up.

"Bill, I have to see Robert. Tonight. I want to help him."

"You'll see him when he's ready. Oh, yeah, he said to give you this." Harper's voice had leveled slightly. He took a watch from his pocket and handed it to her.

Ann couldn't stop her stunned reaction as she grasped the watch, an anniversary present she'd given Robert. "I gave him this watch just before he left." Her voice abruptly went flat, emotionless. "I knew he wasn't happy, that something was bothering him, but I didn't expect him to disappear."

"Disappear?" Harper sounded vaguely interested.

Ann didn't hear him. "I have to see him. I want to set everything straight with him. Tell him, Bill. Or tell me where he is. I never really believed he stole Speed Dancer. If we could just talk, maybe I could help him." She touched Harper's shoulder in a pleading gesture.

"Wait a minute. Wait a minute." Harper swayed slightly. "You're saying you didn't make him steal that horse and leave? That he walked out on you?"

"I never knew what happened to Robert, or the horse. He left, the horse vanished, and four months later I got divorce papers from Mexico." She took a deep breath.

"Why didn't you hunt for him if you cared?"

"I knew he was seeing someone else, and I figured he wanted to start a new life. So I signed the papers."

"You didn't run him off?" Doubt crept into his voice. "You really cared for him?"

"At one time, yes. I never did anything that would have made him leave and I don't think he stole the horse. Not really." She clutched the watch in her hand. "I never knew why he left, but I'd like the chance to ask him."

"You never knew, did you." There was a note of amazement in Harper's voice. "All that time he was gambling and running around with—"

The sharp report of a gun split the night. Harper jerked and fell to his knees. "I'm hit," he cried in disbelief.

Ann dropped to her stomach and crawled to the wounded man. "Where are you hit?"

"Help me!" He writhed in the dirt. "Please, I've been shot!"

Another bullet ripped into the sand by Harper's head. Ann grabbed his shoulders and flipped him, rolling him toward the cover of the spectator stands. If she could get him under the stands, he would at least have a chance.

"Roll!" she urged him, tugging at his clothes.

Harper only thrashed against her efforts.

Just as she reached for his shoulder a bullet bit into her arm. The pain almost made her sick.

"We've got to find cover," she screamed at him, but Harper paid no attention.

Kneeling in the dirt, blood dripping from her arm, Ann was frantic. She couldn't abandon the man to the sniper, but she didn't want to get killed, either.

A loud vibration split the night. Dazed for a moment, Ann didn't understand what was happening. When the bright lights of the large bulldozer nearby blinked on, she knew too well. With a grinding of gears the machine headed straight at her.

"Harper!" she screamed trying to make him see the bulldozer, its blade ready to grind them into pulp. "Run!"

She tried to drag him to his feet, but he couldn't stand. He'd quit yelling, but he couldn't get his legs under him.

With each second the bulldozer got closer. Ann could smell the diesel, taste the rank exhaust. She also tasted fear.

The two of them were spotlighted in the twin beams of the headlights. The machine was enormous, rumbling down on them like an engine of revenge.

She managed to get Harper to his knees, and she pulled his arm around her shoulders, determined to drag him with her to the safety of the stands. Somehow she got him up and moving, but not as fast as the bulldozer approached.

Looking back over her shoulder, she saw it was only twenty yards behind. The stands were a good fifty feet away.

"Hurry," she begged Harper. "Please hurry."

Just as she could almost feel the blade of the bulldozer at the back of her neck she pushed Harper under the stands. She herself dashed madly to one side, then leaped up another nearby wooden stand, trying to divert attention from the wounded man.

The sound of wood splintering and the sudden collapse of the structure Harper was under made her gasp in horror. She turned around slowly, as if time had thickened to slow syrup. Exactly where she'd left Bill Harper the blade of the bulldozer lifted and fell, smashing the stand to bits.

"No!" Ann's scream echoed on the night, high above the roar of the engine. "Stop!"

She started back down the stand she was on, but the bulldozer had turned her way to ram the structure. Soon it was shaking so badly she lost her footing and fell. With a groan she caught herself, and then another tremor shook her loose again. She tried to cling, but with one injured arm her effort was in vain.

The ground came at her hard, knocking the wind from her. She gasped desperately as she rose on an elbow. Somewhere in the night, another shot was fired. The bulldozer paused in its attack, its engine idling and the blade high in the air. Yet another shot followed, and she buried her face in the dirt, sick and scared.

Long moments passed before Ann heard voices. Both were male, both familiar. The beams of flashlight came toward her swiftly.

"Ann!" Her name echoed over the rumble of the bulldozer.

She recognized Matt's voice, and she hid her face in her arms. The movement brought a dizzying round of pain from the gunshot wound, and she couldn't make a sound.

"Ann!" Jeff Stuart's voice reached her. At last she had enough breath to cry out. She called his name, but the bulldozer was so loud she couldn't yell over the noise. Suddenly it was quiet.

"I'm here," she cried out, struggling to sit up.

It was Matt who found her first, Matt who gently tucked her into his arms and carried her away from the stands.

"Bill Harper," she said.

"Where?" Jeff asked softly.

"He's under the bleachers."

"Take her to the car. I'll look," Jeff said.

Matt carried her as if she were a sick child. She had no strength left. It was enough that the terror was over, at least for the moment.

Matt held her in the passenger seat of Jeff's car until Jeff returned.

"Harper?" he asked.

Jeff gripped the steering wheel. "He's dead."

"They crushed him," Ann whispered. "I tried to help him, but I couldn't. He was hurt, and when I got him to the stands I thought he would be safe, but the bulldozer kept coming and the stand collapsed and the blade lifted and fell on him...." Pain was making her dizzy.

Jeff nodded. "Let's get you to a doctor and then we'll call the police. Did you see anything, Matt?"

"I got there just before someone started shooting. Then I heard the bulldozer crank up and I ran toward it just in time to see it smash the stand. I fired a couple of wild shots in the air. Someone jumped out and ran, but I couldn't tell who it was so I didn't shoot."

Jeff made the trip to the hospital in record time. Ann found herself on a stretcher flying through the emergency-room door. Ronnie appeared from nowhere, shooing Matt and Jeff away.

"Take care of the police reports," she urged them. "Let me stay with Ann. She needs a woman now."

Reluctantly Matt stepped back and left Ann in Ronnie's capable hands.

"Don't try to talk," Ronnie said comfortingly to her as she walked beside the stretcher. "They're going to take the bullet out of your arm and then you'll be fine."

Ann barely felt the jab of the needle into her vein. It was as if a warm blanket descended on her from nowhere, covering her safely against the horror of the night, washing away all of her cares.

Strong fingers opened her hand and removed the watch she clutched. She wanted to protest, but couldn't. Something she needed to remember floated past her, a golden, shimmering weave. She reached for it with her good hand, wanting to catch hold of it. It was terribly important. But it slipped through her fingers, soft and silken, and brushed against her cheek. She smiled softly as she fell into a profound sleep.

SHE WAS SO PALE. Matt touched her face, concerned by the coolness of her skin. Only her steady, relaxed breathing reassured him. The nurses kept telling him that patients coming out of anesthesia were always pale. That didn't cancel his concern.

Her cheek was smooth beneath his fingers. He'd come so close to losing her. At the thought, he withdrew his hand, unwilling to disturb her rest with his fears.

Turning to the hospital window, he examined a nearby stand of pines, the fitness course that some farsighted individual had contributed to the hospital. Several women in bright jogging suits were walking the course.

Jeff had been by, his face tight with worry. Bill Harper had been shot, then crushed. He had also been drunk. Why had Ann gone to meet him? Especially alone. It didn't make sense when Ann suspected the contractor of violence against her and her property. A killer was on the loose, and Bill Harper, the most obvious suspect, was dead. Murdered. Matt was consumed with worry about Ann. He knew she didn't believe her ex-husband was capable of violence, but Matt didn't share her doubts. He'd seen the hunting knife stabbed into the car seat. Jeff had identified the watch she held clutched in her hand as Robert's.

He paced the room, his eyebrows drawn together. Time was running out. In another hour he had to go load up Blue Chip and prepare for the drive to Louisiana. He wanted to talk with Ann before he left. He had to talk with her. His only consolation was that she would be safe in the hospital. Well guarded.

Ever since he'd told her of his decision to breed Blue Chip to another stallion, she'd been distant. He couldn't really blame her. Somehow he had to make her understand his point of view. For five years his ex-wife had used money as her most effective tool in keeping his children from him. Plane tickets, inconveniences in her schedule, private schools. All had been held up as insurmountable obstacles to his visitation rights. With enough money, though, Monica would gladly turn her greedy eyes to selfish pursuits. She wanted her own boutique. That was the price tag she'd put on his children. Once she had something else to occupy her mind, she wouldn't care so much if the kids came to live with him, private school or not.

His fingers tightened around the cord to the blinds. He forced his hand to relax, his eyes to focus on the scene outside the window. Blue Chip was his trump card, and he had to play her now, this year. If he waited, the children would be too old to ever reconnect in that loving bond he remembered so well.

Ann stirred, moaning in her sleep. He rushed to her, watching her eyelids flutter as she fought to return to awareness.

"Ann," he whispered.

"Lies!" The one word was startlingly clear in the room. Examining her closely, Matt saw her face contract. She tossed her head, fighting something in her sleep.

Her drugged accusation struck home. He hadn't yet told Ann about the group of investors who wanted to buy her ranch. The group he represented—and had begun to suspect. That he'd never told Ann was just one more splinter in his mind. And now he really had to leave if he was going to get his mare to Covington in time to be bred.

He opened the door and glanced down the hall. Ronnie would be in to sit for a while. He needed to talk with her, to make sure she and Jeff would watch the ranch for the night while he drove over to Covington.

Ann sighed deeply, then opened her eyes. Matt hurried to the bedside, gently taking her hand in his.

"Everything's fine," he said, kissing her forehead. "The bullet's out, your arm's going to be okay."

The vapors of sleep still curled around Ann. She'd been thinking about Matt. Remembering. She smiled. It was good he was here.

"Freddie's going to be all right," Matt continued. "He should wake up soon."

"Bill Harper?" She couldn't remember exactly. Something terrible had happened. It had to do with her arm, the hospital.

"He's dead, Ann."

She remembered. Her body tensed, and Matt put a restraining hand on her shoulder.

"It's all over. There's nothing to be done."

Investors. Gunshots. Deceit. Ann tried to edge away from Matt, but his grip tightened.

"I'm glad you woke up. I didn't want to leave without talking to you."

His dark eyes watched intensely. Ann swallowed, but her throat was dry. "Call the nurse."

"What is it?" Matt grew anxious.

"I want some water."

He fished a piece of ice from the pitcher near her bed. "Take it easy, one piece at a time. The doctor said you might get sick if you didn't."

His fingers touched her lips as he gave her the ice, and Ann wanted to cry.

"I'm going to be gone for a while," Matt said softly. "I don't want to, but I have to. I'm going to take Blue Chip over to the Oakridge Stables in Covington to be bred. I'll—"

"You can't." Ann struggled to sit up, but a sudden pain shot through her arm and she gasped, falling back into the pillow.

"Not so fast," Matt admonished her. "Remember, you've been shot."

"How could I forget?" she angrily fired back. "You can't take Blue Chip."

"I have to get her bred this year, Ann. I haven't explained it all properly, but it's very important. Essential."

"As essential as coming to Dancing Water as a front for a group of investors?"

Watching the expression on Matt's face, Ann felt her heart twist. So it was true. Everything Bill Harper had said was true. She closed her eyes, shutting Matt out.

Chapter Fourteen

Ann's head and arm pounded like drums in a military march. As each moment passed the pain increased. Matt had left the room in a cold fury, but it was nothing to match the anger she'd felt at him. If she hadn't been confined in a bed, she would have been tempted to try to throw him out the window.

Finally she picked up the phone and dialed the ranch. When Mica John answered she didn't waste any time.

"Matt is coming to get his mare and take her to Covington to be bred. Take Blue Chip to your house, Mica." He had an excellent small barn where he cared for two of his own mares. "Then act as if she simply disappeared."

"You want me to steal his horse?" His young voice rose an octave.

"No. It isn't actually stealing. The mare is in my charge, to take care of her the way I think best. This is for her good, Mica. She's already bred to Easy, remember?"

"Yes, ma'am. But Mr. Roper is going to be very upset when he finds out she's gone."

The young groom had a point. Ann chewed the inside of her lip, wishing for a moment's respite from the hammering in her head.

"I know. Tell him I ordered the mare sent away. Don't tell him anything else. That way he'll know it isn't your fault. Okay?"

"If he asks me where she is, what do I say?" Mica didn't like the idea of lying.

"Just walk away and tell him to take it up with me."

"Yes, ma'am." He sounded relieved. "I can do that, 'cause that isn't really a lie."

"That's true." Ann sighed. "I'll be out at the ranch in a few hours, Mica. Just hang on until then."

The receiver rattled back in the cradle as the hospital-room door opened and Ronnie entered. "Well, you're awake. I brought you some clean nightgowns and cosmetics and—"

"Give me some jeans and a shirt." Ann swung her feet over the edge of the bed.

"Wait a minute," Ronnie protested. "They're keeping you a few days. The doctor said you needed to rest."

"Things are happening at the ranch. I'm going home. Don't try to stop me." Ann rumbled through the suitcase Ronnie had deposited on the floor. Finding what she wanted, she started pulling on a pair of jeans. Her arm throbbed like it was on fire, but she ignored it.

"Dr. Zimlich isn't going to like this," Ronnie warned darkly.

"I don't like it, either, but it has to be."

"What's going on that you have to be there?" Ronnie asked.

"Matt's taking his mare away." She pulled off the hospital gown and fumbled with a shirt as she spoke.

"I know. But Jeff and I are going to watch the ranch. You don't have to be there."

Ann stopped. "Matt can't take Blue Chip to be bred. She's already bred. To Easy. I did it yesterday without his permission."

Ronnie stopped with her hand in midair, a pair of socks clutched tightly. "What's going to happen?"

"That's why I have to be at the ranch. Now will you lend me your car? It's an automatic and I can handle that."

"Sure." Ronnie handed over the keys. "Should I get Jeff and come out? He wants some explanation about what you were doing meeting Harper at the track."

"No. I think it's best if Matt and I go over this. We have several other issues to discuss, too." Ann's scowl didn't invite questions. "But thanks, anyway."

"Ann, be careful."

"I will," she promised, slipping out the door and hurrying down the long, white corridor.

MATT'S TRUCK AND TRAILER were in front of the barn, but he was nowhere around. Ann parked by the truck and hurried around the area. She found him at last, sitting in her office.

"Where is she?" His voice was cold, furious, and he wouldn't look at her.

"She's safe, Matt. Isn't that what really matters?" Ann found it difficult to breathe. He'd used her hospitality in the hopes of ruining her. And if Bill Harper was right, Matt or his associates might have been involved in the attempts to sabotage her ranch.

"What matters, Ann, is that Blue Chip is my mare. I want her."

She slipped into her chair. "I'm sorry, Matt. I'm doing what I think is right for the mare."

"Damn it, Ann. I want her."

"And I want some answers, Matt." Ann forced her voice to remain stony. She leaned back in her chair. She couldn't help but feel a pang of guilt about what she'd done, but she suppressed it with a healthy dose of reality. "Who are the men interested in buying my ranch?"

Matt started to ask where she'd heard about the investment group, but he shut his mouth. In business, a tough question was always countered with another question. "Where's my mare?"

"This isn't a bargaining table. Bill Harper was remarkably well informed about your business. Ever hear of Gordon Boswell?"

"Harper *is* Gordon Boswell," Matt replied." I'm positive of it. It took me a few days, but I recognized his voice. The whole thing has been a setup from the start. But there has to be a third party involved. Maybe your ex-husband. We'll have to work together, Ann."

"Like yesterday, when we developed such a close working relationship." She smiled coldly. "Is your working-relationship policy anything like your honesty policy?"

"Yesterday had nothing to do with it." At last Matt saw beyond his own anger, saw the pain that Ann was so careful to hide. He'd hurt her. "Ann, yesterday was something special between us." He rose and started toward her.

"Stop right there." She wouldn't be able to stand it if he touched her. She'd lose all of the control she'd managed to hold on to.

Matt stopped as if he'd been struck. Gauging her fury was like trying to get a temperature reading on a volcano. "I never meant to hurt you."

"Only use me a little," she threw at him. "Was it part of your job to sleep with me? Maybe if I felt something for you then the price would be a little lower. You'd get a better deal."

"That isn't true!"

She stood up. "Well, the mare you brought in here for me to breed is already bred, and I intend to see she stays bred to Easy Dancer. She's safe, and when I'm sure you won't try to destroy the foal, you can have her back."

She ran from the office before Matt could recover from the shock of her words. Blue Chip was bred to a stallion with a psychopathic streak a mile wide, and Ann refused to return her. He swallowed the sudden feeling of doom that came over him. Now he'd never be able to barter with Monica. His last hope to get his children had been trampled at his feet.

ANN RAN TO THE STALLION BARN. Easy's warm greeting only made her heart ache more fiercely. The stallion was docile and eager to see her. The responsibility for his future was as cutting as a blade in her heart. Ann wasn't blind. Easy's life hung by a tenuous thread. Even Ronnie was afraid that he was dangerous. She'd delicately broached the subject, tears shimmering in her eyes. Ann felt as if her support was crumbling from beneath her. She hurried to his stall. Looking at him, she couldn't believe he was capable of hurting anyone.

At least a decision about his fate had been postponed until Freddie could recover enough to tell what had happened. Dr. Zimlich was still very concerned about the possibility of brain damage, but Ann was more optimistic. With each hour, Freddie's chances improved. If only he'd wake up.

Something must have happened each time to provoke Easy. It was up to her to figure it all out. To save Easy, and to prove to Matt that her decision about Blue Chip was the right one.

Easy nuzzled her hand, his velvety nose blowing warm on her skin. The desire to ride him came over her.

She unlatched his stall, slipped on his halter and drew him out to the cross ties. Expertly she began the process of grooming him. Easy stood, occasionally twitching his tail as she worked.

From the tack room she took a worn English saddle and a bridle and quickly tacked up. With a deft leap, she was on his back and walking out of the barn, her injured arm held tightly against her side to hold down the painful shocks.

"Ann!"

Matt's cry came to her. Looking over her shoulder she saw him running toward her. She put her heels into Easy's side, and the stallion burst forward with an amazing flash of speed. Ann leaned into his neck, clutching the reins in her good hand. She wanted to escape, to get away from Matt, the ranch, the lies. She wanted to take Easy and ride forever.

Beneath her the horse was like silky water rushing over smooth rocks. Every action, every move of his muscles was pure magic. His shoulders reached forward as his long strides devoured the ground. Ann held the reins tightly, giving him the support he needed to lengthen out even further.

As they tore down the driveway and across the road, Ann felt a delicious sense of freedom. This horse was everything she'd struggled for, her dream. He wasn't irrational. Someone was giving him something. If not in his feed, then some other way. She'd find out how. She'd defend him. With her life.

She gave him an inch more rein and surrendered completely to the pleasure of the ride.

Matt watched her flying down the driveway, his heart in his throat. At first sight the woman and the stallion were a mythical image, a visitation from a time of goddesses and magic. Ann's tall, slender body blended with the horse as his long mane whipped back into her face. Easy Dancer. What a perfect name for a creature that covered the earth with elegant strides that made it seem as if horse and rider danced a jet-speed, linear tango.

Pushing aside the powerful romantic image, Matt examined the stallion. Easy looked fine, perfectly controlled in Ann's capable hands. Even when the stallion had attempted to attack someone he'd *looked* fine. That was the dangerous thing about him. One moment he was like a lapdog and the next a crazed killer.

Ann was a fool to take off on him with no one to help her if she got into trouble. Matt gave in to his anger for just a moment, then he hurried into the barn, found another horse and saddled up. He had to catch Ann, keep her safe.

With a touch of his heels, he sent the horse flying down the driveway, his gaze focused on the horizon as he looked for some clue to the direction Ann had gone.

Crossing the road, he entered the woods. He searched the area thoroughly, but there was no way to be certain. She had a ten-minute head start, and he began to realize the futility of chasing her. No other horse in the barn could possibly keep up with Easy. As much as he hated to admit it, it would be better to wait at the barn for her. With a softly muttered oath, he turned back to the ranch.

He was surprised to find Cybil's large green truck parked near the barn when he returned. She was sitting inside, a clipboard in her lap. As he rode beside her she rolled down her window. "Got a minute?"

"Sure." He started to tell her that Ann was back, but she sprang out of the truck and went into the barn.

As soon as he unsaddled the horse, he met with her. She was sitting at Ann's desk, a pen stuck in the corner of her mouth.

"I'm glad I caught you alone." She put the pen down on the desk. "I'm worried about Ann."

Matt walked over and sat on the edge of the desk. Cybil's eyes were dark. Her long blond braid hung over her shoulder, thick and beautiful.

"I'm worried about Ann, too," he said. "I think all of this has been too much for her."

"I know." Cybil pushed back from the desk and stood up. "Matt, she's going to have to put Easy Dancer down. There's no other way."

Matt felt as if all the air had been pressed from his body. He'd expected Cybil to be concerned, but a call for putting Easy down was a strong position. Ann would be devastated.

"Ann's not going to agree to that. She isn't convinced that Easy's dangerous. She wants more tests, Cybil."

"That's foolish. The horse is going to kill someone. Look at Freddie." She threw her braid over her shoulder. "I'm doing this because I care for Ann. If that stallion injures someone, or kills someone, she's opened herself up for a lawsuit that will cost her everything she's ever worked for. Even if it isn't that bad, say Easy savages someone's mare, Ann's still liable. She could lose the ranch, the horses, everything in a negligence suit. Those are the hard, cold facts—the facts that we, as her friends, should insist she face. She may recoup the loss of Easy, especially since the insurance will pay. But she will never, never recover if she loses this ranch. She's irrational where that horse is concerned."

Matt said nothing. Breeding Blue Chip to Easy was an irrational act. And kidnapping the horse wasn't exactly a conservative course to take. Those were measures he didn't care to discuss with Cybil. Not yet. She was already over-wrought about Ann's condition and behavior.

"Ann has been under a terrible strain," he said, "but if we give her time, she'll come around and do the right thing. I don't think we should force this on her, Cybil."

"Matt, she's in the hospital. If we took care of this for her, it would be so much simpler when she came home. She would be upset and she would grieve, but she would pick herself up and move on. I'm afraid she's going to get killed by that horse."

Matt couldn't doubt the passion in Cybil. She was wired with worry.

"I hate to tell you, but Ann isn't in the hospital."

"Where is she?" Cybil swung around as if she expected to find Ann in a corner of the room.

"She's riding. She'll be back later."

"With a bullet hole in her arm, just out of surgery, she decided to go for a nice, calm ride?" She swung around, her braid flying in an arc around her head. "She's being irra-tional. It's up to us to protect her. She takes better care of those horses than she does herself."

Cybil picked up her bag from the floor. "Has Easy had any more attacks? Since Freddie?"

"None." Matt tucked his hands in his pockets. "And we don't have any conclusive proof that Easy hurt Freddie."

Cybil dropped a vial of antibiotics and a handful of needles back into her case as she looked at Matt in disbe-lief. "You aren't saying you're going to defend that horse? For God's sake, think of Ann! If you encourage her, she'll never accept what's best."

Matt cleared his throat. "Dr. Zimlich had some concern about Freddie's wound. Though it could have been in-flicted by a horse's hoof, he couldn't verify that."

Cybil cast a furious gaze at him. "So you think Freddie obligingly bonked himself on the head, strolled into Easy's stall and dropped down in the shavings to have his body used for a hoofmat?"

"I'm saying there are several ways the scene could be played, and I'd prefer to wait until Freddie regains consciousness before we try to pressure Ann into making a major decision."

Cybil returned her attention to her medical bag, extracting more vials and needles. "You're right, Matt. This doesn't have to be decided today. It's just that—" she looked up, eyes bright with tears "—Easy means more to Ann than anything in the world. Losing him is going to be excruciating for her. I just wanted to make it as cut and dried as possible. Sometimes that's the easiest way to face something hard."

"Perhaps it won't come to that."

"All I can say is that you can thank your lucky stars you didn't breed your mare to Easy. God, what a perfect match, but with a wild gene like Easy could pass on, it would be stupid. At least you won't lose a year and have a foal you can't get rid of."

Matt's stomach tightened, but he kept his face expressionless. "Are you here to do some work? I'll be glad to give you a hand."

"I need to give some encephalitis shots to a few of the horses, and some antibiotics to Jaycine, a mare that was cut yesterday. Ann's records—" she opened a cabinet and pulled out some files "—are right here. I'll do that, and then I want to have a look at Easy. Maybe there's something I've overlooked."

"You'll have a tough time seeing Easy."

"Why? He's been fine, hasn't he?" Cybil was momentarily flustered.

"Sure. He just isn't here."

A sheen of sweat broke out on Cybil's forehead. "Isn't here? She hasn't sent him away. He's dangerous."

"He isn't today." Remembering the scene of Ann and Easy galloping down the drive, Matt couldn't suppress a smile of pure pleasure. "Today, he's . . . magnificent!"

"Ann's riding Easy!" Shock drained all of the color from Cybil's face. "Matt, she's injured and that horse is unreliable."

"I thought the same thing, until I saw them on the drive, his golden mane flying in her face, her eyes alive with excitement. Cybil, we've got to find out what's wrong with Easy." He walked to her and took her hand. "She counts you as her oldest and dearest friend. Surely there's something we can try?"

"Don't you think I haven't tried everything I know?" Anger glinted in her eyes, and she pulled her hand away. "When I was a girl, every good thing I ever had came from Ann or her father. Every nice dress, every hair ribbon, every trip." She abruptly picked up her supplies and went to the door. "The best thing I can do for Ann is protect her. If you genuinely care for her, that should be your first concern, too." She left, closing the door softly behind her.

LISTENING INTENTLY for the sound of footsteps or voices, the dark-clad figure waited in the tack room of the stallion barn. Daylight forays were dangerous. Deadly. But today, so very, very necessary.

A vial of clear fluid appeared in the hand, for once devoid of a glove. The strong, blunt fingers pulled a syringe from a deep pocket and began drawing liquid from the vial. Increment by increment the liquid was drained. When it was all gone, the medicine was transferred to another bottle, one clear fluid mixed with another.

With great care the full vial was replaced in the medicine cabinet.

The task was completed. A low sound of anger and frustration escaped. This wasn't the plan. Things had gone wrong. Harper, that weak imbecile, had almost spoiled everything. Only extreme intelligence and quick action had saved the day. Now, with her own hand, Ann would seal her fate, and that of her horse.

Creeping from the tack room, the figure eased out the back door of the barn and swiftly crossed through the redtop hedge toward the pasture. A finger of woods offered total protection as the figure darted among the underbrush. In a moment, booted feet found the path that led among the trees toward an old abandoned church.

The figure hesitated at the steps, almost going in but turning instead to go behind the building. At the wrought-iron gate to an old cemetery the figure paused. Slowly the intruder swung open the gate and approached a cluster of graves.

"Time doesn't heal all wounds, does it?" The voice was a rough whisper, a raw nerve of emotion. "When I dug your grave, I thought it didn't matter. I hated you. But now I'm so alone. Why did you have to die?" Sobs were muffled by a thick hat pulled down covering every feature.

Chapter Fifteen

"It would seem I should sit guard over you twenty-four hours a day. What in hell are you trying to prove? That horse is dangerous." Cybil blocked Ann's path, refusing to budge an inch. Her eyes were sparking anger, and her hands were planted firmly on her hips.

"Easy isn't dangerous," Ann insisted calmly. "There's something wrong, but it isn't the horse." Her convictions gave her step a bounce as she shifted to the right, her hands still on Easy's bridle. "Now if you'll excuse me, I'd like to unsaddle him and cool him out. We had a long, vigorous ride."

"I won't step aside and watch you kill yourself because you're too stubborn to admit that stallion has the potential to kill."

"Cybil, I appreciate your concern, but he's my horse. I make the ultimate decisions about him." Ann's words were clipped and cold. "Medical science may indicate one thing, but my heart tells me another. I've always followed my instincts, and I'm not going to change now."

"You're a fool, Ann Tate." Cybil stepped forward and took Easy's reins. "What will it take for me to convince you that your safety is at stake? Perhaps the death of your employees and friends."

"I don't think you can convince me of that, Cybil. Easy Dancer is off-limits to anyone but me. Therefore, no one can be hurt by him except me. I believe I know the horse well enough to be able to judge when he's going to misbehave."

"I wouldn't count on that." Cybil put a hand on Easy's neck. "He's fine now, but any moment he could cut loose."

"You're right about one thing, Cybil. I'm too stubborn to give up on Easy, so this conversation is a waste of time. Now if you'll please get out of my way. . ."

"Certainly." Cybil dropped back against the wall of the barn and let Ann and Easy pass. She remained there as Ann removed the tack and began to groom the horse.

Ann worked fast, ignoring Cybil's continued presence. She felt as if her friend were scrutinizing her every move, waiting for a false step from Easy.

She put her grooming tools away and stepped under Easy's neck to cross to the tack room. Her first warning was a disapproving snort. Suddenly she felt Easy's teeth on her shoulder in a savage bite. The only thing that saved her was the thick padding of her jacket.

"Easy!" She twisted free of his teeth and stepped back just as he reared and pawed the air. His eyes rolled and his ears were pinned back against his head as he charged at her. On the first attempt, the heavy ropes of the cross ties held him. The rope hooks, screwed into the stout timbers of the barn, protested dangerously.

Her arm throbbing, Ann reached for the left cross tie and brought her weight down on it, pulling the stallion to all fours.

"Stop it!" Her voice was fierce. "Easy!"

"This is what you call reliable." Cybil came to Ann's assistance, a heavy-duty lead rope in her hand. While Ann clung to the stallion's halter, Cybil snapped the lead rope through the stout nylon, the chain running over his nose.

When he tried to rear again, Cybil brought her weight down on the rope, jerking the chain across his nose. The pain didn't faze the stallion; it only seemed to anger him more.

"We can't control him," Cybil said through clenched teeth. "If he gets off these cross ties, he's going to kill someone." She took a deep breath. "Matt!" The word echoed off the wooden rafters, reverberating through the barn. "Matt!" she yelled again.

"Leave me alone with Easy," Ann hissed at Cybil. Her efforts to control the horse took everything she had. She felt her arms being jerked from the sockets as Easy reared again. Then the pressure relaxed as a hard body pressed beside her, a strong hand grasped the cross tie and helped bring the stallion's feet to the ground.

For several seconds they battled together, Ann's body pressed firmly against Matt's as they worked to prevent Easy from breaking free. Even though her total concentration was devoted to restraining the crazed horse, she was aware of Matt's closeness. Her stomach tightened dangerously.

Reaching across her, Matt grasped the halter. "Open his stall," he commanded Cybil. When she didn't move, Matt yelled, "Open the damn stall. We'll herd him through the door."

While Cybil stood frozen, Ann leaped at the door and flung it open. With the stallion almost lifting him from the floor, Matt unhooked the cross ties and snatched the lead rope from Cybil. "Get on!" he urged, slapping Easy on the chest and backing him up. With a sudden jerk, he turned him toward the open stall door. Easy raced forward and shot into the stall. Ann slammed the door and drove the bolt home.

Spinning in a tight circle on his hind legs, the stallion threw himself against the walls of the stall.

"Easy!" Ann called, her eyes burning with tears. She turned to Matt. "He's going to injure himself."

"Or someone else." Cybil stood in the middle of the aisle, hands clenched at her side. "That's the perfect example of how dangerous that horse is. Five minutes ago you were frolicking on his back. Five seconds ago he would have killed you without compunction." She turned to Matt. "If you have any influence over Ann, any at all, I urge you to use it. I'm going to the office to fill out some reports. Call me when you've made your decision."

As Cybil's footsteps smacked against the concrete floor, Ann watched Easy with horror. He was thrashing and throwing himself against every wall. "We have to stop him," she said barely louder than a whisper. "He doesn't know what he's doing."

Watching the huge animal hurl himself into the solid wood walls, Matt had to agree, but he had no idea how to stop him. The stallion's past attacks had shown only demented anger. As he swung his beautiful body into the unyielding wood, Matt could think of only one word—insane. If the destruction went on much longer, the horse was sure to do himself permanent damage.

Ann pushed away from the stall and ran into the tack room. A few moments later she emerged with a syringe filled with a clear liquid.

"After what I did with Blue Chip, I don't blame you if you say no, but I need your help. His life depends on it. Can you hold him long enough for me to get this into him?"

Matt didn't have to calculate the risk. Both he and Ann could be hurt in the attempt, but the alternative was to watch the horse kill himself in the stall. "What is it?"

"It's a sedative. In his condition, I'm afraid to give him a regular dose. I want to give him just enough to take the edge off."

"Let's try it," he said.

The lead rope still dangled from Easy's halter. With the right timing and a lot of speed, enough leverage could be provided for Matt to hold the horse. Carefully planning his lunge, Matt waited until Easy spun past the door. In one smooth motion he entered the stall, grasped the rope with a jerk that pulled Easy around, and then he grabbed his nose. Feeling his body forcibly twisting, Matt jerked with all of his strength, turning Easy's head and giving Ann the opportunity she needed.

Ann dove under Matt's arm, finding the thick vein in Easy's neck with a deft plunge of the needle. In another two seconds, the syringe was empty, and she and Matt retreated from the stall.

"Nice work," Matt complimented her as he latched the door. "I don't think I've ever seen a shot administered so neatly or so quickly."

"There wasn't time for a mistake," Ann said. Her legs were trembling and she felt sick. The shot was taking effect, and Easy's self-destructive behavior was slowing. He stopped thrashing. "The sedative will last about an hour," Ann said, answering Matt's unasked question. "After that, I don't have any idea what to do. I'm afraid to give him a stronger dose. In his state . . ."

Matt's arm tightened around her shoulders and he pulled her close to his chest. One hand stroked her hair as he pressed her against him, holding her securely.

"Ann, I'm so sorry this is happening." He kissed the top of her head. "I thought at first that maybe someone was deliberately giving Easy something. I wanted to believe that. But after today I'm not so sure."

Matt's words were distressing but true. Nothing had provoked Easy. No one had been near him but her. He'd been fine, and then had exploded. There was no reason for his behavior. None. And that meant there were no excuses. Like it or not, it seemed she was going to have to have him destroyed.

"I can't deal with this right now," she said, her words muffled in the thick coat Matt wore. "In an hour, let's see how he's doing. Then I'll make a decision."

"That's plenty of time," Matt agreed. "Why don't we take a walk? I noticed a path that leads away from the pecan orchard." Gently he guided her away from Easy's stall.

Ann hesitated. "I feel I should stay here—to watch." The sedative was having a remarkable effect. Easy stood still, nostrils flaring.

"He's resting. I think you need to get away for a few minutes. Besides, we need to talk."

It was Matt's firm grasp on her arm that finally convinced her. They walked out of the barn and into the golden sunlight together. And couldn't help noticing the warming weather. Under normal circumstances, it would have been a perfect day for breeding. The brisk air, the teasing knowledge that spring was only a few weeks away made the horses rambunctious. The promise of spring. New life. Ann forced herself not to think about those things.

For several minutes there were only the sounds of nature. The bare limbs of the pecan trees reached toward the blue sky; it was a perfect day.

"Where does that path go?" Matt asked as they neared the end of the orchard.

"There's a small, abandoned church. A few graves. It was part of the estate when my father bought it. He offered several times to allow the congregation to continue, but they were building a new brick church on a nearby highway. Now this one's abandoned."

"No one uses it?"

"Well, sometimes I go there to relax and think. It's an interesting old building. Plain, but somehow restful."

They walked into a thick maze of woods. Pine and dogwood crowded together along with scrub oak and elderberry shrub. Bamboo briars laced through the thick undergrowth. The trail was wide enough for two and relatively clear. As soon as they stepped into the cool depths of the woods, the temperature dropped several degrees.

"This is beautiful," Matt said, stopping when several squirrels began chattering from an oak limb. "I think we're intruding on someone's private domain."

"It's a good place for the squirrels, birds and rabbits. It gives them a measure of safety. Dad always insisted that we keep this tiny little corner wild. He said it was the duty of each landowner to provide for the creatures who couldn't hold deeds." The memory of her father was suddenly painful. With Freddie in the hospital and Easy virtually on death row, she felt as if she'd lost everything she loved. The pain in her chest grew almost unbearable, and tears threatened. To hide her distress she walked toward the church, Matt only a step behind her.

The white steeple of the building came into sight first. The place was an old clapboard design with wide front steps and a single entranceway. An ancient bell hung in the tower, connected with a new rope. Ann's hand touched the hemp, but she didn't pull it. "Church bells for celebration and mourning," she said more to herself than Matt.

"There will be other celebrations, Ann." Matt's hand covered hers briefly, giving a squeeze of support.

"Nothing like wallowing in self-pity," Ann replied dryly. The tears were so near the surface she had to get a grip on herself. "Please excuse me." She stepped away from the rope quickly and went to the door. Pushing it open, she entered.

Except for dust, the sanctuary was clean and well kept. "About once a year I send the men over to make sure everything is okay. I don't know why, but it would be a shame if the roof leaked." She shrugged, taking a seat in one of the dozen wooden pews that took up most of the room. If she focused on ordinary details, she wouldn't give way to tears.

Matt slid down beside her. His hand picked up one of hers and he brought it to his lips. "I have something I want to tell you."

Ann shook her head and struggled to free her hand, but he held it tightly. When she couldn't escape, she began to talk. "Blue Chip is at Mica John's stable. I made him take her there. I thought I was doing the right thing." She blurted the words, unable to look at him.

"Ann, listen—"

"We can call Cybil and have her abort your mare. She'll be okay to be bred next month. I'm sorry. There's no excuse for what I did." She bowed her head and focused on an old hymnal still in the rack behind the pew.

Matt's fingers gently touched her chin, stroking the sensitive skin and lifting her face so that she had to look at him. He said, "I've decided to keep the foal."

"Why?" She didn't believe it.

"I want you to have it. Maybe it will be another Easy Dancer. Maybe it will be a foal you can love as much as you love him."

The thin sunlight slanted through the church windows, defining Matt's dark curls and amber eyes. She knew his face well, for she had thought about it and dreamed about it since the day he'd arrived. Her fingers touched his lips. From the afternoon in the loft she knew exactly how generous a lover he was, but now he had offered her something even more, an essential element of his future.

"No one has ever given me a finer gift," she said, her voice throaty and low. "I can't accept. Blue Chip is your ticket to your children. It would be wrong of me to let her carry a foal that has a chance of future problems. Wrong for me, for you, Blue Chip and her foal."

"That's an assumption, Ann. Something you're very good at jumping to, by the way. There's no solid proof, yet, that Easy will transmit this disorder."

"No proof...yet! That's not a risk I'm willing to take with your horse. I can't accept the offer, but nothing will ever lessen the importance of it." She stood up and walked down the narrow center aisle of the church to the tall, austere podium. "Maybe we should go back."

"There's something I have to tell you," Matt said. "I did come here to look at the ranch as part of an investment group. When I was in Atlanta, I made some friends who were interested in horses. Somehow a group that was eager to invest in a breeding farm in Mississippi got my name and got in touch with me. They found out I was looking to breed Blue Chip to Easy Dancer, and they phoned and asked me to combine business with business and I agreed."

She hadn't heard his step on the wooden floor, but she didn't object to the feel of his hand on her shoulder or the gentleness with which he turned her to face him. "Investments are your business. I can understand that."

"From the first hour I was here," he said, "I knew this wasn't the right place for them. This is your ranch, Ann. This is your life. I never considered it as a potential sell. That's the truth. Even if you were in distress I could never recommend that it go to some corporation."

He kissed her forehead. "I'm a businessman, yes, but I can see that this place doesn't run on economic principles. It operates on the love you have for it."

A small clump of black near a choir chair caught his eye. He bent over and retrieved a leather glove. "Hmm. One of the workmen must have dropped this."

Ann took it from him. "It's so supple. Quality leather." Something about the glove made her uneasy. It wasn't a workman's glove. It was far too expensive. It was a riding glove. She tucked it into her pocket.

"I don't know exactly the role the Winner's Circle has played in your troubles," he went on. "Harper was involved—I'm positive of that. I'll find out what I can. You have to believe that once I met you, I never again thought of you selling this ranch."

Ann forced a brave smile. "The irony of the matter is that once Easy is gone, there's a very good possibility I'll have to sell. None of his offspring will be able to take his place. At least not for several years until their temperament is proven. The cold, hard fact is that I don't have the cash to buy another stud."

A primal urge to take her in his arms and protect her swept over Matt. He followed his inclination. "Ann," he murmured, "don't think about all of that now."

Matt's embrace was a luxury. Though only a temporary haven, she clung to him fiercely.

She opened her mouth to his kiss, reveling in his hungry exploration. Her hands found their way against his chest, pressing the familiar terrain of his shoulders and torso with eager, demanding fingers.

She gently pushed against him, breaking the kiss. "Come with me," she whispered, taking his hand and leading him down the aisle toward the door.

Matt had to fight the urge to pull her back into his arms and kiss her into mindless obedience. Instead he followed her out the door and down the steps. Almost running, she led him into the woods.

"Come on," she urged, dragging at his hand.

Ann wasn't headed back to the ranch, and Matt had no idea where she was going. When she pushed aside the limbs of a wild bay tree and stepped into a small clearing, he suddenly understood.

A large oak tree sheltered the area, and twenty yards away a small spring pooled in a bay grove. Dry and warmed by the sun, the wild grass that covered the secluded alcove was at least a foot high.

"It occurred to me that this might be a little softer than a hardwood floor," Ann said. She unsnapped her jacket slowly and let it fall from her arms to the ground. "Of course—" her fingers worked on the buttons of her shirt "—if you'd rather, we could simply go home."

His kiss stopped further comments as they sank together onto the sun-drenched grass.

Long after their breathing had returned to normal and the pounding of their hearts subsided, they clung to each other. Ann marveled at the fit of her hips against his, the comfort and strength of his arms as he held her.

The grass offered little protection from the cold, and once the heat of their passion had evaporated, the afternoon was bitter.

"We're going to freeze," she said, snuggling closer to his chest.

"That would be a shame, especially when it's so much more enjoyable when we're both…warm." His brown eyes were filled with a teasing light and he caressed the length of her thigh. "You're cold," he whispered, leaning on his elbow to kiss the spot he'd touched.

Ann shivered, half with desire and half with cold. When he handed her clothes to her, she slipped into them. Their lovemaking had erased her problems, creating a desperately needed haven. Now, though, she knew it was time to return to the farm and face her choices. She was stronger, better able to confront them, now that Matt stood beside her as friend and lover.

The grip of his hand on hers was the only support she needed as they walked back to the ranch. At the edge of the woods, Ann hesitated. She looked back into the dense overgrowth, savoring the memory of the intimacy they'd shared.

As they emerged into the pecan orchard, they were smiling.

Then Ann's smile froze and changed to a look of consternation as Mica John dashed toward them, his young face openly revealing his worry.

"Where've you been, Ms. Tate?" he cried.

"What's wrong?"

"It's Easy. He's down in his stall and no one can get him up. And Freddie has come round. The nurse has been calling here for the past hour. He demands to talk to you and no one else!"

Ann started toward the barn and then stopped, turning on her heel toward the truck. She stopped again, undecided.

Matt propelled her forward toward the barn. "Let's check on Easy and see what's happening with him."

Together they ran across the yard. Ann's heart pounded in her ears as she reviewed the dosage she'd given Easy. It wasn't enough to knock him off his feet. She'd been very careful about that. What had happened? Was it a reaction to the drug?

Breathless, she opened his stall door and hurried in, Matt right behind her. Easy was on his side, his labored breathing moving his golden body up and down in a frighteningly shallow rhythm.

Ann grasped his halter and tugged. "Come on, Easy, on your feet." She turned to Matt. "If he stays down much longer, his respiratory system will collapse."

"We've tried everything," Mica said. "I put in a call to Dr. Matheson, but she's on another call, out of radio range."

Matt positioned himself behind Ann, and together they tugged. "Get a crop and tap him on the butt," Ann yelled at Mica. "If we don't get him up, he's going to die."

The young groom entered the stall. Yet together, tugging and prodding, they made no progress. "Get a winch and a sling. We've got to get him on his feet," Ann said.

For twenty minutes, they worked like fiends. Matt and Mica set the winch on a high beam above the stall. It took every ounce of strength to get the sling worked under the horse, but somehow they managed.

"Thank God," Ann whispered, as the mechanical device slowly pulled Easy to a standing position, "and thank you both."

"What's wrong with him?" Matt asked. "I've never seen a horse react like this before."

"Maybe he's developed a sensitivity to the medication I gave him. I don't know. But as long as we keep him up, he'll have a chance. If he goes down again, I'm afraid we'll lose him."

"He's a fighter, Ann. He didn't give up and he won't quit now." Matt's hand covered hers on the halter and he slowly removed her fingers.

Startled, she turned to face him.

"Do you trust me?" His question was unexpected.

"Yes," she answered, reaching up to take the halter again.

"Then leave Easy with me," he said. "You go and see about Freddie. He needs you, too, Ann, and I can manage Easy."

"Matt, I—"

"Go, Ms. Tate," Mica interjected. "The nurse said Freddie was climbing out of the bed in intensive care. They're afraid he's going to hurt himself if you don't go there."

She reached out to Matt, a gesture so eloquent no words were needed. Then she lifted herself to her toes and kissed the tip of his chin.

"Watch yourself closely," Matt warned her. "Don't trust anyone."

Chapter Sixteen

"We had to give him a sedative." The nurse's voice, which was distinctly disapproving, was as starched and white as her uniform. "We tried repeatedly to locate you."

"After he's been unconscious for days, he comes to and you put him back to sleep!" Ann wanted to grab the skinny nurse by her neck and choke her. She'd driven so fast to the hospital, the speedometer of the old farm truck had pegged out permanently, but it was only to find out Freddie was tucked neatly in a bed, sleeping. The intensive-care nurse wouldn't even let her peek in at him until official visiting hours.

"He was so excited, we were afraid he'd hurt himself. If we'd been able to find you, we might have been able to control him." Her thin nose bobbed with disdain. "He was afraid something had happened to you. He was alarmed for some reason." Her gaze swept over Ann's disheveled clothes, the tiny bits of grass that had managed to tangle in her short hair.

The nurse's unfriendly scrutiny earned a blush from Ann as she swept her fingers through her hair. She eyed the metal name tag on the nurse's right pocket.

"I'll be in the waiting room, Mrs. Welford. Please call me the moment there's a change. I must talk with Freddie."

"And *I* must make certain my patient isn't unduly disturbed." The nurse turned on her white rubber heel with a squeak of authority and padded away.

"Tyrant," Ann whispered under her breath. She hurried out of the cubicle of a waiting room and found a pay telephone. Mica John answered on the fifteenth ring.

"He's still up, Ms. Tate. No change, though."

"That's a good sign," she said encouragingly, forcing the anxiety out of her voice. "Just keep him up. Don't let him have any water right now. He's oddly stiff, and I'm afraid he'll choke himself. I'll call back."

Nervous as a cat on a willow limb, she went to the concession for a cup of vile coffee. She could almost feel the black liquid staining her teeth as she made herself drink it.

When thirty minutes had passed, she called the ranch again. Mica could only reassure her that Easy was on his feet, but only because of the sling. He was no better, and no worse.

Ann returned to the waiting room. When she tried to sneak through into the intensive-care unit, Nurse Welford nabbed her ten feet from the door.

"I want to look at him," Ann insisted.

"You should have thought of that before you sent the other visitor in. The patient is only allowed one visitor for five minutes every hour. Freddie's allotment is done for this hour." She started to turn away, but Ann's hand jerked her around.

"I'm tired of this. There is no visitor authorized to see Freddie. No one. I'm the only one here, and I just went to make a phone call."

"Don't blame me for your inefficiency." Nurse Welford stepped back two small steps as she talked. "I don't make the rules here. I just see that they're carried out."

"Who was the visitor?" Ann's voice was almost a growl as she stepped forward.

The physical intimidation was effective. Nurse Welford thrust a sheet of paper attached to a clipboard in Ann's face. "See."

The name scrawled across the page riveted Ann.

"That's impossible!" The name on the list made her heart beat with a wild erratic tempo. It wasn't possible. She gripped the clipboard and examined every nuance of the boldly scrawled signature.

"If you would stay where you're supposed to be, you wouldn't find everything so impossible." The nurse reached for the clipboard. Ann's glare stayed her hand.

"Did you happen to speak with this man who came to see Freddie?" Ann asked.

"I don't have time to chat with visitors," Nurse Welford replied stiffly. "I have my duties."

"Did anyone see Mr. Harper?" Ann's chest was heaving.

"Possibly one of the aides."

"I insist on speaking with the aides." All pretense of politeness disappeared from Ann's voice. "For someone who is a paragon of efficiency, you've made one tiny mistake. This last visitor, Bill Harper, is a dead man."

The shocking words had the intended effect. Nurse Welford led Ann back to the nurses' station without another question. She gathered the three aides and crisply instructed them to cooperate.

None of the aides, two men and a woman, was very helpful. A short man in a burly coat and cap did visit Freddie's room, Ann learned. He'd stayed several moments and then left without asking any questions.

"Get Dr. Zimlich for me," Ann ordered the nurse. When the woman started to protest, Ann hardened her voice. "I suggest you do it now."

Without waiting for permission, Ann stepped around Nurse Welford and went to Freddie's cubicle. He was lying quietly in bed, smaller than she'd ever seen him. His chest moved up and down so slowly that for a moment she thought he might be dead. The monitors and screens were stacked in a corner, disconnected since he'd regained consciousness.

"We were getting ready to move him to a private room," Nurse Welford explained, appearing at Ann's elbow. "He was doing so much better that we disconnected all of the monitors, everything. Until he became so excited about finding you, he was really doing well."

Ann's gaze swept the tidy room. There was a water pitcher on the table, a glass, and nothing else. Freddie's clothes were apparently tucked in the drawer beneath the bedside table, for there was no sign of them. Everything was perfectly orderly, but there was one thing wrong.

An IV with its glucose drip was hooked to Freddie's right hand.

"Why is he on intravenous," Ann demanded, "if he's awake and able to eat?" The nurse turned and her eyes widened.

"There's no order for any medication," the woman exclaimed. "We took all of the supports out hours ago!" She rushed to the bedside and picked up the clear plastic tubing. "This kind of carelessness is completely inexcusable. If I don't watch my staff every second, this is the kind of thing that happens. And I can't do my job when people keep interrupting me."

Ann reached for the IV shutoff apparatus and twisted it quickly. "I want Dr. Zimlich. Without delay." A dark and frightening possibility was taking shape in her mind. A dead man had visited Freddie's room, and a needle was inserted into his arm. Now he was stretched out in the bed, his eyes twitching and an unhealthy color in his cheeks.

As she bent to brush her lips across Freddie's cheek, she saw a small black object tucked under the edge of his pillow. She pulled it out and saw a finely made black leather glove. Fear struck like a blow to her stomach. The memory of the taste of leather in her mouth rushed at her, a memory made of fear and pain. She had to force herself to breathe as she held the glove. Leather-clad hands. Cruel hands. From her pocket she removed the mate.

Ann swung around on the nurse. "Test that IV for some additive, something that might be a poison or a sedative."

"Yes, ma'am." The nurse removed the needle from Freddie's arm and wheeled the IV stand away from the bed.

She left the room with the IV bag clutched to her chest, mumbling about going straight to the lab.

Alone with Freddie at last, Ann picked up his hand and held it. Every callus was dear and familiar, and she found herself suddenly overcome with emotion. He looked so old and frail against the white hospital sheets. The shallowness of his breathing frightened her. It wasn't as if he was resting peacefully, but as if he was struggling against the wall of sleep without success.

Touching his brow, Ann felt her doubts grow as she noted the coolness of his skin.

"Freddie," she whispered, kissing his wrinkled cheek, "it's me, Ann. I know you wanted to see me and I got here as fast as I could. As soon as you've rested, you'll wake up and we can talk. I'm not going to leave you. Not until you're wide awake and ready to tell me what was troubling you."

There was no awareness on Freddie's face, but it made Ann feel better to talk with him. He might not understand her words, but she felt certain he could hear her voice, would know she was there for him.

She brushed a strand of white hair back from his forehead and kissed his wrinkled cheek. Freddie was a big part of her life. She'd grown to love him like a daughter. "You have to wake up soon," she told him. "I need you."

She heard the doctor's footsteps outside the room and straightened to greet him.

"What seems to be the trouble?" Dr. Zimlich asked as he gave Ann a pat on the shoulder. "Since you didn't return for a checkup, I assume your arm is better."

"I'm fine. It's Freddie I'm worried about. I know he was given something to make him sleep, but he looks so, well, so disturbed." The gloves were balled into a tight knot in her pocket.

The doctor bent over Freddie, his skillful eyes taking in the bright cheeks, the cool skin.

He picked up the chart at the end of the bed and read for a moment. "I'm not the specialist on this case, but I can tell you that the sedative Nurse Welford gave shouldn't be this strong. It was so mild it would have little effect on a restless infant."

"There was an unprescribed IV in his arm." Ann gripped the metal bed railing. "I had the nurse take it out and send it to the lab."

Zimlich's head snapped up. "What kind of IV?"

"The bottle was labeled glucose. I asked the nurse to have it analyzed."

"Wait here with him." He started out of the room. "If there's any change, buzz me. I want to know what was in that solution. I'm afraid there was something more than glucose."

The speed with which Dr. Zimlich departed did nothing to comfort Ann. Her gaze returned to Freddie. Something was very wrong. His eyes moved rapidly beneath the lids. Ann was gripped by a sudden fear that he would die.

"Oh, Freddie," she whispered, stroking his cheek, "hang on." Finding the buzzer that rang at the nurse's desk, Ann pressed it. When one of the aides quickly arrived, she asked for the clipboard where the visitors logged in. When the aide returned with the board, Ann studied the names on the list intently.

There was Ronnie's name, Jeff's, hers and Bill Harper's, the last entry.

The aides said Harper was a small man muffled in winter clothing. The real Bill Harper was a dead man, but even if he were alive no one would ever have described him as small. Ann puzzled over the list, trying to find a rational explanation.

Who would impersonate Bill Harper? And for what purpose? Unless it was to drug Freddie.

Ann clutched at the bed railing to steady herself as the implications sank in. Someone had impersonated Bill Harper because it was convenient. A dead man couldn't be convicted of a crime. But who would want to murder Freddie? Robert? Even before the thought was half-formed, she pushed it aside. Like Harper, Robert was a big man. No one would ever call him small. So who?

It had to be the same person who had knocked Freddie in the head and put him in Easy's stall. The same person who had attacked her and Matt. More than likely the same person who had killed Bill Harper and shot her in the arm.

As pieces began to drop into place, Ann clenched her teeth to keep them from chattering. All along, she'd assumed that Bill Harper was behind the sabotage at Dancing Water Ranch. Now Harper was dead.

Cybil's words about a psychopath on the loose came back to her. It was impossible to find a rational explanation for irrational behavior.

Her thoughts were interrupted by the return of Dr. Zimlich. She'd never seen a man look more distraught. His face told her everything she needed to know.

"There was something in the IV," he said.

Her body felt numb as she stood there, her hand still clutching Freddie's. "What?" She was barely able to get the single word out.

"We haven't been able to determine exactly what, but we do know that it's a paralyzing agent, something that might be used for a particular type of surgery...."

"Paralyzing agent?" Ann couldn't believe it.

"Yes, it works on the major muscle groups. We're going to have to put Freddie on a respirator. There's a chance that his lungs will fail."

"His respiratory system?" Ann sickened at the thought. "If I hadn't stopped that IV..."

"He would be a dead man." Zimlich moved her out of the way as he spoke, and a team of orderlies drew another machine into the cubicle. "Now I want you to leave, Ann. We'll do everything we can."

"How did this happen?" Anger was the only thing that kept her standing. "This is a hospital and Freddie was in intensive care. How did someone sneak in here and do this?"

"Your guess is as good as mine. The only thing I can promise you is that we'll investigate thoroughly. The entire shift has been put on notice not to leave the hospital, and the authorities have been notified. In fact, they'll want to talk to you, I'm sure."

"Of course," Ann said numbly. She caught the doctor's sleeve before he could depart. "This drug, have you ever seen it before?"

"Not exactly in this form. Our tests are very preliminary. In another few hours we'll have it pegged down to the exact chemical composite. It appears to be a combination. Allowed to drip slowly into the bloodstream, it would have killed Freddie without arousing undue suspicions. He owes you his life, Ann." Dr. Zimlich's hand patted her arm in a gesture of comfort.

"I owe Freddie so much more than that," Ann whispered.

The doctor's arm reached around her shoulders. "Don't worry. You caught this thing in time. This isn't such a rare drug. A form of it is often used in certain types of surgery. It's not a narcotic, and we have an antidote. We'll put Freddie on a respirator for good measure. He's going to be fine, I promise."

"There's an antidote?"

"Of sorts. Why?"

"Could this type of drug have the same effect on an animal? A large animal, like a horse?" For the first time since she'd seen Easy down in his stall, his body still and almost rigid, she felt hope. Easy's symptoms were much like those of Freddie's.

"Yes," Dr. Zimlich said slowly. "Why do you ask?"

"I don't know how, but I think someone gave my stallion the same drug. Where can I get the antidote? I've got to get some or I'm afraid he'll die."

"Call your vet..."

Ann shook her head. "She's on another call, too far away. I've got to handle this by myself. I've got to get that antidote."

Zimlich eyed her speculatively. "Your father and I were like brothers. I know how much he loved that farm, how hard the two of you worked to build it up. Because I've known you for so long, I'll give it to you, Ann. I could lose my license, and if you're wrong, you could kill the horse."

"If I'm right and I don't get help, he's dead already." Her hands clenched with the need to get the antidote and get to Easy.

"Okay. Meet me in my office."

ANN SHOWED NO MERCY for the road or the old truck as she sped toward the ranch, the medicine in a syringe beside her.

She drove straight to the barn and jumped out, rushing to the stallion barn, where Matt and Mica stood beside Easy Dancer.

"Get the bottle of medicine that's marked as a sedative," Ann ordered Mica. "I'm certain it has the same drug in it that someone gave Freddie, and I want to have it tested." Finding the vein in Easy's neck, she administered the antidote with a silent prayer. If she'd been giving herself the drug, she couldn't have felt more worried. After she withdrew the needle, she tenderly stroked Easy's neck. His lack of response threatened once again to bring tears. Easy trusted her, depended on her to help him. She had to be right.

At last she stepped back, then filled Matt and Mica in on what she'd learned at the hospital.

They stood side by side as she waited for small, telltale signs of improvement in Easy Dancer. When he started to revive, Ann impulsively put her arms around the stallion's neck and buried her face in his mane.

Matt's dark eyes warmed with relief and pleasure as he watched the scene.

"If I'd been wrong, I could have killed Easy." Ann's voice was muffled by the horse's neck.

"'If' is a powerful word, Ann. We business types don't like to use it." Matt bent down so that his lips lightly brushed her hair. "If I could have saved you from all of this..."

"I've got to get back to Freddie. Can you manage with Easy? Keep him walking, give him a little water if he acts interested."

"Ann." Matt touched her shoulder and stopped her.

She turned a questioning look at him, keys dangling in her hand.

"While you were gone, my assistant called. There is no Gordon Boswell, so Harper told you the truth about being the one who called me. There's also no such group as the Winner's Circle. No record of a Robert Tisdale involved in any financial dealings with my company. If your ex-husband is involved, he's using an alias.''

"YOU LOOK LIKE AN ANGEL." Freddie was still stiff, but his voice was in good working order. "I only hope you're not the Angel of Death."

"Oh, Freddie." Ann was dangerously close to tears. "I've been worried sick."

"Well, I've been a little under the weather myself."

She kissed his cheek and captured his roughened hand. "Quit kidding around and tell me you're going to be fine."

"What? And give up my once-in-a-lifetime chance for melodrama? Never!"

His chuckle was the best sound Ann had heard in what seemed like an eternity.

"Whatever happened?" she asked, tears hanging in her eyelashes.

"Now that, my dear, is what I wanted to tell you before that wicked nurse jabbed me with a needle." Freddie's eyes grew bright, and he looked quickly about the room to make sure they were alone.

"The last thing I remember is hearing a strange sound in the main barn. I went outside to check, and there was no sign of anything at all. The dogs were quiet, but still I was concerned."

Ann's pulse began to race. She, too, was reliving the night Freddie had been injured. The night she and Matt had been knocked unconscious.

"I looked around the barn," Freddie went on, "but there wasn't anything to be seen. Not the first thing out of the ordinary. I went around the main barn and checked the outside. When I couldn't find anything there, I had an idea about Easy. It just didn't seem right for him to be fine one minute and having a fit the next. Even though Dr. Matheson didn't find anything in his feed, I haven't given up that idea. I got to thinking that maybe someone was giving that horse something. Injecting him with some drug that would send him bonkers for short periods of time."

Ann started to interrupt, but she checked herself. Freddie had enough to worry about without knowing that Easy had grown even more erratic. Instead of speaking, she picked up his hand and placed the roughened palm against her cheek.

Freddie smiled and touched the top of her silky hair. "There, there, girl. I'm fine. Anyway, I went to the stallion barn, down from the main entrance. My intention was to get some of those vet books and do a little reading. I walked through and was opening the rear door when I saw you walking into the main barn. My curiosity got the better of me and I watched for a moment, when out of the darkness this figure came and before I could even cry out, you were whacked in the head and on the ground."

"You saw the person? Who was it?" The solution seemed so close. Ann clenched her fist.

Freddie shook his head. "Even now I can't believe it. My eyesight isn't the best at night."

"It doesn't matter. We'll find out eventually," Ann responded quickly. Not for a moment would she allow Freddie to feel he'd failed at anything.

He straightened in bed and reached out a hand to touch her face. "I was frightened to the bone for the first time in my life. Watching the way you fell, the way that person hovered over you for a moment and me unable to do a thing except run to you, I was truly afraid."

"There's nothing to be afraid of."

"Yes, there is, Ann. Something terrible."

From beneath the wall of fear that crashed down around her, Ann clearly saw how much Freddie had aged in the past week. In the jumble of her thoughts, she tried to think of something to say to alleviate his fear.

She kissed his cheek. "I wasn't hurt, Freddie. You know my skull is thicker than a cement block. Now if I'd been hit in the stomach, I would have been a goner. I don't think the assailant meant to kill me."

Freddie's old eyes sharpened. "What makes you say that?"

"Just a hunch."

"Well, when he sneaked back around the barn and hit me while I was bending over you, I have no doubt he meant for me to die."

"You weren't in Easy's stall?" Ann couldn't help her mounting excitement.

"Of course I wasn't in Easy's stall. I've got better sense than to be gallivanting around in the middle of the night in a stall with a horse who's been acting loony." Freddie sat taller in the bed.

"When Matt and I found you," Ann said, "you were in the stall and nearly trampled to death."

Anger sparked the old life back in Freddie's face. "So, the coward put me in the stall so a horse could take the blame for the crime. When I catch Robert I'll skin his hide in two-inch strips. Bill Harper's, too."

"Robert?" Ann repeated. "What makes you think it was Robert?"

"He was wearing that old, leather bomber jacket with the zippers. You know, the one he loved so much."

Chapter Seventeen

A psychopath has no logical motivations.

Watching Easy nibble at the grass, Matt went over the clues he'd gathered again and again. Whenever he tried to logically arrange the clues, he reminded himself that logic was irrelevant. And with Harper dead, there was no other logical suspect. Robert's return wasn't logical. The man had left and divorced Ann. That fact alone led Matt to view him as mentally unstable; therefore, dangerous. But Ann was reluctant to point the finger at her ex-spouse, and Matt had come to rely on Ann's instincts. Ann insisted that Robert could be blackmailed, but was not one to originate a scheme of violence. But if not Robert, then who?

There had been trouble at Dancing Water Ranch before, back when Jeff was trying to pass the racing bill. Could someone be involved in a revenge scheme against Jeff, using Ann as the bait?

He sighed deeply. Anything was possible. He returned to the telephone conversation he'd had with Ann. Freddie had recovered consciousness and identified Robert as Ann's assailant. Robert was involved, that much was definite. But that was as far as he could get. His thoughts spun round and round, but he had no solutions. The only thing he knew for sure was that someone had gone to a lot of trouble to create danger, without actually inflicting real damage on Ann's person.

He and Ann had managed to pull the tiny cogs together, but the mastermind behind the whole plan was missing. Ann was still in serious danger.

The ringing of the telephone pulled him from his thoughts. He grabbed it. "Hello?"

It was Cybil. "I have an urgent message to call the ranch. What's wrong?" she asked tensely.

"The worst is over," Matt said, quickly giving her the details of Easy's near tragedy. Then he paused. "Cybil, you knew Robert, didn't you?"

"Yes." There was no hesitation.

"Would you say he's capable of violent behavior?" Matt asked.

"What are you saying?"

"Come out to the ranch." He paused, weighing his words. "There's something you should know. Robert's back, and he's apparently involved in some of the troubles Ann's been having."

"I'll be right there."

ANN WAS SURPRISED at the number of cars parked at the ranch. There was Jeff's truck, Dawn's little compact, Cybil's truck. She sighed deeply. All she really wanted was a hot bath and some sleep. It was good of Matt to plan a gathering to celebrate the recoveries of Freddie and Easy. Given her choice, though, she'd have waited until the next day.

Pulling one weary leg after the other, she climbed from the truck and started toward the barn. Her smile brightened as she saw the excitement in the eyes of her friends. They'd come to share her good fortune, and she couldn't resist them.

"Sunshine breaks through at last," Jeff said, kissing her cheek with brotherly intensity. "I hear Freddie's talking the nurses' ears off."

"He has a captive audience," Ann agreed. "They'll let him come home next week."

"There's an All Points Bulletin out on Robert. The cops will have him soon, if he's still hanging around." Jeff hugged her again. "Once he's in custody, we'll get to the bottom of it all, I'm sure."

"Easy Dancer is a lot better." Mica John burst through the crowd and grabbed Ann's hand. "He wants to see you. I know it."

Smiling an apology, Ann ran with Mica back to the barn. Easy greeted her with a soft whinny and the nodding of his head that indicated his desire for attention.

"I thought you were a goner," Ann whispered, rubbing his forehead. Mica handed her a carrot, which Easy eagerly ate.

"He's tougher than we thought," the young groom boasted. "He wouldn't quit. He kept trying and trying. When he got the antidote, nothing could stop him."

"We're both very lucky," Ann said with a tired smile. At the sound of footsteps, she turned to find Cybil entering the barn.

"I hear Robert's back in town. Are you sure?"

"I'm sure." That was one topic she didn't want to talk about. "I appreciate your help through all of this."

"Would it make you feel better if I examined Easy?"

"I don't think it's necessary, but help yourself." Ann drew him from the stall and put him on the cross ties. "This last incident confirms my belief that all along someone has been injecting Easy with something. I'm curious that nothing ever showed up in your blood tests."

"My bag is in the truck, would you get it, Ann?"

"Sure thing." She stepped by Cybil just as the vet turned. The long blond braid struck Ann across the face, momentarily blinding her.

"Sorry." Cybil caught Ann's arm.

"I'm fine." Ann blinked and started toward the vet's truck. "I'll be right back."

She was out the door when she stopped, struck by a sudden memory that rooted her to the spot. From a long distance away she saw Matt, heard him call her name and then begin to run toward her. To Ann, his stride was in slow motion; everything was wrapped in a reddish haze, and she felt a paralyzing fear.

There were no clear thoughts, only the sensation of Cybil's long braid grazing her cheek. The cool touch of clean hair, and the expectation of a blast of pain to her head.

"No!" The word exploded from her and seemed to free her body. She ran back toward the barn, her legs churning. Easy! Her horse was in danger. He was standing obediently on the cross ties, a perfect victim.

Gaining the entrance to the barn at last, she saw Cybil's hand, a small, blunt hand, the perfect size for the leather gloves Ann had found at the church and in Freddie's bed, lift the syringe in the air. The drop of fluid seemed to hang from the tip of the needle.

"No more games. It's too bad, but Easy has to die." Cybil's voice was low and raspy, nothing like her normal voice. Even her posture had changed as she crouched slightly and cast furtive looks to left and right. Her face was unrecognizable. It was a mask of hatred.

Ann flung herself forward, hands extended toward Cybil's midsection. Ann's back arched in the air like a swimmer's at the start of a race. She struck with such force that Cybil was thrown into Easy's shoulder just as Ann rolled under his feet.

Hooves jittered beside her head as she found and held Cybil's legs.

The two women rolled under the horse as Easy tried valiantly not to step on them, a wild whinny issuing deep from within his throat.

"Ann!" Matt's stricken voice was right behind her. She felt him grab her leg and pull. Try as she might, she couldn't keep her grasp on Cybil as Matt dragged her from beneath the horse.

Easy saw the vet and sidestepped to avoid her head. There was an anguished cry as his right front hoof landed on Cybil's thigh.

Matt pulled Ann free, then rushed to help Cybil. His hand caught her arm, and in a split second he saw the needle coming toward him. His sudden dash backward caused Easy to rear. Though the horse attempted to avoid landing on Cybil, there was no other place to put his feet. Another front hoof caught her shoulder.

"Damn you all," Cybil cursed, rolling out from under the hooves.

She came up on her knees, the syringe somehow still intact in her hand. She made a jump for Easy, needle aimed for his neck, but Matt was quicker.

His foot caught her arm just at the elbow. The syringe flew from her hand and landed twenty feet down the aisle.

Kneeling beside the now-quiet horse, Cybil glared at Matt. "I should have made sure you were dead. You've done nothing but interfere." She swung to look at Ann. "But then you've always had someone to look out for you, someone who'd risk everything just to satisfy your every little whim. Princess," she sneered. "Every time your father called you that, I wanted to hit you. You were always the little princess, with your fine horses and blue ribbons and fancy clothes. How I hated you."

Ann swallowed, unable to say a word.

Jeff, Dawn and Mica stood in the doorway of the barn, watching the exchange in horror. At last Jeff moved forward, lifting Cybil to her feet. She winced as he touched her, but she seemed unaware of the injuries Easy had inflicted on her.

"We'd better get you inside," Jeff said, his voice amazingly gentle.

Dawn took charge of Easy, leading him out of the barn and into the sunshine.

Mica John moved to Matt's side. "Should I call the sheriff?"

Matt nodded, never taking his eyes from Ann. She was ghost white, her palms spread against the wooden wall behind her. She didn't even seem to be breathing as she stared into Cybil's eyes.

She finally spoke. "I loved you like a sister," she said. "You shared everything I had."

"What you didn't want, that's what I shared. But I shared more than you even knew. I had Robert. We'd be living here now if he hadn't backed out of our agreement."

Looking at Cybil's twisted face, Ann felt sick. "Where is Robert?"

"We were in love. All you ever thought about was the ranch and the horses and your father and money. Robert started gambling, and you didn't notice. I did. I loved him. So I came up with a plan where we could get rid of you and have everything."

"Where is he?" Ann could barely speak.

Cybil pointed out the barn door toward the woods. "He tried to stop me from hurting you. He wouldn't help me. I had to kill him. He's been in the church cemetery there for nearly three years."

Ann was stunned by Cybil's revelation. It seemed impossible that Robert was dead, murdered so long ago. And no one had even suspected.

"Why didn't you kill Easy Dancer? You had plenty of opportunities." Matt's voice was a mixture of loathing and pity.

"I wanted to make *her* do it," Cybil half snarled, looking at Ann, "to make *her* decide he had to die. I stole Speed Dancer. It was so simple. I took him one night, knowing it would kill Mr. Tate. And it did. But Ann was tougher. I knew it would hurt her more if she had to decide that Easy was to die. And then my investment group would purchase the ranch and I'd come back with Speed Dancer as stud."

"You're sick." As Ann spoke, a touch of color at last returned to her cheeks. She stepped forward, slowing only when Matt put a hand on her shoulder.

"Leave it, Ann," Matt whispered.

"No. I want to know why she started all of this now. She had years to torment me. Years. Why now?"

"It was him." Cybil nodded at Matt. "When I read his application for breeding in your office and saw his mare, I knew she was perfect for Easy. I had to stop it. You were going to realize everything you'd ever wanted. Then I decided to use him, too. He was the perfect front man for the Winner's Circle. It would be the ultimate revenge if you killed Easy and had to sell the ranch. When it became obvious that he'd fallen under your spell, it was that much better. You kill Easy, and the man you love is the instrument by which you lose your farm."

"And you wanted it all so much that the thought of murder never even bothered you?" Ann felt the tears start behind her burning eyelids.

"Murder? Killing Bill Harper can't be considered murder. He was a fool. I made him believe your desire to shut him out of the racetrack was personal. I made him think you felt superior to him. He didn't have to die, but he wouldn't shut up, drinking and then feeling sorry for you. He was just about to tell you about me and Robert."

"And Freddie? Trying to kill him didn't bother you a bit? He taught you so much!"

"That tight old man should have died years ago. He always resented every mouthful I ate here, every minute I took of your father's time. He wanted me gone, and I wanted him dead."

"Where is Speed Dancer, Cybil?"

"I'm not a fool. He's at a ranch, and you'll never find him. He would have been the perfect replacement for Easy Dancer, don't you agree?"

Her eyes began to shift around the barn. "In fact, he could be put in Easy's stall. That's exactly what I'll do."

She started twisting in Jeff's hands, but he held her tightly.

"Take Ann inside," Jeff said, giving Matt a warning glance. If Cybil began to fight, he didn't want Ann to see.

"How about some of that endless coffee?" Matt's voice was soft, but there was no arguing with the strength of his arm as he took her to the house.

ANN LEANED ON THE RAIL as Mica led the mare away and Matt held Easy's lead rope.

"That's the last for today. Thank goodness with the breeding schedule you set that Easy made such a quick recovery." Matt uncoiled the rope so the horse could graze. "I hope he gets an extra ration of feed tonight. He's worked like a devil."

"I can't believe a man would call what he does for a living work." Ann arched an eyebrow. "It seems to me that last night you were calling it something else."

Matt laughed. "You're heartless, and too smart."

"I've been called worse." For a moment the smile left Ann's face.

Reading her thoughts, Matt leaned a boot on the fence rail. "Cybil is very sick, Ann. You can't take anything she says to heart. She's been sick for a long, long time. Only her intelligence allowed her to cover it up."

"I know. Still, it's hard to believe she was sneaking around giving Easy injections of amphetamines, trying to make him kill someone. As much as she hated me, I never believed she'd hurt Easy." She drew the black leather gloves from her pocket. "She hated me so much she killed Robert and tried to kill Freddie and you."

"She hates everyone," Matt made sure the gate to the breeding pen was latched before he unhooked the line and let Easy free to graze. He came to Ann and kissed her nose, her cheeks, and then her lips.

"She killed the man she loved." Ann swallowed. "Looking back on things, I think Robert loved her, too. We'd both realized we weren't right for each other. I was too driven by worries, and Robert wanted a woman who would devote herself to him. How could she have done it? And after she shot him, she took his clothes and has been wearing them."

"We'll never understand why. We can only be happy that it's over."

"Will Cybil ever get better, do you suppose?" Ann's voice trembled as she thought about her friend, who'd been taken off in a straitjacket to keep her from doing damage to herself or someone else.

"I can't answer that, Ann. No one can. She steadfastly refuses to tell where Speed Dancer is. Maybe she doesn't know anymore."

"When some of this blows over, I'll begin a search. I do have a question you can answer." Ann picked up his hand, which rested beside hers on the rail. "When are you going back to Atlanta? It's been a week since Cybil's arrest. Blue Chip has been confirmed pregnant. Easy has a clean bill of health, and I suppose my life is as right as it can be, especially since Freddie is home."

She dropped her gaze from his. After everything she'd been through, she didn't want to face Matt's departure. She loved him, pure and simple. But the idea of a stockbroker working in her tiny, rural Mississippi community was ludicrous.

"Are you firing me?" Matt asked, his voice containing a lilt that made Ann look at him.

"Of course not. But you do have a career."

"I sort of like the sound of a wife with lots of money, land, horses, something along the order of a wife who could support a country gentleman."

Ann's heart quickened. Matt was teasing, but there was a hint of seriousness in his eyes.

"You want to stay here?" Her fingers tightened on the rail.

"Yes, but with a few conditions."

"Such as?" She was wary of his teasing.

"Well, first you have to agree to marry me. Then we figure out the areas where I could work effectively."

"Oh, I see." Ann couldn't completely hide the happiness she felt, but she tried. "How about fence mending? That's a good job for unskilled farm labor."

"It's a start." Matt edged closer. "As long as I'm working my way to the top."

"You could do that by sleeping with the boss."

"I'm not above that tactic."

"Oh, Matt." Ann sighed, unable to resist his tempting lips any longer. She kissed him, moving closer and closer until they were twined together. "I accept."

"You'll hire me?"

"I'll marry you, hire you, whatever it takes."

"Excuse me." An embarrassed Mica John suddenly appeared beside them. "Are we through breeding for the day?"

Ann and Matt stepped apart, but their gazes remained locked.

"Yes," Ann said. "You can put him back in his stall."

"Ms. Tate and I have business in the house," Matt said, "so please don't disturb us unless there's an emergency."

Ann didn't hear Mica's answer. She was in Matt's embrace, walking beside him as he delivered promise after tantalizing promise in her ear.

Harlequin Superromance

Here are the longer, more involving stories you have been waiting for . . . Superromance.

Modern, believable novels of love, full of the complex joys and heartaches of real people.

Intriguing conflicts based on today's constantly changing life-styles.

Four new titles every month.
Available wherever paperbacks are sold.